Wild Nines

by A.R.Knight

Wild Nines

Mercenaries One

Copyright © 2017 Black Key Books

All rights reserved. No part of this book may be reproduced in any form by any electronic or mechanical means including photocopying, recording, or information storage and retrieval without permission in writing from the author.

This is a work of fiction. Names, characters, places and incidents either are the product of the author's imagination or are used fictitiously. Any resemblance to actual persons, events, businesses or locales is purely coincidental.

ISBN-13: 978-946554-01-7
ISBN-10: 1-946554-01-4

Visit us online at:
www.blackkeybooks.com

Give feedback on the book at:
arknight@blackkeybooks.com

First Edition

Printed in the U.S.A

To my mother

Also By A.R. Knight

The Mercenaries Trilogy
Wild Nines
Dark Ice
One Shot

Prologue

Marl shaded her eyes from the Sun's glare. The dome over the Martian town cut the light at angles, making seats like her's blinding. There weren't any other open spots in the cafe, typical for the late morning. The usual time to meet the Red Voice, to meet her sister. A crowded place made for harder targets.

"They're here," the man sitting next to her, Castor, said. Normally a suit-and-tie guy, like Marl herself, they both wore the traditional ramshackle rags of Martian tradition. Strips of cloth taken from relatives past and present, stitched together into a motley arrangement. The wrap on her left hand came loose as Marl picked up her coffee, a strand of cloth dipping into the brown liquid.

"About time," Marl said. "They're always late."

"We have an easier route," Castor replied.

True. Alissa would be ducking down alleys, slipping through friendly houses. Marl went right down the street. Still, her sister called the meeting. Not Marl's fault Alissa had to work for it.

A man appeared out of the crowd, pulled out the two chairs across from Marl and Castor. The wraps around this guy were so thorough Marl couldn't see his face, only a shaded slit for his eyes. Bulges along the waist indicated he was armed. His loose grip on the chairs, the relaxed shoulders said he knew how to use those weapons he was carrying.

"Marl. Thank you," Alissa said, sliding into the chair across from Marl, her own coffee in hand. "I know this was short notice."

"I thought you were dead," Marl said. "The footage of that last attack. How?"

Alissa glanced at the man behind her, then nodded to the empty chair. The man took the cue, sat down. His hidden face alternated between Castor and Marl, and she suppressed a shiver.

"Bakr, here, is the only reason I'm alive," Alissa said. "But there's no time. I need your help."

"Alissa," Marl interrupted. "I'm going off-world. Eden wants to move me to a new project, on Europa."

"And you're going?" Alissa didn't sound angry. Strange. Marl expected an outburst, claims of betrayal.

"Mars is lost, Alissa," Marl said. "If I stay, Eden will figure it out eventually. Then we'll both be dead."

"Marl," Castor said, putting a hand on her arm. "Please."

"It's fine, Castor," Alissa said. "She's not wrong."

Her sister took a deep breath. Marl took a long sip of her coffee.

"Marl, this new project, what is it? A settlement?"

"Eventually, yes," Marl replied.

A noise rippled into the cafe from outside, a rumble with a mug-rattling quake. Bakr, the faceless man, stared out through the cafe entrance while Castor swiped away at the comm on his wrist, looking for news.

"When its ready, tell me," Alissa said. "If we can't hold Mars, we'll need a home."

"Eden won't let that happen."

"But you will," Alissa said, her eyes staring right into Marl's. She hated that look, hated the way it twisted her mind into knots, pulled Marl into whatever scheme Alissa had planned. The Red Voice followed Alissa because of those eyes.

"They're attacking the town," Castor told Marl. "We need to leave. If Eden finds you here, you're dead."

"I thought you said this place was secure?" Marl asked Alissa.

Around them, the cafe emptied. People scrambling for the exits, dashing out through back doors. Overhead, through the windows, corporate drones flew. Hunting for targets. Sporadic laser fire blotched the sky, one of the drones erupting in flame as a lucky shot downed the craft. The killing machines returned fire surgically, one precise beam responding to every bunch of scattered shots.

"Stay in touch, sister," Alissa said, getting up from the table. "You may well be the last hope we have."

Then Bakr pulled Alissa away, towards the back of the cafe. Marl moved in the opposite direction, Castor next to her. The outside was ruinous now, laser fire everywhere, smoke pouring throughout the dome as ruptured fuel tanks exploded. Red Martian sand swirled as part of the dome cracked, sucking air towards the hole.

"We'll never get out unseen," Marl said.

"We have a plan for that," Castor replied.

Marl swallowed. Their contingency. A claimed kidnapping, Marl and Castor taken by Red Voice operatives, held for ransom and interrogation, and saved by the opportune attack of corporate forces. There was only one part necessary to make it hold up.

"I'll do it," Castor said, drawing his sidearm.

"No," Marl replied. "It was my idea."

Castor nodded, handed her the weapon. Marl raised the sidearm and pulled the trigger, sending a fiery red bolt into Castor's chest. Behind her, the grind of corporate war machines drew closer. Marl turned the sidearm on herself. Stared down the small barrel, designed to focus electric energy into a concentrated beam of light, hot enough to burn through her rags and into her skin. It would leave a scar, if the laser didn't kill her.

What we did for family.

Marl pulled the trigger.

A Girl and Her Bot

Viola winced as she brought the robot to life. The ash-gray ball on the workbench in front of her, its various plates and parts connected to each other like puzzle pieces. The bot sat in an oval bowl with a cord stranding out from it towards the wall of Viola's room, drawing power from the Sun's solar energy slamming into Ganymede.

"How are you feeling, Puk?" Viola said to the bot. The size of a melon, Puk had small jets, allowing it to hover and float around the room. At least, that was the idea.

"You ever get a new body?" Puk asked. "Cause it's a trip."

"Consider it an upgrade," Viola replied, standing up from the chair. "C'mon, let's see how they work."

Puk didn't have running lights - there wasn't any sign that the bot was functioning. Not until a soft whirring sound, like a fast-moving fan, filled the room. At first, nothing happened. Then, as the whirring built up speed, Puk floated up from the cradle. The bot wobbled as it reached Viola's eye-level and started on a slow loop around the room. Viola followed, stepping over various half-done projects and their attendant parts, coils of wire, or racks of batteries.

"Makes getting around here easier," Puk said, rolling itself forward, so the jets propelled it faster. When Puk zipped near the door to Viola's bedroom, it rolled itself sideways and flew through.

Viola followed the bot and spotted Puk hovering in front of the wall-screen opposite Viola's twin bed. The screen was showing a waterfall, somewhere on Earth, and the surrounding jungle. It was muted, Puk's jets providing the only sound in the room.

"That's on the list," Viola said. "An island, Hawaii."

"Better than a beach," Puk replied. "At least there, I won't get grains in my circuits."

"Speaking of . . . the jets doing fine?"

"Greens all around," Puk said, referring to the systems checks the bot ran on itself. "As for how they control, they could be faster, but I suppose I can make this work."

"Glad you're happy," Viola said, crossing her arms and watching the waterfall flow. The feed wasn't live. Viola, or rather, her parents subscribed to a service that batched these recordings and delivered them to Ganymede a few times a year. Viola waved at the screen and it shifted, switching channels to the outside camera feed from her parent's house. Their bubble.

The screen showed Ganymede's blasted surface, the brown rock and great transparent bubbles. Clusters of homes on sat in radiation-blocking domes on the surface, with underground paths connecting each of them. Larger tunnels, populated with carts that sent passengers back and forth, linked the neighborhoods to Ganymede's nexus, the giant factory and headquarters of Galaxy Forge.

"You can see the storm tonight," Puk said, watching the screen. Jupiter often dominated the sky, sometimes blotting out every inch of space. Tonight, the planet's eternal red storm churned right through their view. Viola shuddered. She'd had nightmares of being caught in that thing.

The door to the workshop beeped. Viola ran over and pressed the keypad's green button. The entrance shot open, sliding into the wall to show a goofy grin on the other side. The bearer of the smile was a slipshod mix of adolescent dreamer and grimed-up shift worker. Roddy split time as the family's personal mechanic and a Galaxy Forge grease monkey, often taking evenings at the house to put in whatever new toy Viola's dad brought home.

"Hey Viola, how's it going?" Roddy said. "You said you needed help?"

"Hey Roddy!" Viola wrapped her arms around the man for a quick hug, then stepped back. "Wanted you to test something for me. It's with Puk and, um, might hurt a little."

"Hurt a little?" Roddy said, coming into the room. The door slid shut behind him. Puk whirred out into the workshop, rotating so that the black circle camera focused on Roddy.

"He's a target," Viola said to Puk. "Go."

Roddy looked at Viola, eyebrows rising into the man's clay-red hat, part of the Galaxy Forge uniform. Puk didn't hesitate. The bot shot forward until, a meter away from Roddy, Puk let loose with a hot white laser. The beam hit Roddy on the forearm, causing the mechanic to jump back, curse, and rub at the spot. Puk darted forward after Roddy, shooting more of the stinging lasers. A lot of them.

"Puk!" Viola yelled. "Stop!"

The bot paused, rotating to look at Viola.

"He's not neutralized," Puk said. "I should keep shooting at him."

"What the hell, Viola?" Roddy said. He'd grabbed a piece of scrap metal and was holding it in front of him like a shield.

"Puk, go back to the cradle," Viola said, though excitement leaked into her voice. "Did you see that, Roddy?"

"I felt it, all right," Roddy grumbled.

"Yeah. Um. Sorry," Viola said, helping Roddy put the metal slat back on the ground. "I didn't think Puk would keep shooting, but it means the threat assessment program works. Are you okay?"

"I'll survive," Roddy took a breath, looked at Viola. His face was straight, tight. Roddy never liked being reminded of why Puk was getting a threat assessment program or why they'd been working at night to build the jets for the bot.

"Still not changing your mind?" Roddy asked.

"I can't, Roddy," Viola said. "If I don't get out of here now, I won't get another chance. After this semester, I'll have the degree, Dad will put me in Galaxy Forge, and I'll be stuck."

"It's not so bad," Roddy replied, continuing to rub his arms where Puk's lasers hit him. "You'd be good at it."

"I'd be trapped," Viola said, turning and walking over to a large console that dominated one side of the workshop. Viola turned it on, accessed the star chart program, and the console projected Jupiter and its surrounding moons into a swirling hologram in the center of the room. Viola pointed at a smaller, bluish one.

"Tomorrow will be a perfect launch day," Viola said. "How's the ship?"

"Good," Roddy said. "Your dad hasn't used it lately. Been too busy. But Viola, I don't think—"

"I know it's a lot to ask," Viola interrupted. "Dad will find out it was my idea. I'll leave a note."

"It's not me I'm worried about," Roddy said. "You don't know what it's like out there."

"Which is the point. We're not doing this again, Roddy. Please, just tell me you'll have it set tomorrow."

Roddy nodded. Viola could see a dozen arguments start and die in his eyes. There wasn't any time for them. Now that Puk's threat program worked, she had to boost the bot's laser so it could do more than sting. Then there was the packing. And the note to her parents.

"I'll make sure she's ready to go, Viola. For you," Roddy said, sighing.

"Thanks, Roddy," Viola gave the mechanic another hug as Roddy made his way out the door. As she moved back to the workbench, Viola flipped the console to the streaming headlines. News around the solar system popped up on the screen. Viola paid little attention, except this time almost every headline included the same quote. Viola waved her hand through one article to expand it.

"You cannot silence the Red Voice," said Alissa Reinhart in a mass-transmitted message today. The leader, previously presumed dead, continued to state that until the people of Mars have their rights restored, there would be no peace.

"Thankfully, Europa's a long way from you," Viola said to the picture of Reinhart. With another wave of her hand, Viola dismissed the image and went back to work.

The Escape

D o you understand the state Europa is in right now? It's barely civilized. There's no atmosphere. Stuck in a base where if one thing goes wrong, we'd lose you.

Viola heard the voices of her parents. That didn't stop her from approaching the bay where her father's private ship sat, waiting for Viola to take it. One by one, Viola debated down the arguments. Sure, Europa was full of profit-seeking prospectors. But so was Ganymede! It was just more refined here, after two decades of colonization.

No atmosphere? Ganymede's was still thin enough, siphoned away by Jupiter's gravity, that if you spent more than an hour outside you got lightheaded. Endurance competitions ran to see who could go the farthest without succumbing. Anywhere off of Earth was harsh.

"Are you sure?" Puk asked. "Cause you do this, it will not be pleasant when daddy finds out."

"Don't care," Viola said.

Puk made a beep, a low sarcastic noise. The little bot could hack the docking bay doors in under ten seconds, because Viola had spent days studying those locks, buying her own and dissecting them. She'd found a backdoor, and coded the keys into Puk's library. There were times Viola wanted to leave the house without her parents knowing. This time included.

A single panel sat on the right side of the door and glowed a dull red. Puk floated within five centimeters of it. These locks sent a radio frequency out and expected a specific response, her dad and Roddy wore badges that replied with the value and the door opened. Puk did the same thing, catching the signal, running it through Viola's backdoor, and sending the necessary response to flip the light green and open the lock.

The opening showed a dim wash of yellow lights silhouetting Viola's parent's ship. The *Gepard* was a 12 meter-long needle, meant to only hold a pilot and a passenger and sprint around nearby space. Her dad took it on joyrides, jaunting up and out of the atmosphere to "remind him where we came from." Viola had gone up in it a few times, seen the stars in their natural habitat.

"Is she ready?" Viola asked Puk, who'd zipped ahead and plugged himself into the ship's diagnosis panel.

"All fueled up and green," Puk replied. "Almost like we planned this."

"I'll owe Roddy so much," Viola said.

"What're you giving him again?" Puk asked.

"I'll find him some souvenir. A rock from Europa," Viola said.

A ladder up to the cockpit was three meters, and every rung landed heavy in Viola's chest. The *Gepard* could get her to Europa, barely. Its design required a large chunk of electricity to charge *Gepard*'s batteries. Small solar panels lined the sides of the ship, enough to keep life support running in an emergency, but not enough to get her anywhere once the main battery ran dry. Unless Viola found her bank account more flush than she'd left it an hour ago, there'd be no way to buy her way home.

Making Viola trapped. On her own on a frozen moon. Easy to argue against going. That things were safe, secure on Ganymede. But Viola could see her future if she stepped away from the ship. Could see the next hundred years of her life playing out, a boring biography. Complete the degree, take the job, work her way up and maybe, one day, run the company. Every year getting further and further away from the engineering she loved and placating it with toys like the *Gepard*.

And that might be okay. Might be fine. Only not now, not when there was still that voice telling her to take a chance. Viola pulled herself into the cockpit and disengaged the ladder.

When the ladder moved away from the *Gepard*, it ran over a pair of sensors in the floor. By doing so, the bay's departure system registered Viola's intent and turned on the rest of the lights. The gate, a thick block of smooth moon rock, ringed with glowing ruby dots warning her it was still shut.

Puk floated beside Viola, hovering above the passenger seat slotted behind the pilot chair. In front of Viola sat the flight stick, followed by a panel of buttons and levers controlling thrust, landing struts, and more. The *Gepard* had few autopilot features. The manual effort was part of the thrill. Viola had been here a thousand times in the family's simulator, feeling her way through a virtual trip. Now, though, when she started preflight and saw the dashboard come up green, the thrum was real.

The *Gepard* chimed when the checks came back positive. Viola flipped the next switch in the sequence, the weighted click bringing her one step farther from home. A countdown scrolled till the craft was ready to launch as energy transferred from the storage batteries to the thrust. The *Gepard*'s design, and most of the ships out away from Earth, leveraged electricity to combat the scarcity of rocket fuel. Carbon propulsion was left to Earth, where the gravity was too intense for large ships to jet away under electric power alone.

"Puk, open the launch doors," Viola said.

"The alarm will go off," Puk said.

"I know," Viola said. "They won't react in time."

"Sweetness. Let's get outta here,"

The doors behind the *Gepard* split open, revealing the huge, billowing monstrosity of Jupiter behind them. The swirling gasses and storms of the largest planet in the solar system blanketed the sky, leaving room for little else. Tonight, Ganymede had moved to the side of Jupiter, so that most of the sky was a bright series of swirling tans and oranges, while the other third was pitch dark, the part of Jupiter catching no sunlight and blocking any view of stars beyond.

"Good omen, leaving on a half-night?" Viola asked, pulling the handle that closed the cockpit in a transparent glass barrier.

"I'm a machine, I don't do omens," Puk said.

"You're no fun."

"Am I helping you run away in a space ship? I believe I am. Is that fun? I believe so," Puk shot back.

The engines beeped that they were ready to go. Viola triggered the hover jets and, two seconds later, the *Gepard* floated free. Ready for an escape. Viola reached for the flight stick to turn the ship around when she noticed someone walk into the bay.

"Roddy?" Viola asked as the young mechanic stepped into the bay, waving at her.

"You know, I don't hear that alarm," Puk said.

"He must have turned it off," Viola muttered. "Dad's going to kill him."

"Better be one heckuva souvenir you get him."

"It will be."

The *Gepard* rumbled to life. Viola eased the ship out of the launch bay and then angled it upwards into the Ganymede sky. A request for a destination came up from Ganymede's flight control, buzzing in over the *Gepard*'s comm unit.

Last chance to take this bad boy back, land it, crawl into bed and wake up to another nice breakfast, another day spent crunching math problems and watching movies. Viola looked up through the cockpit, at the glorious mass of Jupiter, and punched in Europa, Eden Prime.

"Roger that, *Gepard*. You're clear to launch. Safe travels," Flight control said.

"Let's hope so," Viola replied, and shot the ship up to the stars.

The Day Job

"You want to see a miracle? Just look out the window," Castor, Eden Prime's trumpeter-in-chief, said to the assembled crowd of big shots, buzzwords, and bullet points.

Davin followed their glances, out the covering dome of the cruise skiff and towards the swirling white storm that followed Eden Prime's terramorpher as it sifted Europa's surface and turned it into something usable. Despite the base's name, Europa sure as hell wasn't a paradise.

First a series of bubble cities, then an atmosphere to heat the ball of ice to a more livable temp. The bright pillar of light lancing to the surface near Eden Prime was an indicator of those efforts; a large solar mirror orbiting the moon and reflecting concentrated photons to the surface. Most of Eden Prime's power came from that thing, even if it meant never having a true night.

Davin let his hand drift up to the gun hanging over his shoulder, thick with two stacked barrels. Melody had enough kick in her to blow her way through any of these suits if they made a move. Not that Davin was planning to fire it, not while Eden's checks were clearing.

A pair of sidearms hung off Davin's belt, both set to a nerve-numbing level more suitable for people who didn't enjoy death in their new development headlines. The armament drew glances, but those eyes were more comforted than nervous. Davin was their paid protection.

Davin nodded across the skiff to Cadge, a ball of bearded muscle and partner on this joyride. Once a week Eden Prime paid them to 'escort' these show-offs around the terramorpher. A way for the settlement to sell property on Europa to prospective buyers, build up publicity, and bore the Wild Nines to death. But easy money was still money, and Davin figured catching the coin till it stopped raining was the right move.

"You know what's the best about this guy?" Called a burbling voice from the back of the crowd, like its owner had been working up the courage to talk and now was bull-rushing ahead.

Davin located the source, a tall, lanky man who sported the refined suit-and-tie look of the rest of the crowd . . . at first glance. The man moved into a litany of grievances, how Eden Prime was a scam, that they were being played, that Castor didn't want the colony to succeed at all.

Cadge made his way parallel to Davin, and the rough-and-tumble rogue beat Davin to the heckler. The rest of the crowd watched with an interest so mild that Davin felt his stomach curl. The accusations sounded crazy, yeah, but these people weren't phased in the least. Some leaned in as Cadge wrestled the man back from the group, eyes hunting, hoping for a fight.

"At least struggle, I could use some entertainment," Cadge said. Davin pulled the pair of stun cuffs they all carried on these assignments and slapped them on the heckler's wrists. The cuffs blocked the nerves from communicating with the brain, making it real hard to try and slip out.

"They're hurting me!" The heckler cried. "That's the kind of service you get with Eden!"

"Shut it," Davin said. "You say one more word, you'll wake up in a cell with one hell of a headache."

"Do it," Cadge said to the heckler, whose eyes were flipping between the two of them. "It's been too long since I've punched somebody."

Cadge's manic look quieted the man, and the heckler fell into a sulk. Castor drew back the attention with a cracked joke about how there were still crazies way out here. The crowd turned back to the word-smith with a chuckle and sips of their drinks.

"A bunch of softies," Cadge grumbled, keeping one hand on the heckler's shoulder. "Bet not one of them could throw a decent punch."

Cadge's voice was on the grittier side of a meat grinder. It flowed through thrice-broken jaws, out of lungs that'd played sport with most of the deadlier drugs this side of the asteroid belt, and carried with it the dead age of experience. Davin could listen to Cadge curse for days without being bored.

"You're complaining about that?" Davin replied.

"I'm worried my edge is gonna get soft," Cadge sighed. "It's been days, Davin. Days since I've knocked a man's teeth out and hauled his drunk self to the cell. I went to the range this morning, barely knew how to fire my gun."

After another fly-by, the skiff, a transparent bubble strapped to slow engines, docked back at Eden Prime. From the air, the city was a steel snake stretching through flowing shades of ice. The terramorpher grew a line out from the city, marking its path with patches of light green tundra moss, waiting for a stronger atmosphere. Used to be that process took decades. Europa, though, was the pioneer of the grand new machine.

Going by Castor's pitch, the terramorpher would have Europa warmed up and breathable within a few years. Invest in the city of Eden Prime, Castor said, and you'd be setting yourself up for quick returns.

As if you could call Eden Prime a city. The few thousand engineers and their support staff formed the backbone. The nigh-endless stream of crazies that thought a chance at a new planet meant the opportunity to strike it rich sprung out from that spine like random limbs searching for purpose. Most wouldn't find one until the atmosphere solidified, but getting in early on a new colony had the chance of a big payoff, if you didn't die of explosive decompression first.

The suits followed Castor off of the ship, a few thumbing messages into the comms buckled onto their wrists. The bay they'd docked at was covered with gleaming renditions of the glory coming to Europa. Tall, winding towers overlooking paradise. Melted frozen seas pushing against newly-made beaches. Green parks with children playing. All that soil coming from broken asteroid rock infused with nutrients by the terramorpher.

Davin was about to suggest a stopover at one of the few bars on Eden Prime. Get the standard home-brewed disaster they made from lab-grown hops way out here. Given the scarcity of customers, at least it was cheap. Then Davin's wrist vibrated.

"Yeah?" Davin answered the comm, a flexible black and white device that wrapped around his left forearm.

"Hey," Phyla's voice came over bright and clean. "You done out there? There's a message you should see. Important."

The Nines' primary pilot looked through the comm's small screen at Davin, her face set in that stock grimace Phyla used whenever there was something real to talk about. Soft lines pulling in strands of blazing hair, mingling with a spread of freckles earned in a surprise meeting with a solar flare. That lesson bled out into everything Phyla did. Maximize the planning, the preparation, and people don't get fried.

"Mind telling me, then?"

"People could be listening."

"You're being paranoid."

"Do you know me?" Phyla replied. "Just get here, fast."

"I can handle locking her up," Cadge said, referring to the skiff. "Get outta here."

Davin nodded and took off at a fast walk. Running, the Eden contract stated, was one thing that could incite panic. Don't do it. Part of ensuring a calm environment while they tore apart a moon. The Nine's office was right near the skiff launch bay, but Davin didn't bother checking in there. Phyla hadn't placed the call on one of the official comms. It'd come from their ship.

The Wild Nines

The *Whiskey Jumper* had bay three all to itself, a requirement of the Wild Nines' contract. A big box with engines at the aft and a bulge at the bow, left for a cockpit, Davin's ship was a cargo hauler tweaked over the years to be anything but. Four landing struts descended from the large central pod, along with a loading ramp.

Davin walked up that ramp, into a the main cargo bay, two stories high and just as wide. A built-in stair to the right of the ramp led up to the cockpit, while other circular doors and stairs led to the left, right, and rear pods. The inside of the ship was . . . colorful. A standing invitation to make an artistic mark on the inside over the years had covered the walls with paintings ranging from little more than graffiti signatures to rendered landscapes like the red valleys of Mars.

Every time Davin walked in here, history struck him like a hammer. He paused a second to look over the memories from crews long gone. One always caught his eye. A black outline of the *Whiskey Jumper*, lines bleeding everywhere on the metal walls, hovering against a blue and white ball. A cursory glance might assume the planet to be Neptune, but Davin knew it was Earth. Earth as drawn by the *Jumper*'s first captain as he flew the ship into space on its maiden journey. The ship had never been back.

"So what's the emergency?" Davin asked as he climbed into the cockpit.

Phyla leaned back in the co-pilot's chair, decked out in lounge clothes that said leaving the ship today was optional. Her face was glued to the console. Three monitors stuck to each other, the console was a stream of data. With touches and swipes of fingers, the displays could switch as needed. Phyla had the left one set to the comm display, tracking incoming and outgoing messages, the most recent recording front and center for Davin to play.

"Two high-profile visitors. Personal escort. Your favorite kind of job," Phyla said, sucking on a jolt stick.

Davin reached for the stick, Phyla handed it to him. Chemical cocktails wrapped around a sugary twig. Tasted dry and scratchy, but gave one helluva kick. Like eating a spasm.

"Where are they now?" Davin said after a few twitches.

"Landing. Going through the usual harassment," Phyla said.

Eden, the company behind Eden Prime, was hyper-vigilant about taxing any incoming cargo. Grabbing every spare coin they could. Eden Prime boarded and assessed every incoming ship, assigning a value to it. That value determined what level of attention people like Castor and his boss, Eden Prime's overall manager, Marl, paid to the vessel.

"Cadge is going to blow it," Davin said, sitting in the co-pilot's chair. "Just lose his mind one of these days and split someone in that crowd, or maybe Castor, open. Worst thing is that I'm starting to hope he does it."

"Feel like Eden would frown on that," Phyla asked, taking the jolt stick back.

"There are always more contracts," Davin said. "So why'd you have me come here? Escorts aren't a secret."

"They don't want Marl to know they're coming. Or anyone else on the base."

"Interesting. How are they getting around the search?"

Phyla rolled her eyes, a slow motion where Davin could track the pupil as it made its journey from one side of the blue eye to the other. She'd started doing that when they were kids, decades ago. Learned it from her father, Phyla mentioned once, saying it was a warning she was going to be sassy.

"You think I had a nice chat with them? They beamed the ask straight to us. Short-range, hard to intercept. All it said was to meet them and keep it quiet."

"Any idea who they are?"

"The ship is small. Eden-branded. Like, mothership Eden, not Prime."

"Parents wondering what their kid is up to?" Davin said.

"Maybe," Phyla replied. "Either way, for this much coin, does it matter?"

Phyla pulled up the message. At the end of the single sentence was a price. A good price.

"It does not," Davin said. "How much time do we have?"

The pilot flipped the console back to Eden Prime's air traffic. Pointed to an entry.

"Bay seven, scheduled to land in an hour," Phyla said.

That gave Davin enough time to shower off the Eden uniform and put on more comfortable clothes, a jacket with plenty of pockets, pants with plenty more. Boots flexible enough for running, strong enough to keep his feet from getting shot off. One glance at himself in the cabin's mirror, and off.

On the way out of the *Whiskey Jumper*, Davin grabbed Mox from the man's room. The crew cabins were tight affairs: a twin bed with a desk, complete with single-screen console. A locker built into the wall for clothes. Davin looked in and suppressed a flinch. Mox wasn't wearing a shirt, which meant the black metal frame of his exoskeleton was on full display. Like a spider attached to his back, the exoskeleton latched into Mox's limbs, a series of flexible joints and electric motors. Mox himself leaned over the shelf, browsing through something on the console.

"Get your gear on, we've got a special job," Davin said by way of announcing himself.

Mox twitched, looked at the captain. Before Mox swiped away the image on the console, Davin caught a glimpse. A news piece with a familiar title. Not the first time he'd seen Mox looking at that one. An attack on Luna, the main city on Earth's moon, years ago.

"Doing what?" Mox replied, his voice a lava flow, slow and thick.

"Escorting some VIPs. I think it's for Eden. You've got thirty minutes, and we're going hot."

"I'll be ready."

Davin turned to leave, then paused.

"I'm going to need you here," the captain said. "Not thinking about her."

Mox matched Davin's look. Didn't blink.

"I'll be fine," the metal man said. Davin left Mox with that. Davin couldn't stop Mox from crawling through his past. Problem was that Mox was doing it more and more these days. Wrapped up in things he couldn't change. At least this escort could be a distraction.

Opal was aft, near the engines. Davin found her working with Trina, tearing apart the housing on one of the four main thrusters designed to push ionized gas out behind the *Whiskey Jumper* when she made her escapes to orbit. The juxtaposition of the two, Opal, the strapped veteran, taking commands from Trina, the grease-ball mechanic caught in cords, tool belts and goggles made Davin laugh.

"It'll get us another one percent boost on initial acceleration," Trina was saying, with every word spoken as though it was an experiment, examined and displayed on its own. "Should reduce our escape time from this rock to be less than a minute."

"And how much did that cost?" Davin interrupted, disarming the comment with a grin.

"Oh, hey cap," Trina replied, turning her oil-smudged face back to Davin. "Not much. Bought it myself, off my pay. If it works, you can buy it off me."

"I hate it when you do that," Davin said.

"You're a bad liar, captain," Opal ran her words tight, a flow between the ends and beginnings. She held a bunch of screws that'd been keeping the thruster's access plate closed. "You ready for these yet?"

"Almost. Just have to reconnect the circuit," Trina said, turning back to the cluster of wires hanging off the engine's control panel. "Cap, you can't be too mad. Bet I got these for half the price you would have."

"Hey now," Davin said. "I'm not that bad, am I?"

Both of the women gave him deadpan looks.

"Shoulda seen her, captain," Opal said, setting the screws on Trina's wheeled work cart. "Here's this guy, sitting on a stock of these boosters thinking he'll sell them to Eden—"

"Only Eden doesn't use gas for their ships," Trina continued.

"They're all solar, electric now. So he's stuck here with this cargo that he can't sell. Thinks I don't know that and wants to charge me double what they're worth."

"Trina says, you want to eat tonight? I'll give you enough for dinner, and even a drink, cause I know you don't even have that much," Opal said, laughing.

Trina blushed, shrugged.

"Harsh," Davin said, shaking his head.

"The guy broke down. It was pathetic, really," Trina said. "But then I bought four to cheer him up."

"Four that I'm going to wind up paying for," Davin said. "Guess I can cut you some slack though, seeing as you keep the *Jumper* running so well."

"Thanks, cap," Trina replied.

"So what d'ya need, captain?" Opal asked. "Assuming you're not stopping back here just to chat."

"You and that rifle of yours," Davin said. "We've got an escort, and it's chancing to get unfriendly."

Inspectors

Pain. With each step, the scratch of a nerve. Bending fingers, the tug of a joint. Feeling something against his skin every moment of every day. There were many sleepless nights. Still were, years after the procedure. Hundreds of Earth days since Mox planted himself on the slab and growled at the doctors to do it.

To plant bolts inside his skin, to lace every limb of his body with an electric-powered frame. To graft the wires through his spine. They'd offered to hide it. Bury it beneath skin and along bone. An operation with months of recovery, multiple stages, more money Mox didn't have.

So Mox stood near the *Jumper*'s ramp and ran his hands along the meter-long pulse cannon. The weapon ran from the same batteries powering Mox's exoskeleton, batteries that patterned around his waist in a series of small, thin boxes. Batteries that Mox charged nightly, that would get him through two days of use if he had to run them dry. The cannon could discharge over twenty bolts per second, not as fast as projectile weapons, but fast enough. Mox would never lack enough again.

Davin and Opal walked in, bearing their own, smaller, arms. Davin with his shotgun, Melody, and sidearms holstered at his hip. Opal carrying a sniper rifle, its barrel as long as Mox's cannon, but with a thin scope attached. A lot of firepower for an escort job in this tiny base. Mox wasn't paid to understand. Only to shoot when ordered.

"Their ship's coming into bay seven," Davin said. "Let's get walking."

Down the ramp into bay three. They weren't unloading cargo, so Mox wasn't surprised to see the bay deserted. Big enough to hold a ship twice the *Jumper*'s size, Davin had negotiated for the solo space as part of the contract with Eden. The less people running around your ship, the fewer parts that went missing.

As it was, fuel pods, supply containers, and random junk cluttered the bay. If Eden Prime's dock master couldn't fill the bay with ships, he was going to use it for storage.

"Haven't seen you use that since Titan," Opal said to Mox, nodding at the cannon. "Careful you don't blow a hole in this place."

"Davin said heavy," Mox replied.

"I'm saying that for what they're paying, they're either paranoid or know something isn't right," Davin said.

"No Merc?" Mox asked when the *Jumper*'s ramp closed behind them. The stick jockey was usually part of their ground team, or flying cover in the Wild Nine's lone space fighter, a Viper.

"He was on overnight," Opal said. "Has it again tonight. I know I don't want him shooting when he's half asleep."

"Agreed," Mox said.

Stretching along behind the bays was a wide corridor meant for shuttling goods and people. Mox walked behind Opal and Davin, eyes scanning the back and forth movement of small skiffs, a seat or two and a flat bed.

Magnetic repulsion kept the skiffs afloat, signals activating magnets in front as the skiff passed over them and deactivating as it passed to keep from messing with people walking the halls. Of which there were always plenty; merchants, mechanics, and various service bots. Obstacles to be dodged. Or to be kicked out of the way.

The walk meant passing bays four and five, which were in-and-outs. Ships landed, dropped cargo, fueled, and left within a few hours. Skiffs lined up at the gates to deposit or receive cargo. Eden Prime was a taker, needing everything to keep itself alive.

Mox glanced at one skiff going by, its back end laden with crates colored for fruits and vegetables. Less of those lately. Gardens were online now, growing produce with water gathered from Europa's melting surface ice.

"Mako!" Davin called as the trio walked by bay six, one of a few privately owned bays on the small base. As Mox looked at the towering piles of parts, organized in a way he couldn't untangle, a helmeted head poked itself around a column of pipes and waved.

"Davin?" Mako replied, stepping around the column and extending his scrawny, pale hand for a shake. "What're you doing this deep?" Mako took them in, lifted the goggles from his eyes and whistled. "And ready for action."

"A job," Davin said, then waved his arms. "Your place is messier than usual."

Mako turned and gestured at a ship behind the junk piles. A cargo hauler from a generation before the *Jumper*, the hulking series of spheres was being dismantled by a horde of small robots, scratching and tearing at various pieces and hauling the scraps to different piles.

"You see that?" Mako said, squinting at Davin. "Business is good. You ever see this place clean, you'll know I'm done. What job?"

"You're going to have a neighbor," Davin said.

"Five? You know that's an in-and-out."

"Seven," Mox announced. "And soon."

"Seven?" Mako said. "Rare day that seven gets filled. Only Eden corporate, or big shots."

"Any idea who might be coming in?" Davin asked.

Mako shrugged, looking like a puppet on strings, given how light the man was. Mox felt a tug on his frame and glanced. One of the salvage bots, poking at his leg. Mox kicked it away. Mako's eyes followed the stumbling droid, tracking back to Mox, and then looking away. Mox saw the man gulp. Fear. Mox supposed that was the intended reaction.

"Maybe if you kept your ears out of that junk pile," Opal said. "You'd catch wind of things."

"All I know is what comes in pieces," Mako said. "And the parts are selling fast. Most of it to our fearless leader, Marl."

"What's she want?" Davin asked.

"No idea. Don't care," Mako said. "I mean, should I . . . ?"

Davin sighed, pressed a few keys on his comm. Mako's own unit beeped and the junk vendor looked at it with a wide grin.

"It's energy stuff, and shelter gear," Mako said. "Like she's planning on expanding, but not with Eden's help. A new group of people."

Davin glanced at Mox and Opal, but neither one had any ideas. Eden, the super-massive company that was investing in the base, had plenty of coin and supplies to expand Eden Prime as much as they wanted. Marl, the base's director, shouldn't have to go scrap hunting.

"Seeing as I just paid you for that crap," Davin said. "You give us a heads up if it looks like something strange is heading towards bay seven."

"Like you three?" Mako laughed. None of them joined him. "Sure, yeah. You see one of my scrap bots roll by, expect company."

Then Mako went to a pile of small lift jets and dove in, digging. Conversation over. Davin walked out and Opal followed. Mox took one look back at the busy bay, bots building piles of scrap to sell. Tried to picture himself doing that job, sorting through junk for anything good. Couldn't. Mox tested the grips on the cannon as he stepped back into the hallway, firm and ready. His weapon far from belonging in those heaps.

The gate into bay seven was unlocked. Mox glanced to the left, at the blank stretch of blue-tinted wall across from the gate. In there, somewhere, was a camera. More in the halls. Anyone thinking to get fast-fingered with someone else's stuff would be filmed, found, and flung off the moon. Davin held up his comm to the scanner alongside the door which beeped an affirmative.

Bay seven appeared as the gate slid open, vast and empty. No crates, no power cells. As the trio stepped into the bay, Mox felt his neck itch. The walls shifted, slid in his vision. He'd been here before, or somewhere like it.

Mox knew what was about to happen. Past memories too strong to let die. Knew it, and could not stop it.

Strongman's Start

A blink.

The green lunar surface, a verdant product of terramorphing weaving between spiraling glass towers. Low gravity making it easier to arc buildings overhead, or to build off-shoots, architecture as fantastic art. Mox moved through a wide courtyard, smoothed moon rock broken up by those patches of mossy grass. Security's crimson colors enveloped him, a cape hanging off his shoulders.

The first explosion came many meters over Mox's head. It tore through the centerpiece of an arching office, sending ripples of shattering glass across the lunar sky.

Mox tried to press forward, towards the explosions. Workers, business people were going the other way, running and jumping through the low gravity in a rolling surge of panic. As he came closer, Mox saw ruin. The shattered building's foundation leaned, while people scrambled out.

Overhead, the arch split, breaking this half of the building free from its counterpart. The curved tower listed further. Mox waved people away, pointing back towards the courtyard. Countless faces blurred passed as Mox's comm called out with questions, orders, warnings.

Then the floors started falling. Support beams tearing apart, anchors ripping up the lunar surface as the leaning weight proved too much. A woman tottered out of the building as it collapsed, bleeding from her head. She looked dazed, then fell to one knee. Mox ran towards her, pushing against the crowd.

They parted for the red uniform, worth respecting even in crazed flight. Mox picked her up, the woman turning to look at him, her face marred with a hundred tiny scratches from the glass window that'd blown out in front of her. In her eyes, Mox saw the building above them, falling. The woman's mouth opened.

"Yo, Mox, you with us buddy?" she said.

A blink.

Bay seven sat in front of him, no fire. No woman. Just Davin, waving his hand back and forth in front of Mox's eyes.

"We're not there. You're not there," Davin said.

"I know," Mox growled, but the edges of his vision played out the attack, flames still curling, glass still falling. "It feels similar. Open, calm."

"Tell me about it," Davin said, looking around the bay.

"You weren't there."

"Doesn't mean I don't understand."

Mox didn't reply. No point in arguing.

Mox looked and found Opal, set up in the near-right corner. Rifle up and out, supported by shipping crates. Davin leaned against the door. Mox stayed where he was. Dead center, cannon primed. Mox felt the captain's eyes on his back.

"What?" Mox asked.

"Who was it? The woman you say you're seeing?" Davin said.

"I knew her," Mox replied.

"That's it?"

Mox didn't turn to look at the captain, just stared straight ahead at the bay's opening. Resisted falling through he hole again.

"I don't talk about her," Mox said after a few seconds.

"Doesn't mean I can't ask," Davin replied.

"Why?"

"Cause I got a guy wearing a machine running around my ship, think I owe it to the crew to know if you'll ever lose it."

"It won't happen again."

"Feel like I've heard that before."

"It won't happen again," Mox repeated, more to himself than Davin.

Mox raised his arms, showing off the exoskeleton. The cannon, when Mox let go, pulled forward on his torso. The frame tugged back, its batteries pushing energy to keep the big weapon level. Mox felt it, the tight yank on his muscles, the red bloom of pain as bolts in his shoulders tensed. His face tried to move, eyes tried to narrow, but Mox resisted. Showing weakness wasn't a choice. Was not his role.

"This is enough," Mox continued.

"I won't push you," Davin said. "Just don't go day-dreaming if this goes sideways."

"I'll be fine," Mox said.

Bay seven's alarms wailed. Incoming ship. A light blue film covered the big, gray bay doors. A magnetic field, preventing the oxygen and atmosphere in the base from leaking out.

The gray doors opened with a loud chunk, then slid along rails greased to perfection by the endless attention of bots. Europa's dark, bruised sky shown through the doors, a thin wash of blue sheer silk over the endless outer black. At the edge of the opening, a hint of bright lurked, the edge of the solar beam. Jupiter was on the other horizon tonight.

The ship flew into view, floating like a ghost. Electric engines, so quiet and without the burn, the pulse of cruder methods. Mox looked at the sleek oval craft, its matte exterior the color of deep jungle. No logo, any company sign. It was too small to hold cargo. Five, maybe six passengers for any lengthy journey.

The ramp extended slow, like a person's tongue tasting a hot drink. As though trying not to hurt itself. Small yellow lights blinked along the slope to the bay floor.

The first feet appeared at the top of the ramp, followed by the stamp of a cane. A weathered, white-haired man and a kind-faced woman following after. Then nobody. The two of them made their way down the ramp, their eyes casting around the bay. At least, Mox noticed, the man's eyes. The woman's gaze went to Davin, to Opal in the corner, and then back to Mox.

"I will say, the guards here do have flare," the woman said, holding a hand towards Mox. "I'm Clare, this is Ward. We're here because Eden thinks this base may no longer be in its control."

Seen through the Scope

The two of them were easy targets. Their clothes were thin, no armor. Every step methodical, easy to predict. Opal felt the ice forming in her veins. Security wasn't hired if there wasn't risk. If things went wrong, the Nines would have to fire first. The woman talked to Mox and Davin, out of earshot. Davin was making his characteristic shrugs, and Opal pressed her lips together to keep from yelling at them to stay low.

Davin didn't have the experience. He'd found Opal on Miner Prime, that space station sitting between Mars and Jupiter, in the heart of the asteroid belt. Not that those were great times for Opal, not that she could afford to say no, but Davin telling her with that smug grin he was moving from cargo into the protection business told Opal all she needed to know. Davin hadn't ever laid in the red mud on Mars, watched the enemy for hours, waiting for the perfect moment.

Opal had gone to Miner Prime to avoid those situations, to stay out of the sights of someone else's rifle. But here she was, staring through a scope. Finger near a trigger that Opal knew, knew she'd be pulling before the day was out.

Except, not here, because Davin was waving at her to get moving. Opal stood up, pressing a button on the side of the rifle's stock that changed the magnetism holding the various parts together. The weapon collapsed into a small cluster, connected through one strand of flexible metal that ran through all of them. Made the weapon easy to carry, easy to hide.

"We were telling your colleagues we're expecting a ship," the woman said. "It should land in a few minutes, I believe in bay five. We'll want your help to search it."

"For what?" Opal said.

"Evidence that Marl's got more going on than building Eden Prime's business," Davin said.

"She'd have too much to lose," Opal said."Eden Prime's growing. Why risk it?"

The woman, Clare, gave Opal a small smile, and sighed. Opal knew that stance, seen it plenty of times in the military. Meant Opal was missing something obvious.

"Eden has too much invested in Eden Prime," Ward said, his voice a high whistle."We're here to see whether Marl shares that sentiment,"

"Love me a good tale of corporate intrigue," Davin said. "But why don't we get you two where you need to go, so you can leave before someone shoots you and costs me a contract."

"The man has a point," Clare said, putting her hand on Ward's shoulder and giving him a gentle push forward.

This time as they walked into the hall, it was Mox in front and Opal at the rear. The big man covered a large part of the hallway, enough for Clare and Ward to stay behind him. A glance down the long corridor showed only a few skiffs being cleared out by two workers. No crowds. No bustling bots. It wasn't late enough for Eden Prime to be slowing down.

"Ready up," Opal said, pulling her sidearm, a better choice in the tight confines of the corridor, from her waist holster. "It's too quiet."

"Phyla, can you get me any info on why the bays have gone ghost town? I've got a pair of—" Davin spoke into his comm, glancing at Clare and Ward. "Pets here that I'd rather not lose if it's going to get dicey."

"Pets?" Clare asked, turning back to Opal.

"People might be listening," Opal replied.

"I'm digging, but there's no news. No alerts," Phyla's voice came over the comm.

"Love it when bad situations get worse," Davin said. "Let's keep going. Get to the *Jumper* and we can re-assess."

"No," Clare said. "Bay five. Now."

"Lucky for you, we'll go past it on the way," Davin said. "You look carefully, you might get a peek."

They resumed walking forward, Opal hanging farther and farther back.

Ambushes were harder when the targets weren't close together. Think, Opal. Tactics. Here in this base, the atmosphere still thin, explosions were a dangerous game. Ripping a hole would cause the bays to de-pressurize. Cause the breathable air to escape. No trade, no cash flow, for days until Marl could repair the hole. That meant small arms. Direct fire.

Opal could see the corridor, all its polished, empty expanse. Someone would have to run down the hallway to attack, giving the Nines plenty of time to react. Unless the attackers were already in one of the bays.

"Mox, go ahead," Opal said. "I'll cover the hall, you check the bays as we get to each one."

Mox nodded and, with his heavy jog, went forward to bay six. As the metal man approached the gate to the bay, the wide double-doors, Mox gripped the cannon and sidestepped in front. The cannon's business-end pointed through into bay six, and Opal waited for Mox to fire away. Wanted it to happen. When the action started, Opal knew she'd be fine. Now it was ice and nerves.

"Clear?" Davin asked, standing between Mox and their charges.

"Looks normal," Mox said. "Mako's there. Still working."

"Can we trust him?" Opal asked.

The answer to that was always no. Never trust. What if Marl found Mako's button? Some new ship to tear apart, maybe, or a shop on the main boulevard through the base? Something tempting enough for Mako to sell them out.

"He's safe," Davin said. "Don't worry."

Opal shook her head. Stop it. This wasn't Mars. This wasn't the Red Voice.

They passed by Mako's bay, heading towards the gate to bay five. Nobody talked, and Opal didn't change that. Aside from the omnipresent hum of Eden Prime's inner workings, the only sound was the tap, tap, tap of Ward's cane on the ground.

Mox hit the gate first, glancing around the side, then stepping in front of the doors. Davin moved to join Mox, holding up a palm to Opal. No rifle needed. At least, not yet. Clare and Ward gathered behind the two of them while Opal kept her eyes going back and forth down the corridor.

"Open the gate," Clare said.

"What's on that ship?" Davin asked.

"That's what we're here to find out."

Opal couldn't tell. What ship? What was beyond the gate? Davin swiped his badge, and the doors slid open. They walked in and Opal followed, keeping distance. Finally, she turned around the edge of the door and saw a ship that hadn't been there earlier. Bigger than Clare's, but still small for a cargo hauler, this one had the sleek look of a courier craft. Speed and luxury, meant to crate people and their luggage, or a prime piece of product, from one planet to another with minimal delay.

The faint odor of ionized gas, the slight sting to the nose, wafted Opal's way as she walked into the bay. A clear indicator the engines only recently turned off.

"They're still on board," Opal said.

Mox and Davin glanced at her and nodded. They already knew that, but Opal had no such guarantee about Clare and Ward. Unlike bay seven, five stayed busy and the usual necessities littered the area. Fuel cells, a skiff for loading heavier stuff, crates for cargo. Plenty of things to hide behind.

"You two might want to take cover," Davin said, sharing Opal's sentiment. "Or am I getting the wrong vibe here? That this ship isn't friendly?"

"Depends on Marl," Clare said, Ward nodded. They stood loose, calm. If they thought this might be a trap, why weren't they treating it like one?

"Let's play it safe then," Davin said. "How about you go over there?"

Davin pointed to a stack of crates near the bay's corner. Clare and Ward didn't argue and took cover. Opal went to the opposite side of the two, near a pile of fuel cells. Slid her finger along the barrel of the rifle, tapping a button that sent out a magnetic charge, snapping all the pieces into place.

Opal leaned forward, bracing her elbows on the top of one cell, and looked through her scope. Mox put himself dead center, a massive target that could dish back everything and more. Davin took a spot near Clare and Ward, standing between them and the gate.

The waiting was always the hardest part. A sniper, Opal sat for hours, each breath a careful in and out to keep her aim from moving. Ready to fire at any moment. The tension growing with each second until, like a frog being boiled, something moved and the stillness shattered with cacophonous destruction.

The ship made a noise. A grinding sound. Systems powering up. With a sudden jerk, a rectangle two meters tall shifted open in the bottom of the ship. A ramp, thinner and meant for people. And a foot was the first thing that appeared. Booted.

Joined by the second foot a moment later, they descended. Opal saw calves, thighs, no holster on the waist. A snap back up the stairs through the scope, but there wasn't another.

"Stop," Mox announced as the person reached the bottom steps. "Move and die."

The person stood still, hands resting near the sidearm on his waist. He was wearing an older, mismatched uniform. Like someone who'd raided a company's dirty laundry chute. Opal didn't recognize the faded brands, but the style of uniform was familiar. The sloppy getup contrasted with the easy grin on the man's face, the relaxed muscles. The guy stared death in the face and grinned. Opal tightened her finger on the rifle's trigger. No fear made someone dangerous.

"So, is that the usual way you greet people on Eden Prime?" the spacer said. "Cause that's not very polite."

"Sorry," Mox said.

"I didn't ask for an apology, but thanks. Now, I've got work to do, so if you wouldn't mind?"

"What type of work?" Clare asked, stepping out from her cover and moving next to Davin.

"Well, that's just the thing. It's work that doesn't need spectators. Or people asking questions. Why'd you say you were in this bay, again?"

The man's hand twitched, his smile grew a centimeter. A tell. The spacer faced overwhelming odds, but he would draw the minute Clare answered his question. Opal pressed on the trigger when a shot flashed. Lasers were always soundless, except for the screams they extracted from a hit. The spacer fell back, down, smoke rising from his chest. Opal looked up from the scope and saw Clare holding Davin's sidearm, pointing it at the spacer.

"Whoa! Hey!" Davin yelled, yanking his gun back from Clare. "That was a nice conversation."

"You see those clothes?" Clare said. "That's the proof we needed. And now we have to run."

"Proof of what?" Davin asked, but Clare was pulling him along towards the gate.

Ward, the man Opal had last seen plodding with a cane, had picked it up and was holding it like a weapon, aiming the point around like it was going to spit lasers. Which, Opal realized, it might. As Clare made it to the gate, Mox back-pedaling to join them, she paused. Opal expected the doors to open. As they should. But they stayed shut. Trapped.

"Phyla, we need the gate to bay five open," Opal said into the comm on the left wrist.

"On it," Phyla said. As the hired security for the base, they had the codes for the doors. Should've taken only a couple seconds, but those seconds passed and the door stayed closed.

The ship rattled suddenly, its ramp retracting. The engines spooled up. Opal shifted the scope, looked at the contours of the small ship. Deep in those recesses were nozzles, barrels ready to fire. In tight quarters, the ship could fry all of them in seconds.

"Mox! That ship has weapons!" Opal said.

"Phyla, we need this door open!" Davin said into his comm. Clare and Ward shifted away from the captain, towards the crates. The only chance they had was—

Mox's cannon ripped a hole in the world, the slap-screech of the rotating barrels heating and spitting bolts, dozens of them, echoing around the metal walls of the bay. The white lines struck the ship which was now a meter off the ground, and burrowed deep into the hull. Black marks riddled the front as Mox arced the cannon towards the various divots, which were opening as the ship brought its weapons on line.

Opal, looking through her scope, lined up on an opening where a small gray nozzle was shifting forward, and fired. The rifle sent a blue bolt, not as hot as Mox's shots, that struck the nozzle and blew it off in a shower of sparks.

The cannon was doing its job. At this range, and without the ship having time to charge a shield, the front of the craft disintegrated under Mox's waves of energy. A key shot blew apart a piece of armor plating covering the cockpit. Thick glass still sat there, used as a view-port when the ship wasn't being attacked.

Opal could make out someone moving back and forth, arms pressing at buttons. She centered the scope on the figure. One good shot and this was over.

And Ward took it. That cane of his blasting a long, slow wave of red-orange that arced onto the glass of the cockpit and ate its way through it. A plasma sprayer. Opal hadn't seen one of those in years. Old-fashioned, slow, but effective. The ship shuddered under the assault, its jets popping off and on as power cables melted and rerouted.

Mox's cannon paused, overheated and needing to cool itself for the next salvo. Behind the melting plasma, the shape still moved in the cockpit. Crazy to stay there. The plasma would melt through at any moment, destroy the console. But Opal raised her scope, lined up the shape, saw the person raise its arms. Surrender? Opal's finger stayed on the trigger.

Then the person pulled something at the cockpit's top. The repulsor jets burst, swinging the ship around so the engines pointed back at the gate, right at Mox, Davin, Clare and Ward. Opal felt the panic, the certainty of what was going to happen next and the complete inability to do anything about it. Opal saw the telltale lighting, the glow of a primed blast. She dropped the rifle, turned towards the others, to warn them.

Mox was already moving. Even with the cannon, that exoskeleton pushed the man when he wanted to go. Mox jumped, grabbed Davin, and shoved them both to the ground as the ship's engines roared to life.

The light wasn't blinding so much as obliterating. Even through her closed lids, her hand covering, Opal's world went pearl. She fell to the ground, her back so hot, Opal thought she'd caught fire. And then the heat receded, the roar pulled away and Opal uncovered her eyes. Her ears rang, the concussive echoes of a full engine ramp-up in the small bay.

The ground, walls, and containers bore black scoring, some still glowing orange where the direct blast of the engines had struck.

Mox shifted off of Davin, looking at the ceiling, dazed. Opal stumbled her way over to them, looking around but not seeing Clare, Ward. A moment later her heart dropped, fell into that familiar bath of numbness. A pair of charred lumps, flames licking at the clothing, sat near the gate.

Ward's cane, burst and leaking plasma in an instant-cooling puddle, sat next to them. Even if they'd survived the engines, the burst plasma would've immolated them both.

A buzzing sounded in Opal's ears and she glanced behind her to see Davin on his feet, yelling something into his comm. There was nothing they could do for these two, except vengeance. Recoup honor from the contract. Opal went back for her rifle, hot but undamaged.

The gate opened. Phyla's hacks got through. A few bots scurried in and began cleaning up the mess. The deep dark of Europa's night still bled in from outside, the magnetic shield keeping the burnt air close.

Fighter Pilot

Merc was grabbing a mid-nap snack when Phyla's tight voice came on over the intercom, yelling for him to get to the fighter. He dropped the energy bar, whose packaging screamed it had literally every vitamin in existence inside, and scrambled out of the kitchen, down the short hallway, slid over the ladder into the central loading dock and then bounced right for the small fighter bay.

"Got any more info?" Merc commed as he went.

"Davin, Mox, and Opal were on an escort. Things went sideways and the cause is running away. Davin's saying they disarmed it. Wants you to bring it in, gently."

"Davin always wants it gentle."

"Scrap's worth more than ash, Merc."

The Viper Two-Twenty-One was a stupid name for a super cool ship. This baby had aerodynamics that guaranteed a rockstar performance in zero G or more. Merc had the preset for Europa's atmosphere dialed in, the preflight check flipping greens in less than five seconds. The Viper flew electric, a killer advantage when you needed maximum thrust immediately. A disaster for long trips, but Merc didn't fly it without the *Jumper* nearby. He coaxed the craft out of the *Jumper* and towards the opening big bay exit.

"Twenty," Merc said.

The Viper processed the command and spit forward, sliding out of the bay and through the magnetic shield. Going by official time, always Earth standard, it was late afternoon. Below, the ice-tinged moss of the ground around Eden Prime looked caught in a morning fog, bits of blue and white clinging to the foliage, like frozen broccoli.

Beyond the terramorpher's edge, pure blues twinkled. Behind Merc, light streamed from the solar array, Europa's new and always-present sun, a beacon alongside Jupiter's constant presence. Merc hadn't seen a true night in five years, not since he'd left Earth.

The Viper picked out the battered ship, its engines glowing white in the relative dark as it climbed in altitude. Outside the cockpit windows, Merc could only see the ship as a bright ball of light streaking upwards, but the Viper's scanners, as Merc dialed them in, modeled the craft, including broken edges and burned holes from Mox's cannon. Much farther out, and the Viper's interpretation would look like it was getting drunk, and then, further away, a big ol' circle stating hey, there's a ship here.

"Phyla, they're making a break for space," Merc said, angling his intercept vector. "But, you ask me, that ship's not capable of holding atmosphere for long."

"Don't make space do your dirty work, Merc."

"Never crossed my mind," Merc said, releasing the comm. "Fifty."

The acceleration pushed Merc back in his seat, a familiar grin crawling up his face. Speed, man. That was the stuff. Looking through the cockpit, the HUD displayed a few dots and meters where Merc could catch them. On the right, the Viper's energy. The left had its throttle. The middle held a deep blue circle around where the escaping ship sat in the atmosphere. It had a head start, but the ship didn't have speed. Merc figured two minutes till firing range.

Merc's left hand released his double grip on the flight stick and eased towards the left panel where a series of buttons sat with stickers over them. Trina's work. The mechanic messed with the Viper when the *Jumper* didn't need her, adding weapons and toys so every time Merc flew the fighter there was something new waiting for him. He found the toggle on the far left. He pressed the switch forward and felt the slight click. The noise, like coins falling into place, echoed through the cockpit.

The Viper had lasers, and they were devastating if you were sure your target had no shields. Or any reflective plating left to bounce your molten bolts off into space or, worse, right back at you. Slugs, those weren't so easy to toss away. They would chew through the ship like toothpicks through cheese. Make it impossible for the craft to leave the planet.

"Hey, sitting ducks!" Merc announced through the short-range comm to the ship. "Flag yourself for surrender and I won't fill you full of holes."

"You think I don't know you'll do that anyway?" The reply came, the voice strained, high-pitched.

"Dunno what you're talking about, man. Except that you keep heading to the stars, you're going to do it as a fireball here in a sec."

"There weren't supposed to be extra people there, in the bay," the man said. "It should have been simple. We'd already be gone by now."

"Say again, ship? And cut your engines," Merc replied. "You getting this, Phyla?"

"Hearing it, don't understand it," Phyla replied through their secure channel. "Hey! Heads up. *Jumper*'s picking up a new player in your game."

A moment later the Viper's own sensors beeped. New craft, coming from orbit. Hot. Far enough out that the scanners showed a plain circle, but it was going fast. Another few seconds and there'd be a picture.

"Shields maximum," Merc said, the voice toggles mimicking hard switches, but he didn't want to take his hand off the stick right now. Slotting the energy to the shields meant losing some of the Viper's potential thrust, but it wasn't like Merc needed it to keep up with the slow-burn wreck of the enemy.

"Ship, you got a new bogey coming in fast. Suggest you tell me what it is, you got any info," Merc commed to the enemy ship. "Then suggest you turn around, high-tail it back to base all nice and easy."

"Stick jockey, threatening a man whose already dead won't get you very far," the guy on the ship replied, before breaking off in sad laughter.

The ship started swinging left, turning away from the inbound craft, but it wasn't moving nearly fast enough. Merc saw the new ship adjust its line to match. At the speed it was going, the new ship was going to overtake in ten, fifteen seconds.

"Ten percent," Merc said, cutting the throttle. No sense getting between the new guy and the old one. Especially when he didn't know what the new one was going to do.

The Viper beeped twice. Deep tones. Missiles launched, but not at Merc.

"Ship, you got a pair of bugs incoming," Merc said.

"They weren't supposed to be there, man," the guy said. "Supposed to be in and out. Can't say we didn't do the job though. Can't say that."

The missiles, their bright ends just visible like a pair of fast-moving stars, lanced through the air in front of Merc and struck the ship. The explosion started small, then crackled into an enormous cloud of fire and arcing electricity. Electric engines would blow big, but that was something more.

"Phyla, there was a bomb on board that ship. Or something that goes up real nice," Merc said, watching the fireball collapse on itself, shards of wreckage plummeting like meteors towards Europa's surface.

"Just get back here," Phyla said.

"What, don't want me playing tag with that new ship?"

Speaking of, the attacking vessel was adjusting course towards Merc, but also towards Eden Prime behind him. Merc pushed the flight stick forward, tilting the nose of the Viper straight. At its velocity, the other ship couldn't twist sharp enough to get a clean shot. Even in Europa's thin, developing atmosphere, the air resistance would rip the craft apart. Once Merc sped underneath the other ship, he could turn around and, if he needed to, light up their rear with all kinds of goodies.

"Hello there!" Crackled Merc's short-range radio. "Just calling to confirm we've got no designs on you, mate!"

Sure they didn't. Merc wasn't going to put himself in their trusting hands anyway.

"Why'd you toast that guy?" Merc replied into the radio, keeping his comm open.

"Put him out of his misery," the voice on the other end fell flat, a player tired of the game. "He was a dead man. Not that it matters for you."

"Kind of you to tell me that," Merc said.

The larger ship blew by overhead, continuing to head for Eden Prime. Merc detected no missile locks, no warning shots. Apparently they were one-and-done killers.

"What do you want me to do, Phyla?" Merc said. "We're supposed to be providing security, and they just wiped a guy on our turf."

"Come back home, Merc. Till we know what's going on here, I don't want you out."

Merc almost complained, wanted to protest. Maybe take the Viper after that new ship. But instead he plugged in the docking routine, curled through the sky and went back to base.

Contract Disputes

The headquarters of Eden Prime sat a ten-minute walk from the bays. That walk went along a wide, open space everyone called the Boulevard. Like a cylinder sliced in half, the curved roof collected solar energy and gave a stellar view of Jupiter and the surrounding stars. Stores bought space along the sides, building bubble shapes from the outer wall.

Marl's government building wasn't any different, except in design. Made from blue swoops, with not a straight edge in sight, the building evoked the waves in Europa's soon-to-be-thawed oceans. At least, that's what Marl said.

The front doors, tempered glass inlaid with swirling drawings of fish, currents, and kelp, opened as Davin approached. Business hours were over for the day, but Davin pushed through the door anyway. Marl had to know what'd just happened in bay five, had to know about the ambushed execution of the ship Mox had shot to pieces.

No ship could land at Eden Prime without permission from flight control. The Wild Nines were the de facto police for this place, and nobody bothered to let them know a suspicious vessel with a bomb was coming. Nor that there was another ship entering the atmosphere loaded with heavy weapons.

"Bay seven's locked," Opal's voice came over the comm. "Can't get in. There's some weird people there though. Looks like they're trying to get in Clare's ship. Don't recognize their uniforms."

"It's fine. Don't push it," Davin replied.

No getting back to the inspector's ship for any hints. Just another twist in this great day.

Davin stood in the lobby of the Eden Prime building, glancing at the twin stairs curling up around either side of the entrance hall. They both led to the same second-floor landing, a balcony that gave you an eye-level view of a dangling chandelier. The lights in that fixture cut sharp, long and thin, like the frozen shards decorating the wasteland beyond the terramorpher's mouth. Lit, as it was now, the chandelier cast a pure white light around the interior. Eden Prime, it said, was beautiful. Was open for real business, real class. How long that impression would keep with a pair of people burned alive in a docking bay, Davin wasn't sure.

He took the left stairs, walking up the steps to the landing. Short hallways on either side ended in doors. During the day, the first floor held the business application work, the tour groups full of prospective investors. The doors up here were labeled 'Eden Prime Staff Only'. Davin tried one. Not locked. The only light on the other side coming from windows, Jupiter's reflection. Empty cubicles guided Davin towards Marl's office.

He itched for Melody, but the only thing he had was a sidearm. The same one Clare had used to blast that guy an hour ago. Davin kept a hand on it. Marl's office was walled off with a darker blue than the rest. As big by itself as the rest of the cubicles.

The door to Marl's office was the first one that, when Davin pressed on it to open, stayed shut. The badge scanner on the right beeped a low tone when Davin swiped his card. No dice. Suddenly Davin, without knowing why, hammered his fist on Marl's door. Pounded it once, twice, three times. The metal didn't bend, didn't even give a satisfying thwack. Instead it took the punishment and sat there, solid.

Davin didn't know Clare or Ward, didn't know what they were looking for, or why they'd requested the Wild Nines give them a shot at getting out alive, but they had, and Davin had failed. But he hadn't failed alone. The killers had help.

"Davin Masters," said Marl's voice, a calm, dead weight, over the office comm. "Isn't it past your shift?"

"Everybody's working late," Davin replied, his eyes scanning up and around the door, looking for the camera and not finding it.

"You know me, I live for the job," Marl said. "What can I do for you?"

"Open this door for starters."

"Are you going to shoot me if I do?"

"Depends," Davin said.

The lock next to the door flashed green and the metal barrier slid right and opened. Davin stepped through into Marl's office, a set of chairs, a desk, and an endless view out onto Europa's surface. Standing off to the side, gun drawn, was Castor, the PR man and Marl's unofficial bodyguard.

"Castor," Davin said as he stepped into the room. "Always a pleasure."

"Davin," Castor said, his voice a straight level tone that avoided any inflection. Whether Castor was getting ready to murder him or wish him a happy early birthday, Davin couldn't tell.

"Who were those two that hired you?" Marl asked. "I'd like to know whose ashes my crews are sweeping away."

"I was hoping you could tell me," Davin said. "We didn't get much time to talk."

"I wonder whose fault that is?"

Davin knew it was bait. Knew it. Marl trying to get him angry, to say something stupid. Davin had seen her do this to a dozen people before, manipulate their emotions with a carefully placed sentence or three and then come away with coin or blackmail while the other person struggled to hold on to their dignity.

"Why was bay five sealed, Marl? Why couldn't we get out?" Davin said, walking closer to the desk, his voice rising as he spoke. "Why was that ship allowed to land?"

Davin took another step, was between the chairs now, when he felt Castor touch his arm. Davin shook the bodyguard off, but stopped his forward march. Marl half-turned back from the view, looked right at Davin, her eyes flashing fire in the dim light. Davin couldn't deny that Marl looked powerful, her chin lofted so her eyes stared down at him. Decked out in official Eden uniforms, but, unlike the drab green worn by the grunts, Marl had dresses and suits that fit. Not a spare wrinkle, a sleeve too long. Their green shades were deeper emeralds, matching the flora growing now on Europa.

In this light, Marl was a black silhoulette as she stood over her desk.

"Doors malfunction all the time," Marl said. "I'll look into why the ship landed. It's possible they lied, hid their weapons from our scanners."

"So you know nothing," Davin said.

"I'm sorry,"

"You're not,"

"No, but then, I shouldn't be. You and your team failed to tell me an escort hired you. Failed to tell me why those two were here. Failed to keep them alive. Failed to capture the ship that attacked them," Marl placed her hands on the desk, thin, bony, but strong. "In fact, Davin, what I should be is angry. And I am."

"Hey—" Davin started.

"Which is why," Marl waved him quiet. "Effective immediately, I'm ending your contract with Eden Prime. You and your Wild Nines have a day to put yourselves together, but then I want you off this moon."

"And whose going to keep this place from falling apart? Captain flack here?" Davin said, nodding at Castor.

"We are," said a new voice behind Davin, full of cocky pride.

The voice came from a built man in the doorway. He looked like a retired fighter, stood with the rugged wariness of someone who'd earned his gray hair. The man's clothes caught Davin's eye. The same set, a loose collection of dusty red and blue, that the man back in bay five had been wearing.

"Ferro and his team are your replacements," Marl said. "And the important thing, Davin, is that they're better than you."

"Really?" Davin turned to the new man. "Where'd she find you, Ferro? Just hanging out waiting for a contract?"

"Marl and I, we go back to Mars—" Ferro started.

"Quiet," Marl said. "Davin, you have a day to get your things together. Then I want you gone."

"You look at the camera feed from bay five, you'll see this guy and the one that tried to blow up your base have a very similar fashion sense," Davin said. "Might want to reconsider."

Davin stepped away from the desk, back towards the door.

"Pleasure to meet you," Ferro said as Davin went by. "I am sorry my coming means you're going."

"Sure you are," Davin said. "Enjoy this pile of trash, it's a real winner."

"Twenty-four hours," Marl said to Davin's back. "Then you're gone, or you're dead."

"Always a sweet-talker, Marl," Davin said as he walked by Ferro, out the door, out the office, out of the building.

Terms of Deception

As soon as the door shut behind Davin, Marl glared at Castor.

"You didn't catch the transmission," Marl said. "You didn't intercept it and warn me, warn Ferro that they had hired bodyguards."

Castor, always the model of military training, didn't flinch under Marl's stare. Stood straight. As though this was an official ceremony. Like they weren't on a backwater world trying to scrabble for survival.

"Direct signals are almost impossible to intercept unless you're listening right in between them," Castor said. The even tone, the march of logic. Just once, Marl would love to see the man show emotion. "What's done is done. We need to move on."

"My men are not police," Ferro said.

"They are now," Marl replied. "Alissa asked me to take you in, and I've done that. You can do this for me. Eden Prime isn't big enough to cause much trouble."

"There is another problem," Castor said. "The inspectors are dead, and Eden will want to know why."

"I suppose we can't tell them it was a botched assassination?" Marl said. "Or it was an accident that a ship turned around in a docking bay full of people and ignited its main engines?"

"Sarcasm?" Ferro asked Castor.

"I don't think either of those will hold up," Castor said, ignoring Ferro. "The recording won't back them."

The recording. Eden Prime was full of cameras catching everything, like everywhere else. They stored the recordings here. Video that could be altered. Nobody had even seen the playback yet, outside of Marl and Castor. There were no witnesses, only Davin and his crew, and who would believe a few hired guns when the evidence was so damning?

"We adjust the video. Change it," Marl said. "The Red Voice has a specialist right? For the media?"

"We could do it," Castor said.

"Quickly?" Marl said, then she pointed to Ferro. "For this to work, you'll have to arrest Davin. Prevent him from leaving. Then, when Eden's next force arrives, we can hand them their prize."

"I'll send the recording," Castor said. "Ferro, give your men a few hours. Then strike."

"Go, get them ready," Marl said to Ferro. "Castor, one more minute please."

Ferro left the room.

"Davin won't let this play out," Marl said. "They will fight."

"We can't let them win," Castor said. "Call him."

"I don't like owing one man so many favors," Marl said. She sat back in her chair, stared at her comm.

"You won't have to repay them," Castor said. "He'll be dead before he can collect."

"Let's hope so," Marl said, and punched in the number.

Bar Nights

It was way past her bedtime. The cockpit of the *Gepard* whooshed open in bay four of Eden Prime after twelve hours of spaceflight. Viola hadn't checked the route before she'd started. Hadn't realized that she launched at the exact wrong time in the moon's orbits to make the transfer. Not that floating along the stars, Jupiter's giant bulk dominating the view, was a bad thing. Meditative, quiet. Especially when she'd made Puk turn itself off for a while.

Approaching Europa meant a slew of conversations with Eden Prime's flight control, along with a quick pause in the approach for a scanning. Viola had slowed the *Gepard* to wait in line behind two larger cargo haulers, rounded boxes with engines. When it was her turn, a swarm of bug bots surrounded her ship.

Some blasted the *Gepard*'s small hold with x-rays. Others crawled along the exterior, tapping into the fuel line, probing the airlock to make sure there wasn't a hidden bomb or other undisclosed items. The whole thing was claimed to be for security, but Viola's dad had spent more than one dinner complaining how it was an excuse to find more cargo they could tax.

The landing into Europa was the easiest part, a matter of punching in the docking command to the *Gepard*'s auto-pilot and letting it handle things. Current practice frowned on any manual piloting, even prohibited it entirely if the ship had an automatic choice available.

The moment Viola touched down and popped the hatch, the dockmaster was there demanding coin for the slot. Viola paid a large chunk of what she had and the dockmaster tucked the *Gepard* away to the side of the bay where it wouldn't interrupt the constant traffic of more important ships.

"How many messages so far, Puk?" Viola asked as they walked the quiet corridor into the promenade.

"Only ten, but they're increasingly frantic," Puk replied. "Your father's showing an impressive range of emotions. We're talking anger, sadness, desperation. Man deserves an award."

"He'll get over it," Viola replied.

The curving central walk of Eden Prime brought Viola by a hotel and, suddenly feeling tired, Viola swerved towards it. A mash-up of Greek architecture with space-age curls, the hotel bathed in purple cast from surrounding spotlights. *Cosmagora* blinked at Viola on a scrolling pink neon banner. The price blaring out below in that same neon made Viola's stomach lurch, but there weren't a lot of options.

"Classy place," Puk stated as Viola reached for the door.

"Didn't hear you suggesting anywhere else," Viola replied.

The human manning the desk looked like she was coming from, or about to go to, a party Viola would expect at a place called *Cosmagora*. She wore suit full of sharp angles and flashing color, flipping hues whenever she moved. It took Viola a few seconds of staring to realize the receptionist was already talking to her.

"A room?" the receptionist said, her voice full of placating boredom.

"If you've got one," Viola managed. When the receptionist leaned to check her console, the entire suit flipped to shades of blue, from ocean depth to cartoon teal. Viola bit back the urge to ask where she could get one of her own.

"Right now, we've got plenty. You walk in an hour ago, you'd have to leave," the receptionist replied.

"It's like you're begging us to ask why," Puk said.

The receptionist glanced at the bot, raised an eyebrow. Then looked back at Viola and waited.

"Why?" Viola said after a moment's awkward silence.

"Changing of the guards. Literally," the receptionist said. "Guess people aren't fans of murder, so we've had a lot of cancels."

"Shocking," Puk said.

"Murder?" Viola asked.

With each drip-fed detail, Viola's eyes crawled wider and wider. Exploding space ships, new arrivals burned alive in a bay by their own bodyguards? Perhaps Europa hadn't been the best choice.

The walk and elevator ride up to her room was like taking a psycho-active trip through a madman's mind. Viola couldn't make sense of the random artwork, picked from heaps of scrap metal and blasted with colors designed to clash with each other as possible. The room itself wasn't much better, its bed a sprawling mess of intermingled sheets, wrap-around pillows, and a ceiling screen that showed a time-lapse birth of the universe on repeat. Viola turned that off first. Then, after dropping their stuff, they fled.

"What next?" Puk said as they stood on the boulevard again, the local time now edging into the deep night hours. "We going to steal a bunch of stuff? Try to meet ruffians?"

"Ruffians? Who taught you that word?" Viola asked, walking the boulevard, away from the bays.

The street wasn't crowded, but it wasn't empty. Wandering pockets of people shifted in and out of the mixture of starlight and multi-colored lamps posted. Conversations carried, but their words washed each other out, like murmurings across a cafe. The occasional burst from a ship lifting off bled light throughout the boulevard for a few seconds at a time. Most people, Viola included, were wearing coats, her breath misting with every exhale.

"I've been on a classic literature phase lately," Puk continued.

"But, don't you know every book ever written?"

"I back-up the book I want to read, then go through it nice and slow, re-installing it to my live memory. Then delete the backup."

"How long does it take you?"

"I've only finished five today, with all our crap going on."

"Glad you're paying attention."

Ahead, across the boulevard, an aggressive series of sapphire letters formed *The Bitter Chill* along with outlines of cocktail glasses. Her father never took her to the working bars on Ganymede, for Galaxy Forge staff. Parties happened, sure, but to go into one of these places? By herself?

"Terrible plan," Puk said, following her look.

"Why am I here, Puk?" Viola replied.

"Because you've made a horrible mistake?"

"You're no fun."

"You programmed me."

"So what will you do now?" Viola said, starting towards the bar. It took a few steps, but then Viola heard the little bot, jets whirring behind her.

"If anyone looks at you funny, I'm just going to start shooting," Puk said.

First Mate, First Round

Trying to find a booth big enough to fit Mox was a frustrating exercise. It was why, months ago, Phyla had asked the owners of *The Bitter Chill* to tweak one for the Nines. In exchange, Phyla promised they'd stop by multiple times a night to provide security. That the Nines weren't the peacekeepers of Eden Prime anymore hadn't filtered to local news yet, which meant the five of them could have at least one more night throwing back beverages and forgetting their problems.

"I can't believe you didn't see the engines coming," Merc was saying to Opal, leaning back in the booth with a beer in hand. "Classic maneuver to fry your opponents."

"Classic maneuver?" Opal countered. "It's a suicide move. That bay could have exploded. Everyone dead and the base heavily damaged."

"That's what I'm saying!" Merc said. "Those guys clearly had nothing left to pull."

Opal's squinted eyes said she wanted to take the fighter pilot and choke him right there. Merc was trying to use that idiot grin of his to disarm the comments. As though slapping a smile on a problem made it go away. Cadge and Mox were talking about something to each other, while Davin was at the bar getting another round.

"Merc," Phyla interjected. "Stop being stupid."

"Think that's impossible," Opal said.

Merc threw up a hand, took a sip from his beer.

"So," Cadge said, returning to the table's talk. "Now that we're a free band again, what's the next job?"

"Captain's at the bar," Mox said.

"He's the only one that gets a say?" Cadge replied. "Thought this was a group effort. The way Davin told it, we've got a day to get off-world. I'm just looking to know where we're going."

Cadge looked at Phyla, the others following his glance. Surely the *Jumper*'s pilot would know their next job. What the back-up plan was in case the contract fell apart. Problem was, there wasn't any back-up plan. No reason for one, with the indefinite contract from Eden Prime staying active as long as they wanted to keep locking up drunks and banishing scammers from the frozen frontier.

"We'll figure it out," Phyla said, hating that she didn't have an answer.

"Now that's what I'm looking for," Cadge said. "Choices. Allow me to vote for the most violent one."

"Cadge, the hell's wrong with you?" Opal said. "Give me another job like this. Where I can breathe."

"Just because you sucked red sand and shot innocents doesn't mean the rest of us have to die of boredom," Cadge replied.

"They weren't innocents," Opal said, her voice a knife's edge. "You were there."

"Clean-up crews don't make the messes."

"Cadge," Phyla said, holding up a hand towards the man, whose face had an evil little smile that showed he knew he had a sore spot and was ready to pick it.

"That's a good idea," Merc said. "Mars. It's still a mess, right? They'll need help."

"You don't want to go there," Opal replied.

"We know, thanks to this guy, that Luna's off limits," Cadge said, allowing Mars to slip away. "Which means, what, we try Earth? Bounce to Saturn and see what's there?"

A tray set on the table, the crowded mugs on it clanking together. Davin, his eyes showing wandering redness from an order that came with a couple extra shots, shots that didn't make it to the table. Cadge and Mox shifted, giving Davin room to collapse onto the plastic cushion.

"Team," Davin said, casting his eyes around to each of them. "As your captain, I hereby order all of you to drink."

"You heard the man," Merc said, laughing.

Phyla took a gulp from the mug. True to the bar's name, the beer was bitter. Cold. It ate its way through her throat and into her stomach like swallowing an ice cube.

"Davin," Phyla said. "They're wondering where we're going togo."

"Don't think there's another bar in Eden Prime," Davin said. "Unless another one opened and you've been holding out on me."

"Hah," Mox said.

Silence. Eyes moved to Davin as he took a long drink.

"The thing is," Davin said. "I'll have an answer for you. Tomorrow. There's some things that I'm working out. Calls I've made. We'll see what comes through."

Phyla was about to ask Davin what calls, but held back. She hadn't seen Davin back at the *Jumper* since, a few hours ago, he'd come back to say Marl canceled their contract. There wasn't anywhere else Davin could've sent transmissions off-world. Not without paying for it.

As for what Davin was working on, Phyla'd heard that one too. A favorite tactic of Davin's when he didn't know what the hell they were going to do. But the rest of the crew sipped their drinks, moved on to other conversation. Phyla met Davin's eyes, the captain gave her a slight nod.

"Now, you see that? I could use one of those," Merc said, looking across the bar. A woman had walked in, on the young side to be here. Followed by a small floating bot, buzzing around her head like a moon.

"You be real nice to Trina, and maybe she'll make you one," Phyla said.

"That girl doesn't belong here," Opal interjected. Phyla agreed. Too many questions on that girl's face as she looked around the bar.

"Don't worry, guys," Davin said, standing. "I'm on it."

Phyla watched the captain stand up and walk, tottering, away from the table. Escape one problem by jumping right into another. Just what they'd always done.

Two for One

The *Bitter Chill* had a vicious set of neon surrounding a double-door that looked pristine. New. Hanging next to those doors, laminated and plastered to the wall, was a short one-sheet that started with THINK. Below, a pair of paragraphs stated that doing stupid things on Eden Prime, like fighting, killing, or just being a nuisance could get you kicked off the moon on the next freighter. No court, no trial. A clause at the end stated this was Eden's standard policy for all of their locations, no matter which world.

"Sounds fair," Puk said. "Not open to abuse at all."

"Ganymede is the same way," Viola replied. "Gotta love the Free Laws."

Through the door there was, somehow, more neon hues spiraling around the interior, casting bubblegum pink, grape purple and lipstick red shadows along the curving roof. The bar, sitting central, was a cascading waterfall of blues. Bass vibes interlaced with wandering instrumentals accompanied the light show, backdropping to the constant chatter coming from a collection of tables and the long loop of a bar.

Viola hunted for an empty seat, but they were all taken by a motley arrangement. Some looked like Viola's father, business sharks waving cocktails, while others looked like they'd stepped out of machining parts and into the place with nowhere in between.

The only opening was at the bar itself, a lone small-backed stool, next to a pair of men in thick work suits that looked like they'd tromped from a clean-up where the mess won. Viola wasn't sitting for over ten seconds before a bartender locked eyes with her and, without a word, asked what she wanted.

"Something strong," Viola said, aping a line from a movie she'd watched a year ago.

"Good move," Puk buzzed, hovering a centimeter from her ear. "Asking for a stiff drink when you're alone on a moon you've never been to is a smart decision."

"I didn't know what else to say," Viola whispered. "I've never done this."

"Hi, I'm Puk. I have literally a million recipes and reviews of various drinks at my beck and call. How may I serve?" Puk replied.

Viola rolled her eyes and settled for staring across the bar at nothing in particular. She'd made it here, but what did that mean? Sure, it was more interesting than sitting at home imagining being here, but still . . .

"That your bot?" said a man whose palm appeared on the bar between Viola and the zoned-out workman.

Puk whirred to the other side of Viola's head while she looked at the man. He was pressing hard on the bar counter, depending on it to keep him up. He rocked back and forth. But the bright eyes and sloppy smile looked genuine.

"Puk's a friend," Viola said.

"Have some of those myself," the drunk replied. "Friends. They're good in a pinch, you know?"

"In a pinch?"

"Yeah," the drunk paused, blinked a couple times, Viola wondering just how far his train of thought had derailed. "You won't judge me, will you?"

"Judge you?" Viola said. "I don't even know you."

"Fair enough," the drunk replied. Then, to the workman, "You mind moving over a seat? Else I might fall on you."

The man didn't argue, shifting over a spot with a nod and giving the drunk a chance to flop on the stool. The bartender slipped Viola's drink in front of her, a tumbler full of something a pale shade of brown.

"Don't trust him," Puk buzzed. "He's drunk."

"Really," Viola replied.

"So anyway," the drunk said, resting his elbows on the bar. "Here's the deal. Today, I lost my job."

Viola caught the man's eyes flick towards her, judging the reaction.

"And?"

"It was boring as hell, so I don't mind."

"Okay."

Viola took a sip of the drink. Cool at first, but the liquid torched its way to her stomach. Viola found herself sweating. Holding back a cough. Every ounce of concentration went into keeping the drink down, to not blowing it here, in this bar full of people who probably guzzled this stuff by the gallon. You can do it, Viola. This is the real world.

"Here's the kicker, and this is why, as you might be able to tell, I've been a little ... liberal with the drinks tonight," the drunk said, waving his finger in a circle towards the bartender. "Two people died today under my watch. Burnt to a crisp."

What was she supposed to say to that? Her father had talked about accidents in the plant. She'd had relatives who'd passed away. Didn't sound like that's what was happening here. The hotel receptionist and her comments about murders floated back through Viola's mind. Was this guy involved?

"And now my crew and I have, oh, 22 hours or so to get ourselves off this moon," here the drunk leaned in, as though compensating for Viola's caution. "But here's the thing. I'm pretty sure she was in on it. The two people that died."

"She?" Viola asked.

"Marl. The woman running this place," the drunk said, then lapsed into silence.

"The bar?"

"Eden Prime," the man said, attempting to spread his arms and nearly knocking over his glass. "Marl's a nasty piece of work. Don't go near her, is my advice."

After another sip'n'shudder of her drink. Viola examined the drunk, noticing that he wasn't wearing the same workman's clothes as the others in this place. Not a suit, either. More accessories. A belt with an empty holster. The comm on his wrist a higher-end model. Who was this guy?

"So what are you gonna do?" Viola asked.

"Leave it," the drunk said. "Take off in the morning, tell Europa to go screw itself and never come back."

"You're not going to try and figure it out?"

The drunk started, took a drink, then turned to Viola with his hand stretched out. Viola took it, and the drunk gave her hand a single shake.

"Davin Masters, captain of the Wild Nines," the drunk said. "I happen to like living so no, I will not be trying to figure it out."

"Viola Allouette," Viola replied. "And that sounds like you're being a coward."

Davin laughed.

"You look over there?" Davin gestured across the bar to a corner table where five others sat drinking. "That's my crew. They'll go where I tell'em, but that means I got responsibility. They die, it's on me,"

Davin leaned in again towards Viola.

"That's why," Davin whispered. "There's going to be no grand investigation."

A hand tapped Viola on the shoulder. A frosted-over pair of hard faces stared at her, greedy eyes bubbling up beneath their glowering looks. Both seemed to have just walked in from a survival expedition, sporting visible nets, batons, and guns on their hips.

"Your name Viola Allouette?" the trapper asked.

"What're you doing, Whelk? More importantly, what are you wearing? You look like a homicidal dog catcher," Davin interrupted.

"And you finally look like the trash you really are, Davin," Whelk said. "But I'm not here for you, especially now you're just another drunk like the rest of us. I'm here for her, and the reward."

"The reward?" Viola said.

"Daddy wants his little girl back home," Whelk said. "And we're taking you there. Now."

"How much coin?" Davin said.

"A hundred thousand," Whelk replied. "Don't even try to step into this, Davin. You've got no right anymore."

Davin slid off the stool, looked at Viola, then winked at her. Everyone saw the punch coming. Davin's drunk swing flew wide left, and Whelk's companion pushed Davin back into his seat. Whelk, shaking his head, stepped towards Viola and reached for her.

Puk flitted from Viola's ear and, near Whelk's arm, shot its laser. Whelk yelped, just in time for Viola to throw her drink at him. The glass shattered, spraying booze into Whelk's face, causing him to stumble back.

Then Whelk's companion threw Viola off of the stool and she hit the ground, hard. The breath left Viola's lungs in a rush. Her head exploded in pain as it bounced off the floor. Viola struggled to breathe, to roll away, to stop hurting. The club lights glowed down at her, a dizzying rush of color. As Whelk's friend bent down to grab her by the shoulders, Viola only had one thought:

Leaving home was a mistake.

The Real World

Things looked different from the floor, a plastic mess of tiles overlaid with the sticky grime of spilled booze. The neon lights in the ceiling faded out as Whelk's companion leaned over, reaching for her with arms outstretched. A reflected glow from the floor showed a straight face, exasperated. The sight pushed a burst of adrenaline through Viola's veins. Like this guy had any right to be annoyed.

So sorry for making this hard for you.

Viola kicked out, hard, at the man's ankle, her foot bouncing off of the strike. The man paused, laughed, and grabbed Viola's shoulders. She tried to wriggle, but the man's grip pushed into her muscles, her joints, and trying to move sent pain whistling through her nerves.

"She's a fighter, Whelk," The companion said.

"We'd hate for this to be boring, wouldn't we, Gat?" Whelk replied.

"Then you oughta love me," Davin slurred, once again stepping off his stool launching into a sloppy tackle.

Davin fell into Whelk, pushing them backwards into another table, beer spilling everywhere. Gat picked Viola up, pressing her back to his chest, and lifted her towards the exit. His wrists and hands were too low for her to bite. Viola's heels broke on the stone slabs of Gat's shins. Puk whirled in front of them, trying to find a shot. Gat paused, glared at the little bot.

"Poke me with that laser, and I'll break her leg. Reward said nothing about bringing her back in one piece," Gat said. Puk hesitated and Viola shook her head. This wasn't worth a broken leg. Puk floated back, and Gat continued his march to the exit.

Viola tried to yell for help, but her lungs were still having a hard time catching breath. Stare after stare slid away from Viola's eyes. There were no friends here. Nobody cared what was happening to her. Other than Puk, and the drunk captain behind her, Viola was alone on the moon.

"Problem with me," Davin announced from the floor behind them. "Is that I'm a package deal, see?"

"With who, other washed up losers?" Whelk, coming up alongside Gat, shot back.

"Nah, Whelk, my crew,"

Viola didn't see the big man until Gat dropped her to the floor. She caught herself on the wall of *The Bitter Chill* and turned around to see the giant man standing over Gat, daring him to fight. The newcomer was one of Davin's crew, one of the bunch who'd been at the table a minute earlier.

The giant man had ripples and bulges beneath his clothes, and not in the usual spot for muscles. As she looked at him, the man looked back at her, his face inscrutable in the shadows of the bar's lighting.

"Now might be a good time to run," Puk buzzed next to her.

"Agreed," Viola replied.

As she back-pedaled, Viola glanced over at Whelk, who was standing very still as a woman with lava-red hair pressed a jagged glass edge up to his throat.

"Phyla," Whelk said. "You know this is just business."

"Yeah, but now it's our business," the woman, Phyla, replied.

Whelk raised his hands and Phyla, after a slight press with the glass to remind the man how close his day had come to ending terribly, backed away. Viola turned to head out the exit, and stared right at a grinning dude wearing a full flight suit.

"Now, lady, you weren't thinking of skipping out on your rescuers without even saying thanks, were you?" the man said.

"Uh, thanks?" Viola said, trying to get around him. She just needed to leave this place. Right now.

"Merc, leave her alone," another woman, sounding tired, said. "She's scared enough without you talking to her."

Viola felt a hand on her shoulder. Davin's head swung into view, his right hand sweeping up in a grand gesture.

"My crew, right on cue," Davin said, before running Viola through high-speed introductions. Between the lights, the adrenaline, and the growing realization that Viola's father had put coin on her capture, Viola barely kept track of the names coming her way.

"For as many times as we save your ass, cap'n, it'd be nice to see a bonus," Cadge, still holding a couple beer glasses and drinking out of both of them, said.

"Keeping your captain alive is just part of the contract," Davin said, voice adopting a sage inflection and draping an arm over Cadge's shoulders. "To warrant a bonus, well, you'd save me before the fight started."

"There's an impossibility," Phyla said, eyes rolling.

"Davin's been nice enough to introduce us to you," Opal said, leveling a very sober look at Viola. "Maybe you can return the favor, tell us why they were after you?"

"Because I ran away and my father wants me back," Viola replied, adding her and Puk's names. The bot was hovering over her shoulder, tracking its camera on each of them. What Puk could do if they took Viola, she didn't know, but the little bot was trying.

"Putting a bounty on your own daughter? That's cold," Merc said.

"One way to get the job done," Cadge said. "Enough money, he'll get her back."

"I'm standing right here," Viola replied.

"Stop. Go outside," said Mox, nodding towards the other side of the bar, where Gat and Whelk were now talking to another crowded table. "Safer."

Nobody objected, and the group escorted Viola out of the bar. Viola was in the middle, with Mox and a wobbly Davin in front. The boulevard was even quieter now, the hour getting close to morning. Exhausted, hurt, Viola still noticed the ten people standing in the through-way. Because they were staring right at her.

Fisticuffs

Oh, look at these bastards in their dirty reds and blues. Matching uniforms like little kids. Cadge slipped his hands into his pockets, ran his fingers through his stunner mitts. The gloves took the kinetic energy off the punch and shocked the victim, blasting their nerves into a spasm. Cadge had seen their original owner knock jaws loose with the mitts, was scaring everyone in the place. Until he forgot Cadge was behind him. It would've been a shame to leave these toys.

"I get the displeasure of seeing you twice in one day, Ferro?" Davin slurred at the lead trooper.

"Unfortunate, yes," Ferro said. "It seems your circumstances have worsened. You are a murderer now."

The captain was a lot of things, but Cadge knew he was too goody-goody to ever straight-up murder someone. Wasn't Davin's way. Wasn't Cadge's way either. Killing a man was fine, but doing it without a fight? Where was the fun in that?

"Murderer's a new one," Davin replied, standing straighter. "Where'd you heart hat?"

Cadge noticed the new girl, Viola, was edging towards the back of their group, her little bot hovering next to her. Whelk had been talking about a bounty, but here Davin was treating her like a new friend. Bet the girl's bounty would be able to keep them paid till they found a new job. He'd have to talk to Davin about it, assuming they didn't all die right here.

"You, and your team, killed two inspectors. The ones who landed here earlier today," Ferro said.

"Liar," Mox said.

"I have no wish to start our lives here with violence," Ferro continued, eying the big man. "Come peacefully, and perhaps we will find redemption together."

Cadge suppressed a laugh as a few of the troopers looked at Mox and stepped back. Cowards.

"Ferro, you seem like a good guy," Davin said, stepping forward. "So I'm sorry for what's about to happen."

Cadge felt the smile as Davin threw the punch. As soon as Davin's fist connected, Cadge sprinted towards the closest trooper, his feet skipping across the floor and then leaving it as Cadge dove through the air and hit the man in the chest. They fell to the ground, Cadge working his arms into the man's ribs, each jab knocking volts through the clothes.

Flashes, white ones, flitted through the air as Cadge moved the trooper's body to keep him in the way of the stunning lasers. The secret to surviving a scrum was to stay low. Go for the knees, ankles, stomaches.

Throwing the first trooper to the ground, stunned into oblivion, Cadge rushed a pair of panicked enemies. To his right, he saw another trooper fly by, sent by Mox on a one-way trip to pain. Only problem was that none of the Nines had their real weapons. A brawl was one thing, but as soon as these troopers got themselves composed, it would get ugly.

Cadge jumped towards the pair of troopers as they raised their rifles. Each hand grabbed a shoulder and Cadge pulled both of them to the ground with him. Elbows flying, knees jabbing, Cadge worked every muscle he had in a frenzied dance. When he felt the troopers go limp, felt them stop trying to hit him back or run away, Cadge looked towards the fight.

Mox was carrying Phyla in one hand, Opal in the other, both of them hanging on as the metal man ran out of the tangle of bodies. Merc was trying to cover their retreat - the pilot had picked up a rifle and was spraying stunning bolts at the remaining troopers, which were diving into cover and taking pot shots. Davin dodged a looping haymaker from Ferro by falling flat on his back and rolling away.

Ferro took the opportunity to talk into his comm. Cadge couldn't hear the words, but could guess what was being called. The new girl was gone.

"Back to the *Jumper*!" Davin yelled, scrambling to his feet. Mox broke into a run while Merc back-pedaled, still shooting. Several troopers were coming out of cover, aiming their shots. The Nines were going to get picked off. Nobody was looking at Cadge, though.

A big mistake.

"You're all a bunch of cowards!" Cadge yelled, running towards the trio of aiming troopers. They turned as one, but the cocky jackasses overestimated his height and their shots flashed over Cadge's head. Or singed it, the smell of burning hair breezing into his nose.

Cadge hit the first trooper low, in the abdomen, bouncing off the charge into the next one. That trooper was aiming his rifle low, and Cadge grabbed the barrel, shoving the gun straight back into the trooper's face. Two down.

Cadge kept his legs pumping towards the third trooper, and took his stun shot right in the chest. The lasers had no actual force, so Cadge kept moving forward even as he stopped feeling any of his muscles. Like watching a movie where his head was the camera. The trooper that hit him didn't have time to get out of the way, and Cadge slammed into him, crashing them to the ground.

Above Cadge, the great mass of Jupiter glowed in the sky. A fixed feature. Lights along the boulevard were coming up to simulate an actual solar cycle. Would've been pleasant, if Cadge could've felt his own body. A pair of trooper heads poked into his vision, staring at him. Cadge tried to spit, but his mouth wouldn't work. Still, if the bastards were watching him, that meant they weren't chasing after the rest of the Nines. Mission accomplished.

The effects of the stun bolt were immediate, but also slow-moving as it worked its way through Cadge's body. Lost the fun extremities first, consciousness last. Cadge felt his brain slag as Ferro came into view. The man was talking, words not making it into Cadge's mind. The view changed as troopers picked him up. Carrying him somewhere, maybe to be shot or dumped out an airlock. But hey, at least he wasn't bored.

Run and Hide

As soon as Davin's fist hit the lead trooper, Viola ran. Puk followed.

"They're not evening following you," Puk said, buzzing up alongside her. "Which, given the effort to rescue you from those clowns, strikes me as a waste."

"Shut it, Puk."

Viola risked a glance back and yeah, Puk was right. The two groups were brawling, with bright white stunning bolts flying out. Mox, that big metal man, was throwing a trooper into another pair as easily as Viola would throw a ball, bowling the troopers over with their own man. Who were these people?

Viola kept running, past the hotel and to the large doors leading into the bays. Through those doors and past the ever-present cleaning and maintenance bots combing the corridor. Past bay one, bay two, and then Viola pulled up short. Ahead in the corridor, outside bay four, where Viola parked the *Gepard*, was another set of those uniformed troopers. Three of them, rifles in proud display. Gesturing into the bay at someone Viola couldn't see. One turn and they'd see her.

"Are they searching my ship?" Viola said, pausing by the open door to bay three.

"Can't tell," Puk replied. "Given your luck with people today, though, I'd hide."

A single large cargo carrier dominated bay three. The ship looked like it had a disease, modules sprouting from the original frame in blocky growths. Different paints coated the parts, as though the crew assembled the whole thing at once from a random collection.

The ship's ramp was lowered, touching the ground. Open door at the top. If she stayed here and those troopers came by, she'd be caught. Viola started towards the carrier.

"You're not," Puk said. "There's crates right over there. Hide."

"They'll see me if they come in here. The ship's the best hiding place," Viola said, continuing towards the ramp.

"And if man-eating pirates own it?"

"Those odds have to be worse than waiting out here."

Viola picked up the pace. A quick jog up the ramp and into the ship's cargo bay. A few scattered metal containers sat around. Too sparse for a ship in active use. Graffiti coated the walls. Drawings of abstract landscapes, faces. One looked like Earth. Another, made up of swiped reds, must have been Mars.

Circular doors led to other modules, and Viola picked one of those at random. Walked up to it, and as she came close, the door spiraled open. Not locked. Whoever owned this thing really trusted nobody would take it.

A small hallway, barely wide enough for two people. Hanging on the walls were maps, charts, diagrams of shipping routes and trade laws for various settlements. After those came a series of …trophies? One resembled a piece of fur, brown and thick and cut in an intricate arrangement with swirling versions of Saturn's rings. Another a dustwork, made from grinding and scattering Mars dust in spots on sticky fabric. This one made fragile and textured work of a Martian mountain landscape.

Several doors branched off, Viola peeked inside them while Puk hovered behind, watching for any sign of the owners.

Crew quarters, each room holding a small bunk. Enough for four crew members on this level, but, going by Galaxy Forge requirements, a ship this size would need at least double that to run well. The first room had a calendar with pictures of Earth on it, landmarks that Viola recognized from classes when she was younger. Pyramids, the fjords of Norway, the regrown Amazon jungle. There was a temptation to dig further, but Viola stopped herself. Maybe she'd get pity hiding back in the engines, but not if she rooted through their stuff.

Further down the hallway Viola hit a fork, one way leading to the engine panel, the other leading to a small launch bay. Which way to go . . .

"Is someone there?" came an older man's voice, scratched and strained.

"You could run," Puk said as Viola took a step towards the sound. "We could get out of here. There's no telling what this guy might do."

"And go where, Puk?" Viola said, then kept walking towards the sound.

In front of the large console and metal access hatch to the left engine sat an older man, his white beard clotted with blood that spread across the cream coat and pants he wore. Despite the wrecked state, the man's eyes tracked up to Viola's, alert and fiery.

"You're not the one I was expecting," the old man said.

"Neither were you," Viola countered.

"Fair enough, I suppose."

"What happened?"

"These thugs in uniforms. They said they'd destroy the ship if we didn't lower the ramp, and then they just about did it anyway," the old man said, then coughed hard. "Much as I'd like to talk, it's rather painful. If you aren't going to kill me, would you mind helping me to the medical bay?"

Viola hesitated a second, Puk's warning dangling in her ear. If she tried to carry this guy somewhere, there'd be no running if someone found her. But then, what other choice was there? Leave the old man to suffer?

"You'll find I'm not as heavy as I look," the old man said as Viola crouched and put his arm over her shoulders. "I'm mostly hot air, you know."

"Was that a joke?" Viola said. Picking up the man reminded her of how long she'd been awake, her legs exhausted and twitching with the extra weight.

"I find it's the dire situations when humor is most necessary," the man said. "And I suppose since you are attempting to save my life, introductions are in order. I'm Erick."

"Erick's clearly crazed," Puk buzzed in Viola's ear. "I say we ditch him and run."

"I heard that," Erick replied. "Though I can't fault your little mechanical friend much if, indeed, you came to this ship under suspicious circumstances."

Viola managed to walk back to the stretch with the crew rooms on either side.

"I'm just trying to hide."

"Oh? And who is pursuing you? Perhaps we share a foe."

"Someone named Davin? He had a crew with him."

Erick laughed, a weak, coughing thing that did little for him making it through the injuries. Viola couldn't stop moving forward - she worried that as soon as momentum stopped, Erick's weight would crush them both to the floor - but she wanted to ask what was so funny.

"What's your name?" Erick asked as the laughter died.

"Viola."

"Viola, it seems you've met my captain," Erick said.

"I told you!" Puk said, buzzing ahead and looking out into the main entryway of the ship. "It's still clear! Drop him and go!"

"Tell me why I shouldn't," Viola said, nearing the end of the hallway.

"Don't worry, Viola, Davin's never made it a point to hurt young women. I wouldn't be here otherwise," Erick said. "I'm sure it was a misunderstanding."

"He didn't hurt me, really," Viola said, replaying the bar scene in her mind. None of the crew had done anything to her, except help, now that Viola thought about it. But there'd been distractions. When he wasn't being attacked, Davin might focus on that bounty.

"If you're having doubts, I can personally guarantee your safety," Erick said. "Davin will let you walk right off this ship if I ask."

"That's a lot of trust," Puk said.

"I'm not going to leave him to die," Viola said.

"And your generosity will be repaid," Erick replied.

They lurched back into the ship's entry bay. It was empty, but Viola could hear noise outside. Erick gestured to the left, a door leading to the med room. Somewhere Erick could patch himself up. Viola stayed silent, trying to keep the easiest escape route clear in her head. That and her legs were burning from keeping Erick upright. One more step, one more step.

"What I'm trying to say, Viola, is that, as you're helping me right now, so we might be able to help you," Erick said, then sighed. "Especially as it seems this ship won't be going anywhere in the near future."

Heal Thyself

Home, a cramped three meter by three meter med room. Seeing the bed, the countertop covered with tools laid out in strict order, labeled cabinets and the bright surgical light took the edge off Erick's constant jarring ache in his stomach. All of the equipment gained in bits and pieces. Junk here and there re-purposed to keep the crew alive. And now it would do the same for him. Hopefully.

"I'll need you to put me on the bed," Erick said. Viola shuffled over to the thin-cushioned apparatus, a sickly gray plastic covering and yellowed rails forming the bed's accents. Viola twisted her body, allowing Erick to slip out of her grasp and fall onto the bed. The cushion felt cool, but then, Erick had the hot stickiness of blood over the lower half of his body right now. It only made sense.

"Are you ready?" Erick asked. "I know I am asking a lot of you, but I think you'll be disappointed if you dragged me all this way only to have me expire upon this table."

"Puk?" Viola asked. "Can you run the diagnostics?"

Erick watched the little bot hover over the wound in his abdomen. With proper cameras, even small bots like Puk could measure a pulse, track his breathing and pupil dilation, among other things. Still, bots were at the mercy of their programmers. One error and the readings could be wrong, fatally so. Erick preferred the personal touch.

"Looks like a nasty fist fight," Puk said, buzzing around Erick and scanning him with its lens. "And you didn't win it, doc. I'm reading bruises all over the place. The blood from the mouth is coming from a split lip, nothing serious. But the stomach, ouch. Did you take a hard kick there?"

"Did I? Possibly," Erick replied, hearing the sound of his own voice, its faintness alarming. "The man's boots were sharp."

"That's what I'm reading. Six-inch laceration, deep. Viola, that's where we need to focus."

Viola stood up, glanced around the room.

"Talk to me, Erick," Viola said. "I don't know where anything is here."

"I'm sorry, my dear, but you're going to have to learn quickly. The scissors are in that top drawer on the left, along with the stitching supplies," Erick said. "But before you close the wound, you'll want to make sure that, um, that . . ."

Erick tried to stay focused, but the world decided to swirl. To dim and lighten at random. The blood loss was causing the problems. But Erick hadn't seen this side in person before. Experienced the loss of control that came as his limbs, his mind started shutting down. It was horribly fascinating.

"Hey, Viola, he's crashing here. Since you want to help this guy, we have to move!" Puk announced, the words echoing and fading, coming to Erick's ears from another world. "Lift the shirt away!"

Erick felt his shirt being pulled. So sticky there, around his stomach. The snip of a scissors on the fabric.

"It wasn't a good shirt anyway," Erick mumbled. The girl ought to know that. So she wouldn't feel bad ruining it.

"Now what?" Viola asked. Erick wasn't sure what she meant.

The ache was diminishing, a battery of agony quieting to the smallest of pinpricks. A bad sign. Come on, Erick, it's not time to quit yet. Erick forced his eyes open, focused on the bright light.

"I don't think he got that from a kick," Puk said. "Looks like a knife wound."

A knife wound. Were they talking about him? They might be. Back to the present.

"At least it looks clean," Puk said. "Relatively anyway. Organs beneath look OK. We're just dealing with a lot of blood loss."

"Oh, is that all?" Viola said.

"Count your blessings, sister," Puk replied. "Now, let's get to stitching."

The first stitch felt like a poke. A second poke. The girl was moving quickly. Doing well. A third poke. Every tiny lance through his skin felt like a stride towards life. A fourth poke. Lacing the skin together was always his favorite part. It meant the job was nearly done, and it was only necessary if the patient lived. A sign of success. The fifth poke was hard, sharp. Erick sat up. His eyes tracked down, saw Viola and Puk leaning over his stomach. Her hands, gloved, were so red.

"That doesn't look good," Erick said.

"Just hang in there, Doc. We got this," Puk said.

The pokes continued. One after another. Erick laid back, darkness flashing at the corners of his eyes. But he held onto those pokes. Each one another rung in that ladder leading up to sanity. He could let go, fall back into that endless chasm. But then, when had he, doctor on a mercenary ship far from the comforts of Earth, chosen the easy route?

An infinity later, Erick's eyes fluttered open. An IV tube led into his front wrist. His stomach felt tight, the pain muted. Viola over there in the corner, sitting in the chair looking dazed. The sound of boots on metal echoed through the ship. Either the good guys were back, or enemies coming to finish the job. Ironic, if it was the latter. All this to save an old man just to have him gunned down.

The door to the cargo room opened, and Davin's face appeared.

"You alive, Erick?" Davin said, stepping into the room.

Viola's face twitched. Erick could see her muscles tighten. Thinking about a run for it. The little bot was out of sight, no doubt planning some sneak attack to buy the girl some time.

"Thanks to the girl, yes."

Davin glanced at Viola, but continued to Erick, looking over the stitch work and the IV.

"Not bad," Davin muttered. "What's your timetable?"

"A few hours. Maybe less."

"We're going to move in twenty. After everyone gets geared up."

"Move?"

"They have Trina. And Cadge, now. If we want to get the *Jumper* off the ground, we'll need Trina back."

Of course they took Trina. Of course he'd been unable to prevent it.

"I'm sorry, Davin."

"Not your fault," the captain said. "Now, Viola. What're we going to do with you?"

What It Takes

Davin walked Viola out of the med room, had her throw away the bloody gloves and shut off that blinding light so Erick could sleep. The central hold was empty, the others getting a hot minute to take a breath before the real fun started.

Looking at the painted walls of his cargo hold, Davin realized his vision wasn't swimming anymore. He wasn't listing from side to side. Amazing what getting punched and shot at will do for sobriety.

"So what are you running from?" Davin said. Viola and her floating bot shied away from him, her back to a wall.

"I'm not running," Viola said.

"Oh really. Just came alone to this frozen hellscape of a moon as a vacation?"

Behind Viola, painted on the wall, was one of Mox's works. The gray towers of the lunar surface, a dot of blue in the sky for Earth. Always amazed Davin how the big man kept perspective,

"I was bored," Viola said. "It sounds stupid, I know. But that's what it was."

"You're talking to a guy who just started a fight with the police. Stupid is very familiar," Davin let her have the wall, stood a meter away towards the center of the room. Spend enough time on a spaceship and personal space gets to be a big deal. "See, what I'm trying to find out is whether you're a problem or an opportunity, why don't you help me out."

"I'm not trying to be anything," Viola replied, folding her arms and staring at the ground.

"So you're open to ideas, then?"

The girl looked up at him. Dammit if Davin wasn't a sop for a hope-filled face. Phyla should be here, ready to throw the cold bucket of reality on the star-faring fantasy Davin was going to offer.

"I'm not a fan of bounty chasers," Davin continued. "Those guys at the bar. It'd feel good to stiff them. Take you out of their reach."

"Meaning what?"

Viola was looking Davin dead-on now. Good. The girl had a spine.

"Meaning I'm not a fan of freeloaders either. Or rich kids that don't have anything to contribute. You want to ride with us, you have to make it worth my while."

"Who says I want to come with you?"

"You don't, I'll let you walk off this ship right now. Ramp's right there. Take your chances with Whelk. He's real nice once you get to know him."

The bot buzzed Viola's ear. Davin didn't eavesdrop. If he was reading the kid right, if she had the guts to fly here on her own and walk into that bar tonight . . .

"That man back there? The one you punched?" Viola said. "He called you murderers."

The words hung there in the air, the silent question tied to them.

"And what do you think?" Davin replied. "We look like a bunch of killers to you?"

"Puk ran your name. There's a charge."

"Let me guess, from today?"

Viola nodded. A universal Free Laws registry synced recorded crimes in a database across satellites, available to anyone. People looking for coin could chance bringing someone in for the reward, otherwise Free Law-signing cities would arrest anyone on the list.

"What'd they put us?"

"Three-hundred thousand," Viola said, and Davin couldn't stop a whistle. An amount over five thousand brought the hunters out from the shadows. This high, the Nines would attract the real rough customers.

"We must be dangerous then. How about before that? Anything?"

"Nothing like this," Viola said. "Small stuff."

"See? We're harmless."

"Uh huh."

"Look," Davin said. "I was where you were. Stuck in a place I didn't want to be and offered an out. We need another member."

"I'm not a mercenary," Viola said, spreading her arms as if to show she wasn't carrying a dozen weapons.

"Did you program that bot?" Davin said, eyes moving to Puk.

"Yeah. Went a little overboard on a class project."

"Then we can use you," Davin glanced at his comm. "I have to get my gear. You want to leave, the ramp's right there. You think you want to stay, go up to the cockpit and talk to Phyla."

Davin turned and left before Viola could ask another question. The girl looked like she would fit in nicely if she stayed. Bonus, she'd come cheap. And if she didn't work out, there was always that bounty.

Davin's cabin was the largest on the ship. Ramshackle souvenirs from a dozen spaceports littered the room, from stick-figure statues of the first native Martians to swirling balls of gas literally captured from Jupiter's atmosphere.

Towards the head of the bed, near his own pillow, Davin had a lamp that filtered light through a blue slate of Europa ice. In the locker on the right side was his objective, hanging on a hook.

Melody was the deadly parting gift of the last captain, along with the *Jumper* itself. The departing captain didn't say anything about it, and Davin found Melody on his first walk through the ship, no note except a full supply of charged battery packs for ammo. Davin slotted a fresh charge into Melody right then, slipped a couple more into his pack.

Next to Melody was the same series of sidearm everyone on the *Jumper* carried. Gotta love bulk discounts. The weapons weren't much in a big fight, but they'd knock a man out cold if Davin shot him close.

"Mox, Merc, Opal, you ready?" Davin said into his comm. "And hey, we're marked at three hundred thousand. Be ready in case there's a surprise."

Three clicks came back. The universal affirmative. Time to stage a rescue.

Video Evidence

Phyla ran her hands over the three consoles that made up the *Jumper's* cockpit. A pair of cushioned chairs nestled in the middle, one of which she occupied. The view closed off now, the armor shades blocking outside light. She was busy checking to see whether their visitors had left any nasty surprises. The idea that someone had been pushing these buttons, adjusting her settings had Phyla feeling ill, violated.

"Hello?" said a voice behind her. Phyla jerked around and tried to put on a neutral expression. Viola, wasn't that her name? The girl was staring past Phyla, at the shifting updates on the consoles as they ran through their checks of the *Jumper's* systems.

"They change based on what the ship's doing," Phyla said. "Because we're resting, it's telling us all the things we'd be interested in for a maintenance stop, or a cargo load."

Viola nodded and Phyla reached her hand towards the central console, then gestured, sweeping the status updates away. An overlay of choices appeared, words beneath simple icons. Flight, cargo, life support. Tap and Phyla could get a second-by-second update on every part of the *Jumper*.

"All of these are different sets?" Viola asked.

"You got it," Phyla replied. "Davin trusts me to keep the *Jumper* running, and I start by keeping the systems as advanced as possible. It's how we know that if we tried lifting off, even if we could get the outer bay door open, they blocked the cooling systems. We'd be in the air a few minutes, then the engines would overheat. We'd be a firework."

"Is it because they think you killed somebody?"

"Maybe," Phyla said, watching the life support checks come back green. One system that wasn't sabotaged, anyway. "I think we're being set up."

"For what?"

"Eden's upset they lost a pair of inspectors, so Marl pastes us with the blame. Why they canceled our contract. But what I don't understand is why Marl gave us twenty-four hours to leave, and then ambushed us outside of a bar," Phyla continued. "And tried to kill our doctor, kidnapped our mechanic."

"She changed her mind?" Puk said.

"But why?" Phyla bit her lip. Eden was a business, an entity that moved slow and evaluated all the options before targeting the most profitable one. Why shift out a security contract so fast when evidence was on the Nines side?

"So," Viola said. "Davin said to come talk to you if I wanted to stay."

"He tell you why?"

"To come to you? No."

"Watch this," Phyla said.

Phyla waved a hand over the center console and the display shifted up and appeared over the closed windshield. A much larger screen. Tapping an icon of a camera, the panel shifted to a display showing several recordings taken over the last few days. The first box listed a time only a few hours old. Phyla touched it and the video played.

Trina, a tiny with blue hair - her color of the month - knotted into a bun, was digging through a supply container in the *Jumper*'s main bay. A few seconds in, Trina paused in her rummaging and glanced towards the ramp. The angle caused the back of Trina's head to face the camera, the boarding ramp visible on the right side of the frame.

"That's Trina," Phyla said. "Our mechanic. There's no sound in these, unfortunately, so I have idea what she's saying down the ramp."

Trina edged closer to the boarding ramp and then jumped past it to the control panel on the wall. The mechanic pulled a small lever and the boarding ramp retracted. On the low edge of the ramp, an arm appeared, then a head. A trooper climbed his way up the ramp as it swung closed. Trina saw the guy too and reached back into the crate for one of the metal tools. Holding it out in front of her like a club, Trina backed away.

"You think she's running, but Trina knows every inch of this ship," Phyla said. "That panel there, put enough weight on it and it'll give. Just a bit, but enough."

The trooper took a step towards Trina and stumbled as his knee dropped farther than he expected. Trina leaned in, swinging the metal club. The trooper moved his left arm in the way, taking the hit and falling right. With his other arm, the trooper pulled out a small object that flashed. Trina froze, the club dropping from her grip. She fell after it, lying on the floor.

"She's only stunned," Viola said. "The color, it's based on the make-up of the energy triggered. The white, it's more electrical, locks up the nervous system."

Phyla glanced at Viola. The girl knew her colors. It was a start.

In the video, the man walked over to the control panel and reversed the boarding ramp's course. He turned and shouted something down the opening. Then an orange blast from off the screen lanced through the cargo bay and into the trooper's side.

"Erick?" Viola said.

"Better shot than you'd think," Phyla said. "I've never figured out where he learned how to fight so well."

The trooper stumbled onto the ramp, then fell to his knees. Erick walked into the feed, towards the control panel, but a flurry of guns from out of sight launched lasers up into the ship, driving Erick back. The doctor settled for reaching Trina and dragging her away. Two seconds later and more troopers appeared on the ramp, moving upward in a crouch, guns ready and pointed. Erick and Trina weren't in the shot any longer.

"The next few minutes is Erick and Trina playing cat and mouse with them," Phyla said. "His mouth keeps moving, like he's trying to reach us over his comm, but they had at least one localized jammer."

"I don't understand why they'd be doing this?" Viola said.

"That's the million coin question," Phyla replied.

Phyla reached over and swiped forward. Now Erick and Trina, still motionless, were in the left engine room. Erick stashed Trina in a corner, then took up a covered position next to the room's entrance. For a bit there was nothing, only Erick staring down the hallway. Then something made him jump, and Erick looked back at Trina, closed his eyes for a breath, then leaned around the corner and fired. Erick kept shooting, targeted and steady, until the gun flashed a red laser, a marker that there was only one more shot left.

Erick took another look back at Trina, aimed the gun at her, then shook his head. Pointed the weapon back off screen.

"He thought they'd kill them both, or do something worse," Phyla said. "I can't even imagine feeling that hopeless."

Erick fired the last shot. A chorus of replies blasted at the doctor, who ducked away from the lasers. Then a few troopers ran into the room, grabbing Erick and throwing him against the engine housing. When Erick tried to throw a punch, one of the troopers whipped out a knife and slashed Erick along his stomach. Phyla paused the video there, then wiped it from the cockpit display.

"You don't need to see the rest," Phyla said.

"So they took Trina, but left Erick?"

"Maybe they thought he would die anyway. So they compromised our ship. All while we were out at the bar, helping you."

"Wait, this wasn't—"

"I know it's not your fault," Phyla said, looking away. "But we should have been here helping them."

"What are you going to do?"

A speaker on the left console crackled. Davin's voice came over, telling everyone to come to the cargo hold.

"We're going to get our friends back,"

Rescue Mission

Opal sat on the bench, sipping coffee and watching the morning shifters heading into their stores, offices, wherever. Across the boulevard was the one place Eden Prime built to house any offenders it couldn't immediately banish. Ten cells, laser-locked and arranged in a circle. A lot of effort for drunks that needed sobering up. Getting here was too expensive to risk doing something stupid enough to get exiled. A trooper stood in front, holstered gun visible, though the man spent most of his time staring at his comm.

"You think that's where they took Trina and Cadge?" Davin's voice came over her comm.

"I'm going to get a better angle now, see if I can spot their heat signatures," Opal said.

The prison jutted out from the wall of Eden Prime, stretching to the center of the boulevard that ran the course of the station. The outside walls looked three stories high. Automated security meant nothing so old-fashioned as guard towers stood on the ramparts.

Above the front door sat a row of windows looking in at the prison's command center. Tinted, the windows prevented anyone from seeing what was happening inside, but gave a clear view out. A problem for most would-be spies. Opal, however, preferred to play with the less visible spectra.

With a twist on the left lens of the goggles sitting on her face, Opal tweaked the view to capture infrared rays only. To save on heating costs, Eden Prime built the ventilation to leak into the boulevard, filtering out towards air scrubbers in the ceiling and floors. The prison leaked plenty of heat straight towards Opal, and the two bodies working consoles in the prison command center stood out in red. The hallways behind, where the cells sat, were murkier. Body heat blended with other sources to make a hazy picture.

"Can't tell for sure," Opal said. "If I had to hunch it, though, I'd say they aren't creative enough to put her anywhere else."

"Calling for a break-in on a hunch isn't exactly my favorite thing," Davin replied.

"No time for anything else," Opal said. "Make the call, captain."

Opal braced for a snap back. A reprimand. Attempting to order a captain on Mars with that tone would've had her getting crap assignments for a week. Possibly worse.

"Have to roll the dice sometimes. Get set on the entrance," Davin commed. "We'll be there soon."

"On it, boss," Opal said. This wasn't Mars. Remember that. Now get in position.

Not that there were great sniping options in the open boulevard. The closed store behind Opal had a second story and a few windows. Perfect, if only she could get in. The one window on the first floor peered into a blank interior, everything of value removed to pay the owner's debts. Still, Opal figured the window tied into the station's alarm network. A smash and she'd have troopers swarming her within a couple of minutes. The door, however . . .

Opal stood and went to the door. The flat metal sheet had a red light on the right. Key card access, programmed to allow the new owners in and nobody else. Thing was, the Wild Nines had cards that gave them emergency access anywhere. Necessary if they were policing the whole station. Opal still had hers. Maybe they hadn't been deactivated yet.

"Can I help you?" said a man's voice behind Opal. "This store's closed, and I noticed you've been out here for a while."

"Sorry, I used to come here. I was trying to figure out why it was shut down," Opal said.

"Sure. I scanned you, and it looks like you have quite the weapon in your pack. Want to talk about that?" The voice said.

Opal stared at the trooper. "No, I don't think I do."

"Too bad," the trooper said. "Cause I'm going to have to confiscate it. Not allowed on Eden Prime, you know."

"That's Eden for you. Always changing their rules," Opal said, slinging her pack off of her back. "Can I get it back when I leave?"

"I'll submit it to holding. When you leave Europa, you can go ask for it from them at the entrance to the bays. You don't cause any problems, they'll give it to you," the trooper said, keeping one hand on his sidearm.

The trooper wasn't accosting her, the guy was only doing his job. Which made the next part tougher. But random chance had no mercy. Taking out the jumble of parts that made up her rifle, Opal handed the armful to the trooper, who took it.

"Oh, you'll want to be careful with this part," Opal said, reaching towards the guard and pressing the rifle's magnetic assembly button. The charge kicked and the parts slotted together, matching their precise strengths, and pinching the guards fingers, and arms in between pieces.

The trooper screamed and shook his hands out of the rifle, which finished snapping together, just in time for Opal's kick to land in the trooper's chest. The guard fell backward to the ground, groaning, and Opal reached for the rifle. As her hand came close, a bolt screamed from the prison and glanced off of the floor in front of her.

Screams rang out along the boulevard as people ran away for cover. Opal dove, rolling behind the bench and sneaking a look at the prison. The tint across the windows had changed color, a filter to let the lasers through. Behind it, at least two more silhouettes aimed at her.

"Captain, about that help," Opal said into the comm, her eyes tracking to the rifle, sitting meters away, out of reach.

"Yeah?" Davin's voice.

"I'll take it now."

Outnumbered

The guards didn't bother shooting at Opal behind the bench. Not that the metal was much protection, but the troopers were probably waiting for their friends to flank her. Opal could see the one she'd kicked climbing back to his knees, favoring his hands.

Opal reached into her waistband, along her inner thigh to where, wrapped around, was a beam knife. Her fingers flipped the tiny latch and the band curled around itself, rolling into a small cylinder and clicking together in her waiting hand. The knife emitted a small, direct laser a few inches out in front. Good for poking an eye out, or severing ties.

"Davin," Opal said into the comm. "Where are you?"

"On our way,"

"I have a little knife, and a bunch of troopers with guns coming. I wasn't planning to die today."

"You won't," Davin replied.

She'd hold him to that. The front door to the prison opened with the audible whoosh of air moving from one spot to the next. Opal peeked through the gaps in the bench, saw four troopers running towards her, and took a deep breath. They'd be on her in a three-count. Opal watched the shadows on the closed store, broadcast there from the prison's bright lights.

One. The tops of the trooper's heads appeared, rising up the wall like ghosts. The sound of their boots hitting the floor of the boulevard was audible, a mismatched pattering of thumps.

Two. Beneath the noise, Opal thought she could hear them talking to each other. The shadows split, a pair to either side of the bench. Close now. Opal tensed her legs, shifted her feet to give maximum lift. A single chance at surprise.

Three.

The first guard sliced by Opal's beam knife in his hands yelled and backed away. The other three paused, keeping a meter of distance between them and Opal, who stayed at a crouch behind the bench.

"It's just a knife," one of the troopers said. "Stun her."

As though flipping a switch, the troopers seemed to remember that they had that setting on their guns. Opal, watching the shadows, saw the trooper behind her slip the gun from his holster. In a single motion, Opal turned and swung her right arm around, letting go of the knife just as her arm passed the apex of her swing. The beam blade turned in the air for second, before bouncing off the trooper's face, hilt-first.

"Crap," Opal said as the trooper guard rubbed his face, looking confused.

Opal felt the arms of the other two guards grab and pull her to the ground. The binders went on, clasping around her wrists and dialing to a tightness that prevented movement but still allowed circulation. One trooper pressed her face hard into the floor, the icy metal biting up through her cheek and into her teeth. And then the pressure vanished as the trooper pulled Opal to her feet, turned her around to face him

"I think I recognize you," the trooper said. "You're one of the Wild Nines, right?"

Opal said nothing, stared at his face. Breathe. Ignore her racing heart and pumping adrenaline. Stay calm.

"Hope you called your friends," then trooper continued, a loopy smile crawling on his face. "Sooner we nab all of you, sooner we can stop trying so hard."

"You're in way over your head," Opal said to the guy pushing her.

"Says the one in cuffs," the trooper retorted.

Opal's comm buzzed, a single clicking noise.

"Not for long," Opal muttered.

Dashing

Merc saw the bright lights of the prison flooding into the boulevard and, as he ran, pulled a pair of small discs with rubber caps in the center from clasps on his belt. With a press of the button in the center of each one, Merc primed the discs. Electric current running through and building up energy in the center of each one.

As Merc continued around the curve, the scene came into view. Five troopers, one a meter away from the prison door with Opal in tow. The other four standing around, watching, weapons holstered, at ease. Hope they liked surprises.

Still in stride, Merc side-armed the two discs, releasing the button as he threw. The discs bounced and slid along the ground towards the four troopers. A hot second after that, as the troopers were looking at them, the grounding rubber on the discs retracted and lightning struck.

Charged bolts of electricity leapt from the discs at the troopers, arcing through the air and into their guns, their hands, any possible conductor to try to reach the ground. Lightning struck the four troopers in milliseconds, overloading their nerves and causing them to collapse, twitching, to the ground.

The trooper holding Opal stared, open-mouthed, at his companions, and kept his mouth open as Opal elbowed him in the stomach, then turned, sweeping low with her leg, and tripped him. He hit the ground hard and didn't bother trying to get up. Merc caught up to his discs, their currents discharged and sitting inert on the ground. The surrounding troopers were moaning, eyes closed and curled up, nerves still twitching. If the residual shocks worked as advertised, these guys should be out for the next thirty minutes or more.

"Am I awesome?" Merc said, grabbing the discs. "Cause I think I'm pretty awesome."

The laser from the prison window caught Merc full in the chest. The burning sensation of the blast hit and spread through his body, fire crawling over kindling. Nerves roasted. His arms and legs went numb. Merc fell to his knees, trying to put himself back together.

There were things he should be doing. Should get up, cut Opal from those cuffs, should get the second disc and then break into the prison. Save Trina. Oh man, Opal would be so pissed he'd been shot. Always telling him not to show off. Reminding him every second that fighter pilots didn't know how things worked in the trenches. That training was nothing compared to the real thing. Guess she was right.

Opal was right next to him now. Merc looked at her, and realized he was on his side. When did that happen? Tried to ask Opal how bad it was. Couldn't tell if his mouth was moving. Things were starting to hurt now, twinges of pain coming in from all corners. Just, everywhere. Opal was pulling him behind a bench now. Another laser flashed nearby.

"Sorry," Merc said, or thought he did. It was too hard to tell.

Assault Tactics

This was why Davin didn't want heroes on his crew. Get themselves shot and ruin it for everybody. If Merc wasn't so damn good in a Viper …

Davin and Mox moved along the outside of the prison building, working their way to the front door. It came out from the side of Eden Prime like a bulge, the curved wall slick and polished Europa rock. A few cameras dotted the two-story top, black eyes peeking out. No windows, save the big one in front. Cheaper to put screens inside than drill holes in the structure. A normal morning, the shops around the prison would already crawl with perusers. Laser-fire had a way of keeping things clear.

Across the boulevard, Opal had Merc cowering behind a bench. Shots lanced out from above the door every few seconds when a trooper thought they had a shot. The cameras would show Davin and Mox coming along beneath, give the troopers time to prepare for a frontal assault. One that wasn't coming.

"Let's say hi," Davin said.

Mox, without his cannon for mobility, crouched. Then, rattling the ground, he jumped the three meters up to the large front window. Mox, at the top of his jump, swung his right fist forward and shattered the glass. The big man was sporting thick work gloves, meant for welding spaceship hull together, but good at keeping those hands safe from the razor-sharp shards that scattered.

Davin stepped to the side as Mox crashed down, shards shattering all around the metal man. Man, Davin ought to look into one of those exoskeletons. For now, though, he'd have to make this throw with his puny human arms. Davin unclipped a small sphere from his belt, pressed a button on it with his thumb, and arced it up through the window.

"Good throw," Mox said.

A hot second later, the orb exploded in a crackling flash of bright light. Mox jumped again, this time grabbing hold of the window and pulling himself in. Davin waited for the sounds of gunfire, but there was only banging. A chair flew back out the window, bouncing through the middle of the boulevard.

"Clear," Mox's voice came over the comm.

"Opal, get him back," Davin said. "Phyla, Erick?"

"We know," Phyla replied. "Already prepping the bed."

Davin watched Opal pulled Merc out from behind the bench. There was no way she'd be able to lift the pilot. Drag him back alive. It was lose Merc, or let Mox handle the prison by himself. Davin looked at the troopers lying on the boulevard ground, still stunned from Merc's electric discs. If that was the best they had, Mox could handle it.

"Together!" Davin said.

Opal nodded, and the two of them held Merc up between them and started the long walk back to the bays. Merc's pilot jacket, a relic from his Earth training days, was charred around the chest, the burned black looking wet next to the dyed dark of the rest of the clothes.

"Mox, you're on your own," Davin commed. "Bring Cadge and Trina home."

"Will do," Mox replied.

Ready to Leave

Viola repacked in record time, Puk spending every second juicing up on its charger. Was she really leaving with Davin and his band of mercenaries? Then again, what else was there to do? The clothes finished falling in the suitcase and Viola pressed the vacuum button. The sunflower-yellow suitcase compressed on itself, forcing the air out. Essential for the tight spaces on ships.

"You're doing this, huh?" Puk said as it came awake.

"I know, as a bot, the concept of mortality doesn't play with you," Viola said, hefting the suitcase and walking towards the door. "But as a person, I have an urge to feel like I'm making something of myself before I die."

"The way to do that is joining a bunch of killers after they're accused of murder?"

"Accused doesn't mean convicted."

They went to the hotel lobby. The souls staying there were rising, and the entryway was full of bleary people grabbing coffees, waters, and scattered breakfast food. Viola snagged a raspberry danish - the fruit filling lab-grown in Eden Prime's own greenhouses - and shoved it in her mouth as she walked out the door.

"Your father would send the coin to get you home, you know," Puk said as they weaved through to the exit.

"I don't want to—"

Viola heard the shouts on opening the door. To her left, a stream of people was running back towards the hotel, towards the bays. Early workers, cast in the murky beige of dawn, Eden Prime adjusting itself to let in more bright light. The solar satellite, beaming its power to Eden Prime, glared above Viola.

"Think that's Davin's doing?" Viola said, pointing towards the crowd.

"Let's bet on it. If it's them, you go home. If it's not, I'll shut up."

"Tempting, but we're going the other way," Viola moved towards the bays. Phyla had said that if Viola wanted, the Nines had an extra spot. They'd let her go along with them as gratitude for helping Erick. Phyla coupled the invitation with a time check, the Nines wouldn't be waiting for Viola either. Once they were in space, Viola would send a message to her father, tell him where he could get the *Gepard*.

"Their ship's broken, remember?" Puk said, gliding along behind her.

"I'm an engineer, and you're full of all of human knowledge," Viola replied. "Can't be that hard to fix."

"I will play that back to you when it blows up in our faces."

"That happens, I probably won't be around to hear it."

A few minutes walk brought them to the main bay doors, crowded with bots and people shuttling goods in and out. People were talking about a fight, but their tones were curious. Less worried than amused at their friends who'd skipped out of going to the office for fear of a stray laser.

As Viola walked through the main doors, a man wearing a tall, thick coat and wide-brimmed hat brushed against her going the opposite direction. The contact was hard, no give, and Viola stumbled to the side.

"Hey, watch it," Puk said, buzzing near the man's head.

The man paused, and Viola noticed that though he was leaving the bays, he wasn't carrying anything. No luggage. At least, nothing outside of that coat. His head turned and, in the shadow cast by the brim of his hat, Viola could see the wild grin. The man's teeth shone. Gleamed in the light.

"Uh, never mind Puk," Viola said. "I'm fine."

The man stared at her for another second before jerking forward and walking away.

"What's up with that guy?" Puk said.

"Don't know, don't want to know," Viola replied. "Now let's go before anything else happens."

Prison Break

Jumping into the command center, the two troopers Davin incapacitated with his flashbang were stumbling around, holding their ears. Mox walked up to the first one, took the sidearm on the ground, swapped it to stun, and blasted him in the face. The second guard tried to run away, but tripped on a chair and fell, smacking his head on a console. Mox checked the man, there was breathing.

"Clear," Mox commed.

Leave them alive. Davin's command as they left the *Jumper*. They think we're murderers, let's not prove them right. But these troopers, they had already shot Merc. Taken Trina and Cadge. Sabotaged their ship. Mox wasn't sure when the line to kill was crossed, but the troopers should have crossed it by now.

The door to the command center opened, another trooper.

"What the hell is going—" the trooper said as she stared at the shattered glass.

Mox blasted her with the stunner. Taking two quick strides, Mox caught the woman as she collapsed. On her belt dangled a red keycard, one of those that could open a cell. Mox tore the card off, set the woman in a chair and went hunting for prisoners. The main hallway, on the first floor, wrapped around the prison like a circle, with cells every four meters. The first three were unoccupied, their laser-gates sitting open. Spare beds unruffled.

As Mox approached the fourth, around a bend in the hallway, he could hear a pair of guards talking. Debating whether to run or fight. To keep the prisoner.

It wasn't their choice.

Mox didn't so much step as bound around the curve, using the exoskeleton to run nearly two meters a stride, so that when the troopers turned to see what was coming to wreck them, any fight was already lost. Mox struck the closer guard with his shoulder, leaning into the charge, and knocked the trooper into his comrade, sending them both spilling to the ground. The cell to the left held Trina, lying on the bed. But only her.

"Where is other one?" Mox said to the cowering guards. "Short. Angry."

"We don't know!" the trooper Mox hadn't hit said, holding his hands out in front of himself. "She's the only one here, promise!"

"Are you lying?" Mox said, standing over them.

The panic in their faces told more truth than their blubbering denials.

"Then run," Mox said. "And I will not break you."

Both of them, the one Mox hit going gingerly, rose to their feet and ran. When one tried to keep his gun, Mox reached out, grabbed the weapon and tore it from the trooper's hands. Mox slammed the gun into the wall until it was little more than broken plastic. The only sound after that was their boots as the troopers ran.

Mox pressed the card to the cell door and the laser gates cut off with a fizzle. On the thin bed in the cell, a woman lay unconscious. Still stunned. Still breathing. Mox picked her up from the bed, blanket and all, and walked from the cell.

Not Gone Yet

Davin and Opal held Merc over their shoulders and ran back towards bay three.

"I have Trina," Mox commed. "Cadge is not here."

"Mox," Opal commed. "Don't forget my rifle!"

"I will get it," Mox replied. "You will owe me."

"Can't you get another one?" Davin asked Opal between breaths.

"You make me leave it, you buy me a new one."

"How much do they cost?"

Opal said the amount like a curse, and Davin replied in kind.

"Davin?" Phyla's voice over the comm. "What's the status?"

"Mox has Trina and we're comin' home. No Cadge though. Is Erick better?"

"He's moving, but it's not good."

"Then read up on laser burns, cause we're going to need a doctor."

The doors to bay one and the shipping corridor loomed large in the growing morning. Yellowed lights projected on the large, dark gray slabs that would move aside when Davin approached. Eden branded the doors with the intertwining greens that made up their logo, echoing to rainforests Davin had never seen. The entire plaza was empty, not a good sign for what should have been a busy rush of morning lift-offs.

As they approached the entrance door, it didn't open.

"Ah, crap," Davin said.

"Figures it won't open," Opal said.

"Phyla?" Davin commed. "I need you to see what's holding the doors shut to the bays. We can't get in."

"We don't have access to Eden Prime's internal network anymore," Phyla said. "They cut us off when—"

"That ever stopped you before?" Davin interrupted. "We need these doors opened now!"

"On it," Phyla replied.

Setting Merc near the edge of the doors, back against the big bay walls, Davin handed Opal his holstered sidearm. She took it with a nod, then dashed away from the doors and into the shadows near large stacks of crates waiting for outgoing ships. Connecting the dots; the locked door, the boulevard empty of crowds during a busy part of the morning, and it wasn't hard to see the outline of a trap.

"Davin Masters!" Ferro's voice poured out of nowhere. "We meet again, and this time it will not go well for you."

Davin tried tracing the sound, but stopped when Ferro walked out into the boulevard, keeping plenty of room between them. He must have been waiting in a store. More proof they were triggering a trap. Davin hated traps, especially when he was caught in them.

"Great," Davin said. "Glad to hear it."

"I appreciate the attitude," Ferro said. "More fun to wipe the smile off of a face than a frown."

Ferro raised a hand and Davin felt something drop on his shoulders and knock him to the ground, breath flying from his lungs and a sharp crack sounding in his chest. His face kissed the floor. The hell was that?

"Oh, I'm sorry. Did that ruin your comeback?" Ferro said. "Then I think what happens next will leave you at a total loss for words."

"Don't think comedy's your thing, Ferro," Davin wheezed, trying to gather enough strength to lift whatever was on top of him away.

Melody, black and wicked, sat a meter away. Close enough to roll to, grab, and squeeze the trigger. Burning Ferro to a crisp would make a solid punchline to this surreal conversation.

Opal must not have a shot. Or she thought Davin could take it. Either way,

Davin had to get this thing off his back.

"Good thing you are a captive audience," Ferro said. The man wasn't moving any closer. Wasn't pulling a gun. Why?

Ribs hurting, Davin collected his hands and pushed. Off of his back rolled something in a thick body bag, something with lumps and blunt edges. But Davin couldn't spare a look. He rolled to Melody, picked it up, and fired it straight up towards where the drop had come from. A pair of troopers watching on the second floor walkway leading to flight control. Waiting for something.

Davin wasn't going to play their game. Melody spat out six balls of grass-colored fire that struck the troopers and the bay wall, bursting into small fires on impact. The troopers fell, rolling on the ground to put out the flames.

Davin heard a surprised shout from behind and knew Opal caught her cue. Ferro was running away, ducking away and out of sight.

"Missed him!" Opal whispered over the comm.

"Getting sloppy, Opal," Davin replied, backing towards the bay doors and Merc, who was lying there, chest rising and falling in shallow breaths. "Where are we at, Phyla?"

"Almost," Phyla commed.

Davin suddenly remembered the thing that'd fallen on him. It was a large bag, with something in it, something moving. If he had Opal's beam knife . . .

"Davin, that you?" called a muffled voice inside the bag. "Cut me out of here, man!"

"Cadge?" Davin said. "You're . . . in the bag?"

"Congrats, you win the prize," Cadge said. "But you only get the reward if you get me out."

"Don't have a knife," Davin said. "Give me a minute to think."

The sound of a door opening up above. Davin looked at the walkway where the troopers had been burning, and saw nothing. Following their commander into the dark. Cowards.

"What wrong with you people?" Davin yelled at the space. "Who drops a person on somebody?"

"I did not drop her," Mox, holding Trina and with Opal's rifle slung over his back, stomped around the curve and into view.

"Nice of you to show," Davin said. "You see Ferro, any troopers come your way?"

Mox shook his head.

"I've got the doors," Phyla's commed. "Marl may have locked us out, but Eden Prime's security is as crappy as ever."

"I am profoundly thankful for their incompetence," Davin replied. "Open'em."

The bay doors lurched open, revealing the corridor beyond, and a person, leaning against the wall, sporting a thick and tall coat that covered his entire side. A collar that nearly touched the brim of the hat. The person didn't turn, didn't react to the sudden reveal of a wounded pilot, a metal-framed man holding an unconscious woman, a squirming bag, and Davin aiming Melody straight down the corridor.

"Now, who are you?" Davin said.

The person's head turned towards him. At ten meters, Davin couldn't see the man's face. But something glinted in that dark space. Teeth, maybe?

"Mox, cut Cadge out," Davin said, keeping the gun aimed on the person. "I'm not getting any warm and fuzzy vibes from Dark'n'Quiet over here."

"Davin, what's the problem?" Phyla commed. "I've got our bay doors unlocked, but I don't know how long that'll last."

"There's someone in the corridor," Davin said. "Will keep you informed."

"Mister Masters," the shape said, its voice a meandering whisper. "You and your band have been charged with a crime. A grievous one."

Davin heard Mox tearing open Cadge's bag, the little man coughing up a storm as he breathed in fresh air.

"Never thought of us as a band. More like a company. A squad," Davin replied, taking a step towards the man. Putting distance between himself and Trina, Merc.

"Murder, Mister Masters," the person continued, still leaning against the corridor wall. "The given punishment by the Free Laws is death."

"The Free Laws?" Davin laughed. "Those are a bunch of crap."

A product of the corporations to govern outer space. No government, no votes by any populace. Just a bunch of people in a board room deciding how they wanted to punish peons they didn't like.

"Androids do not judge," the person said. "We are merely an instrument of justice."

The androids, impartial enforcers of Free Law punishment, provided a company would pay for one. That Eden coughed up the coin wasn't exactly surprising. That Davin's hands were sweating, his heart pounding, that wasn't surprising either. Androids, he could do without.

"Guess I'll take you as a compliment. Didn't know we were worth that much," Davin said, then, to Mox and Cadge. "Get going. I'll distract him till you get by."

The android didn't reply, turned to face Davin straight on. Mox and Cadge, the former carrying Merc and the latter holding Trina, edged away.

"You got this captain?" Cadge said. "Guy looks a little messy."

"Just go for the ship when it comes at me," Davin said. "I don't want to worry about you."

The android broke into a run right at Davin. Its coat billowed out behind, and as the android ran, its arms pumped forward and a pair of nasty looking knives appeared in its palms. Up close and personal, then. The kind of fight Davin wanted. The captain raised Melody and, backpedaling back to the boulevard, pulled the trigger.

Melody's six green bolts converged on the android, who, just before the shots struck home, jumped off of the corridor floor, pushed off of the side wall, and flipped over the bolts. The android hit the ground running. A helluva move. Only meters between the two of them.

In his peripheral, Davin saw Mox and Cadge make a break down the corridor with their precious cargo. Davin had to last long enough for them to get away.

The android passed the bay doors, went out into the boulevard lights. The android's face had a rigid exactitude to it. A perfection to the skin, the bones. Lacking life's nicks and scratches. A man's face, but not a man. And it was about to kill him.

The laser shot out at an angle from the shadows to Davin's right. The aim was dead on, striking the android in the chest. It barely flinched, keeping its stride moving, a molten black mark just below the shoulder where Opal shot it. Davin saw the android's right hand slide back, knife pointed, and swung Melody in the way. The android's arm pumped, the blade striking Melody's barrel with a metallic screech and sliding off. Then the android ran into Davin. The two of them fell to the ground, Davin underneath, Melody in the space between them. In a second, Davin was going to get very, very stabbed.

The android's left arm drew back while Davin struggled to throw the bot away.

The android didn't look that big, but was it heavy. Arms pushing against Melody pushing against the robot, Davin couldn't get an inch. Then another bolt came from the shadows, this time striking the android in the head.

It hesitated, the left side of its skull a molten goo, and Davin, using Melody as a brace, slid out from beneath the robot. The knife stabbed a moment later, tearing through the sleeve of Davin's coat and sticking the floor. Davin pulled Melody out with him and, as the android turned its half-face to look at him, Davin fired.

This time there wasn't any room for the android to move, and the bolts blasted its chest. It stumbled backwards, gouts of green flame rising from its burning clothes. Both knives dropped, bouncing off the floor as the robot's hands tried to pat out the fire.

"Time to run!" Davin yelled, but Opal was way ahead of him. Already disappearing through the bay doors. Davin set off after her. Clear the bay doors, slam them shut and they'd have enough time to get away. A red bolt seared past Davin's head, scoring off of the corridor ceiling. Only a another few strides till he was through. Opal, in the corridor, turned and aimed past Davin, squeezing off shot after shot over Davin's shoulders.

"Shut the door now!" Davin said into the comm and, a half-second later, the sound of the doors clanging shut behind Davin's back brought immense relief. A cold shower of hope. Davin looked over at Opal as they walked the corridor and she gave him a nod. She'd saved his life. Not for the first, probably not for the last, time.

"You make it?" Phyla commed.

"I'm in. We'll be there in two. I want to be gone by three."

Picking up Pieces

Trina shook awake, feeling droplets all over her face. Blinked into the bright light of the med bay. Erick stood over her, and Trina felt pressure on her wrist. The sensation came slow, her muscles soft, eyes and ears muffled, like coming awake from a deep dream. Except her heart, which beat like she'd sprinted a kilometer.

"Don't worry," Erick said to her. "I had to spike you with adrenaline, then gave you a spray with the mister to shake you out. The numbness should fade in a minute. Normally I'd wait the stun effects out, but the ship appears stuck without your help."

"Davin would leave with me unconscious?" Trina said. A headache thudded beyond the edges of her eyes, She noticed Erick had a long series of bandages along his abdomen, that the doctor looked pallid. "You ought to lay here."

"Not a luxury I have," Erick said. "If you're feeling better, then I have to check on my other patient."

"Other patient?"

"Merc took a laser to the chest."

Mox walked into the med bay, his giant frame making the space crunching between the bed and the medical lamp. He looked at Trina and, seeing her awake, nodded.

"Good?" Mox said.

"Capable enough to assure the engines run," Trina replied. "However, I shall need assistance to get to them, as my legs seem to be beyond my ability to control."

Both Mox and Erick helped Trina out of the bed and stood her up on the floor. She was wearing the same clothes, the light shirt and work jeans, that she'd been captured in, only now Trina felt as though they weighed a thousand kilos. Her legs were like the engines she ran, Trina knew they were there and how to use them, but could not feel what they were doing.

"You will need to carry me," Trina said to Mox. "I give you permission."

"Then we will run," Mox said. He scooped Trina up, cradling her in his arms. Trina watched the hallways speed by as Mox clomped. Noticed, on the floor, a streaking red stain.

"Whose is that?" Trina said.

"Erick," Mox said. They took the left at the T past the crew cabins, heading towards the engines.

The bandage on his stomach. The trail was thick.

"He dragged you. Back here," Mox said. "Tried to hold out."

Trina entered the box room where the left engines and their control panel sat. Scuffs and more blood stained the metal, but not the blast marks Trina expected.

"They didn't try to shoot him?" Trina said.

"Didn't want to damage the engines."

"Why not?"

"Trap," Mox said.

Ah, right. Because if the troopers ruined the engines, the *Jumper* wouldn't takeoff. And if they didn't take off, then their trap wouldn't trigger. They could have just dismantled the ship, kept them from leaving. But Trina had to think about where she was. Eden Prime. New business ventures didn't play well if they were violent and left a bunch of people dead in their bays. And after the inspectors, Marl didn't want corpses dropped on the news headlines.

"Easier to call it a malfunction on launch," Trina muttered.

"Hmm?" Mox said.

"Nothing," Trina replied. "They would not have had much time for a complex adjustment."

Trina moved over to the engine panel and reached into a brick-sized storage cubby. A multi-tool, some screws, adhesive, and a quick reference book for all the various alarms the engines used, a book that helpfully added the estimated time until the ship would explode.

Looking at the main engine panel, there were four screws holding in the faceplate. On that plate was a screen reading out simple figures on whether the engine fuel,whether sensors reported clean pipes for thrust, connection to the ship's computer, and so on. A series of dots and symbols. That they were green meant the troopers hadn't messed with anything obvious.

Trina's eyes went over the screws. And there it was. Each of the screws twisted to a different angle, wound in without proper precision. You couldn't have that on a space ship, especially not on the engine housing. One pops loose in flight and there'd be catastrophe.

"Amateurs," Trina said. "Look at this, Mox. They failed to cover up their work."

"Or you are too good," Mox said.

"Perhaps."

Then, with a few quick presses of the multi-tool, Trina had the engine panel off and was staring at a nest of wires. Wrapped around a pair of them, the ones that monitored the engine's cooling, was a small band. A black strip, and Trina knew what was under it. Metal teeth, designed to cut into the wires as the *Jumper* went through atmosphere and warmed up. Interrupt the circuit. The metal teeth were flimsy, though. Cheap. They'd keep the circuit together for a few minutes time before falling apart. Then, boom.

"I'll give them this much," Trina said, slicing through the band and cutting it off the wires. "They had the right tool in the right place. They were close to killing us."

"You'd have found it."

Wide awake and full of energy? She would have. Now, though, better to do it without the stress of actual flight going on as well.

"I will tell Davin to shift the camera, or buy another, to watch the panels."

Mox nodded and left Trina to prepping the ship for launch. First, Trina removed the sabotaging band, then sagged against the wall, closing her eyes. If those screws had been right, Trina wouldn't have caught it. Would've assumed they'd blown the job. Given up the sabotage and hoped Davin wouldn't leave without trying to rescue his crew. All of them vaporized twenty kilometers out of Europa's atmosphere when the left engine overheated, a short-lived star in Eden Prime's sky.

A Fresh Start

"They're saying we're cleared for launch," Phyla laughed. "Funny, cause I thought they were just trying to kill us."

"Still think we're rigged," Davin said. Phyla looked at the captain, sitting in his chair, holding his side.

"Why haven't you gone to see Erick?"

"Because my ribs won't matter if that android blows us away before we get out of here."

"Nobody's getting through."

At least, not till they performed some heavy maintenance on the computer code controlling the shipping doors, which would be one helluva task. Phyla sent the go command to flight control and the bay three launch door opened. The blue brightness of day flung itself in, washing out the artificial lights in the floors and ceilings.

"We ready to spool up?" Phyla commed to Trina, in the engines.

"All greens," Trina said. "There's always a chance they committed a second sabotage, but the odds are against it. Though I must admit I am not at one hundred percent."

"What do you think, captain?" Phyla said. "You trust your mechanic?"

"She's been stunned, concussed, and hasn't slept all night?" Davin said. "Completely. Let's go."

The *Jumper* sat on a series of landing struts, and when Phyla pressed the pre-launch button on the console, those struts raised a few centimeters off of the ground. A series of small jets triggered, firing at the bay floor and shoving the *Jumper* up. From there, Phyla used the flight stick, a twin-pronged beast of a thing covered with quick-access buttons tied to commands. She could talk to the ship's computer, of course, but Phyla preferred the speed of touch.

With a few taps, the landing struts retracted, the engines warmed up for space travel, and a final series of checks on hull pressurization, fuel load, and more fun things essential for life in the stars, began.

"Ready to say goodbye to this place?" Phyla said.

"I never want to come back."

That tone. Davin slipped into it whenever he was making a promise he knew he couldn't keep. It used to be whether he and Phyla would be back in time for dinner, or wouldn't go to one of Miner Prime's upper levels.

"But we will, won't we?" Phyla said.

"Marl tried to kill us," Davin said, staring out the cockpit as Phyla wheeled the *Jumper* around. "Took Cadge and Trina hostage. Sent an android to murder me. Hell, she probably had those inspectors killed too. It's personal."

"But we're running now?"

"Look at us, Phyla," Davin said, glancing at his own left side. "They hit us by surprise. Half of us are hurt. Merc's a mess. He's sitting in the med bay now, probably will be there for days. I won't get us killed."

"They'll be ready for us, next time," Phyla said.

"There won't be a next time," Davin said. "Things go as I hope—"

"Which they never do."

Phyla slide the throttle forward and the *Jumper* slid out of the bay, its engines emitting the gentle churn that said all was well, and they were ready to blast to another world. The pre-flight checks came back positive. Green and good to go.

"I'll never get tired of it," Davin said. Europa fell below, disappearing as Phyla angled the ship up towards space, towards Jupiter. No pursuit registered on the console. Still waiting for their trap to spring.

"Tired of what?"

"This. Launching. It's a fresh start, every time."

"Funny, cause this time, I feel like we're not getting that at all," Phyla said.

"The first time I left, you remember why?" Davin said, still staring straight through that window.

"You never said. All that talk about getting away, and then one day you're just gone. Lina and I figured you'd died."

"That I'd died? I wanted to find a ship and leave and you thought I'd died?"

"You took days to send a message. Your parents were hysterical. We were going to hold a funeral," Phyla said.

"I was excited," Davin said. "Caught up in it."

"Glad somebody was having fun."

"Point is, we have a chance," Davin said. "And I kept my promise."

The atmosphere bled away as the *Whiskey Jumper* shot out of Europa's atmosphere. No explosion, no problems. Life support recycling air. Artificial gravity keeping them stuck to the floor. No hull breach alarms. The flight path sent by Eden Prime's flight control kept them away from incoming ships, so they went into empty space. A great spot for a bomb to go off without collateral damage.

Ahead of them, Jupiter spun in place. Its swirling beige majesty filled the cockpit with churn and chaos. They watched it for a minute, because what else could you do with something like that except stare?

"You did come back," Phyla said. "Guess I can trust you one more time."

"You pretty much have to," Davin said, leaning back and stretching. "I am the captain, and this is my ship."

"Are you ready then, captain?" Phyla said, shaking her head.

"So ready."

"So where are we going?" Phyla said.

"Home," Davin said.

"Home. You think Lina can help, or do you just want to see her?"

"Can I say yes to both?"

Phyla punched in the route and a yellow line shot out from the front of the *Jumper*, a projection on the cockpit windshield. The route the autopilot recommended to get them to the largest space station in the solar system, Miner Prime.

"Yes," Phyla said, pushing the throttle to full flight speed. Seven days to get to Miner Prime. Seven days to get ready to go home again.

Post-Mortem

Cosmetic damage. No critical functions impacted by the woman's - Fournine checked its memory, the mission bios - Opal's shot to his head. By Davin Masters' resistance. The supply of plaskin the android had brought with it to Europa should suffice to repair the cosmetic damage.

So Fournine ended the mission report, beamed out through its integrated comm to the stars. Fournine looked up at the sky. One of those black specks against Jupiter's bright wash was likely the *Whiskey Jumper*. Where would the Wild Nines be heading now?

"You failed," a man said. Fournine turned to him, Its eyes running over the man and scanning his face, his clothes, his scents. Not much there other than a name, Ferro, and a home location: Mars. Obviously, an outdated entry.

"Their combat abilities surpassed expectations," Fournine said. "As I'm sure you would agree."

Eden Prime's local media, what little there was of it, had already reported on the number of injured troopers and damage to the outpost's prison. Fournine's analysis of the language used made it clear the reporters weren't holding back their condescension.

"It is true. We were not ready for them," Ferro said.

The boulevard picked up as people returned to normal. Lasers weren't flashing. Explosions and screams were non-existent. Society resumed functioning. Fournine detected several glances Its way, even as It picked up and put on Its hat, pulled up its collar. Anyone who looked, who noticed, walked a little faster. Android reputation held, even out here.

"Are you planning a chase?" Fournine said.

"Marl says you will do that. We are to secure the city," Ferro said.

"I am surprised. An analysis of your team's abilities thus far indicates Marl should not trust you with that task."

"I didn't see you help."

"I was operating according to the plan. If it failed, it was due to your team's inability to incapacitate, or to hold, those promised," Fournine said. "In fact, were I to conduct a more thorough analysis, I might find enough to conclude an intentionally weak force posted at the prison."

"Never."

"And if I deemed it so, that could be construed as aiding a fugitive. Under the Free Laws, that mandates the same punishment for you," Fournine said. The android shifted a hand to one of its knives.

"No," Ferro said. "You will not deem it so."

"Why?"

"Because we will help you," Ferro said. He glanced up at the sky. "They disarmed our trap. But they have not found our trace."

Fournine flagged its file on Ferro. Updated to include potentially clever, even duplicitous maneuvers. It re-ran the current conversation in its head, picking apart Ferro's responses and searching for double-meanings, tells, things that may give away a less-than truthful telling.

"So you know where they are heading," Fournine said.

"A deal," Ferro said. "We will give you the destination, help repair and outfit you and your ship, you will not tell Marl anything . . . negative."

"I have filed the report," Fournine said. "But not with Marl. I accept your proposal."

An hour later Fournine sat in the cockpit of the single-person starship made specifically for androids. No life support. No comforts besides the lone chair to access piloting controls. An engine capable of sprinting through the solar system faster than any other ship, including the *Whiskey Jumper*.

"You'll wait until after they land and are separated," the voice on the other end of the transmission said. "I don't want a destructive fight on my station."

"As ordered," Fournine replied. "Be careful, as they are not as simple as they would appear."

"So your failure proved once," the voice said. "Let's hope it does not again."

The Wild Nines were going to Miner Prime. And Fournine would follow.

Banter

"You shoulda seen what I did," Cadge said, sitting at the long table that served as the centerpiece for the *Jumper*'s dining room, the splotched cream top meshing with the battered pots and scratched plastic plates in a nonsensical fashion that Cadge always found relaxing. It wasn't perfect, but it worked damn fine. Kinda like Cadge himself. "Three of'em, trying to jump me and I'm throwing punches faster than a tornado."

"Sure," Mox said. The big guy overwhelmed his chair, sprawling around the armrests and looming over the table's surface. But Cadge saw the crinkle at the edge of Mox's mouth. The lug would sit there and listen to Cadge spin stories the whole journey.

"Then they stunned me, the cowards. Shot me in the back."

The food littering the table was mostly dried stuff that made up the ship's stores. Packets full of what Erick called "flavored calories". Sprinkle on recycled water and they'd stiffen into a paste that was as appealing as it sounded. Cadge preferred the strawberry shortcake, and he had two those packets poured into a bowl in front of him now, stuffing his face with spoonfuls in between beats of story.

"Woke up a few minutes later, cause no stunner's gonna keep me out for long, and there's this guy standing over me. Like he's studying me. Like I'm one of those rats."

Mox was having his usual; a shake full of protein powder and vitamin pills.

The man seemed to live on powdered substances. Sure, from time to time Cadge would dose himself up too. Had to keep the strength out here. Every meal though? No thanks.

"And I'm thinking what, is this guy going to open me up or something? Stick some tracing device in me? So I start talking, throwing my words in his face like nothing you've heard before. Even you would've been embarrassed. I had to throw him off his game, you understand?"

The door to the pod opened and Cadge glanced up to watch the bounty herself, Viola, walk in, looking around like she'd never seen ship's kitchen before.

"Anyway, he kicked me, knocked me out and then I woke up in the bag," Cadge said. Mox grunted, cocking his head to the side. So sorry, big buddy, but a more interesting conversation just walked into the room. "Viola. Can I call you Vi?"

"Vi?" Viola said.

"Shorter," Mox replied.

"Exactly," Cadge said. "Now, you might not think that's a big deal, but wait till you've got a bunch of thugs taking shots at you. I call out Vi, it takes a second and you're moving. I call out Viola and you're dead by the time I finish."

Vi looked at Cadge, mouth hanging open. Like the girl was lost or something.

"Hungry?" Mox asked her.

"A little," Vi replied, a program jerking back into motion.

"This is all we got, Vi, so I'd get used to it," Cadge said. "You can find all the flavors in those cabinets. Limit of two per meal, so we don't eat ourselves to death."

Mox gave a low rumble of a laugh, Vi looked confused. Which was great. Worth money, and not even able to hang with casual conversation. Why Davin wouldn't take them to Ganymede for a hot minute to collect the coin made no sense. Cadge would even take her in himself, if Davin didn't want to. An android after them and they were turning down free coin.

"So tell me," Cadge said to Vi's back as she dug around the cabinets. "Your dad, he really have that much money?"

"He runs Galaxy Forge," Viola replied, as though that answered the question.

And it did. Galaxy Forge, that was one of the big ones. Making ships, robots, whole space stations and scattering them around the solar system. Cadge had heard they were making a millennium ship, one of those big ones designed to go for years and years until they hit another star. Get that reward, Cadge could probably afford a ticket. Maybe even a little extra, once he informed Vi's dad of the trouble the man's daughter had brought with her. Bar fights, Davin taking a punch in the club.

Lotta different stories he could tell.

"So, let me get this straight, your daddy is mega rich, and yet you're here with a few space jockeys about to eat some," Cadge glanced at the packets Vi selected. "Powdered turkey and tomato basil. You thinking this is a good call? That you made the right choice?"

"No idea," Vi said, giving Cadge the old straight stare. "Tell you this much, the conversation's a lot more interesting here."

Hey! What do you know. Vi can talk after all. But coming to the table doesn't mean she could play the game.

"Mox, what one word would you say best describes what we do?" Cadge said.

"Dangerous," Mox replied.

"Dangerous. Girl like you, easy to get hurt out here," Cadge said. Turn up the heat, see if she folds. A volunteer run to Ganymede, coin in the pocket.

"What about Phyla, or Trina?" Vi said.

"They're used to it. Grew up with this. You, you've got the golden ticket," Cadge replied. "We could still change course, drop you at Ganymede?"

"I can't go back yet," Vi said. "There's still so much more to see. Back on Ganymede, I'd be bored."

For the first time, Cadge felt the grin slip. That wasn't what she was supposed to say.

"Bored," Mox said. "Worse than danger."

Vi nodded. That was it then. No game set match here.

"Yeah, well, if you stay, then no whining," Cadge said. "You want to play in space, you got to earn your right to be here. Starting now."

Cadge finished the remark by pushing the last spoonful of shortcake paste into his mouth, staring at Vi as he chewed it. Just because they didn't go to Ganymede now, didn't mean he couldn't get her there eventually. The coin would still be there. Might take a bit of time, but he'd been cruising the stars and bars for years already. He could wait a little longer.

Alive

On Earth, going through the repeated drills necessary to become a fighter pilot, Merc had his fair share of rough-and-tumble moments. Ejected once. Had a ship go dead more than a few times, leaving him stranded and staring at the blue marble until help arrived. Each one hurt, physically, emotionally. Meant he had to do better next time.

This, man, this was different. Opening his eyes took too much work. Coming back to reality meant dealing with the fiery claws ripping their way through his chest. Erick mentioned he was trying to blunt those rending tears. But sleep was the only real escape.

"Merc?" Opal's voice plunged into his psyche. Kept him out of the darkness.

Merc opened his eyes and saw a hazy world too hard to interpret. Looking at him, a brown and black smudge that, after a few blinks, turned into Opal.

"Hey there," Opal said.

"Hey," Merc said. His voice raspy, rusted gears grinding into motion.

"Thanks for coming. For saving me."

"Sure thing," Merc replied. "Not like you needed it."

"I was only cuffed and disarmed," Opal said, her mouth quirking into a smile. "Still plenty dangerous."

"Figured I could help out. Never get the chance to use those discs, you know?"

Opal slid her eyes lower. Merc couldn't follow, his head too heavy to lift. Knew what she was looking at, though.

"I saw," Opal said. "A lot of friends get shot on Mars. From sidearms, some recovered. Others took hits from rifles, from bigger things and never made it back. Thing was, that was a war. When things like that made sense. So I took it, for a while."

"For a while?"

"They don't go away. The ones who don't come back," Opal pulled Merc's covers up, rested her hands on them. "I started to see their faces at night, and then during the day. I'd be looking through the scope and hear one of them beside me, talking. Sit at the mess and one of them is there, next to me. So I left."

"That's when Davin found you?"

"Booze is cheap in Vagrant's Hollow. It didn't make the voices go away, but they were easier to deal with," Opal said. "Then he gave me something to do. A purpose that wasn't quite so violent."

"Sorry for ruining that. Didn't mean to," Merc said.

"It's all right, because you came back. Erick works miracles."

"Speaking of that, how'd I get back here anyway?"

Opal's face brightened. He seen the same look on some of his friends back on Earth. Some who'd been to Mars, who'd been in other fights. Take them away from their souls for a second and give them a chance to tell a good story. Opal jumped right in, going through carrying Merc back to the bay doors, fighting the android, Mox breaking into the prison. Cadge in the body bag.

" . . . and Mox carried you into the ship. You should've seen Erick," Opal said. "Doctor's half-dead already, but has you on the bed acting like he's ready for a twelve-hour operation."

"Man's a saint," Merc replied.

"Know what he said to me, after you passed out the first time?"

"The first time?"

"Oh," Opal pressed her hand to Merc's forehead, gently. Like she was feeling him for a fever. "You haven't really been awake for a while, have you?"

"Nothing since taking the hit. What'd he say to you?"

"That fighter pilots never stay down long, because they never like believing they've been hit."

"I didn't get hit. Here on the ground? That doesn't count."

Merc tried but couldn't keep his eyes from blinking closed. His mind wanted to say awake, but his body couldn't handle the idea.

"Whatever you say, Merc," Opal said. "I should let you sleep. Erick wouldn't be happy with me keeping his patient awake."

"It's good," Merc said. Those fiery claws were falling away as Merc fell deeper into dreamland. Couldn't stop it, didn't want to stop it. He felt Opal's hands wrap around his own, warm gloves. They were nice.

"Goodnight, stick jockey," Opal whispered.

"Goodnight."

Wanted

"What's the charge?" Davin said. They were sitting in the cockpit, the Sun a distant spot far, far in front of them. Jupiter loomed, but it was behind the *Jumper* as it sped towards the interior of the solar system. A few days coasting up to speed, then a few days slowing and they'd be at Miner Prime.

Phyla was scrolling through news on the pilot's console. Every tap she made followed by a lag, sometimes only a few seconds, sometimes minutes. A stream of satellites, running on solar power, chained the routes from Earth to Saturn. Soon to Uranus and Neptune. Each one cached data, building up wads of text from companies, news agencies, and other sources.

The most common stories were locally stored and sent fast, deeper queries required hours as satellites bounced the search to and from comprehensive databases on Earth and Mars.

Pictures, movies were non-existent. Too much data.

"I'm looking through today's database," Phyla said. "There's more than charges than usual."

"They're learning they can abuse this thing."

The Free Laws. No sovereign body in space, so here's this loose set of rules to keep people in line. Including a lovely section where any interested party could pay to list a wanted person, and a reward. The ones with real motivation paid to send an android after you, either catch or kill. Getting a bot to murder a target required approval from a council of judges, but they were all corporate stooges. If you wanted to live in space, you stayed friends with the big companies.

"They waited till people invested out here. Now they're turning the screws," Phyla said. "There's a couple in here for failure to pay on time. Really? You're going to send an android after someone late on a bill?"

"It's their playground, they can make the rules. Anything on us?"

"Here," Phyla said. She swiped on the article, bringing it up on the cockpit glass. With the Sun glaring through part of it, the display adjusted the text color, the blue words flipping to white on the black background of space.

"Pre-meditated murder," Davin muttered, reading. "The Wild Nines, a mercenary group formerly employed by Eden Prime, is accused by same of plotting to eliminate two inspectors."

"It says there's video evidence, but we can't get it out here."

"What'd they record?"

"More like, what did Marl make?" Phyla said.

The rest of the piece was commentary about how the Wild Nines were dangerous, unpredictable, blah blah blah. Same stuff could be said of any mercenary outfit. The real question was why Marl wanted this whole thing done to begin with? Why not just cancel their contract if she wanted them gone?

"I have an idea," Phyla said.

"That she wanted the inspectors dead," Davin said.

"You stealing my thoughts again?"

"Only when there's something useful in them," Davin replied. "Doesn't happen too often."

"Watch it, captain. I can still turn this thing around."

Davin looked up from the news, out through the window. Took another deep breath of that recycled air. A few people he'd met, from Earth, said the stuff had a tang to it, a taste that lingered in the throat. Body's way of saying it wasn't natural. Davin hadn't ever felt that. Then again, he'd never breathed real, pure air.

"Our parents came from Earth," Davin said. "Went to Miner Prime. Started families. They knew they could've gone back home if they ever had the money."

"They didn't."

"But they could've, Phyla. You look at this," Davin glanced back at the console, the murder charge. "We'll never be able to land. They'd shoot us on sight."

"That's why you're upset? Cause you can't get to Earth right now?"

"Guess you think that's a stupid reason?"

"Not if you have more behind that. Like not getting killed by androids. Or starving because nobody's going to hire us."

"Phyla, that's why you're the pilot," Davin said. He leaned back in the copilot's, the captain's chair. "Lets me be the dreamer."

"You always were," Phyla said.

Davin closed his eyes. A few more days till they reached Miner Prime. A murderer's homecoming.

Space Work

A couple weeks in space felt like an endless span of time. Viola kept herself busy, or rather, Trina, Davin and Erick kept giving her things to do. The doctor, impressed with Viola's stitching abilities, grabbed Viola whenever he saw her and go over how something worked. Erick's favorite, and an apparent necessity of a frequent space-farer, was the DNA Restoration machine, or the D-NAR.

The high doses of radiation coming in from the outside world required the occasional extraction, repair, and then injection of small nano-bots that swarmed damaged cells and put them back together. Then a beacon in the waste system collected the bots. Erick would bring them back to the D-NAR to be reset for the next person.

Trina gave Viola things more in line with her classes. Keep the engines primed, monitor the systems if Trina was asleep. Clean the Viper of any atmospheric gunk Merc got on it during his flight on Europa. Trina said the pilot would normally do this himself, but seeing as Merc was barely awake these days, that wasn't happening.

Davin was the worst, though. The captain found the most menial tasks. Shunt the trash out into the void. Inventory the food supplies so Phyla could restock on Miner Prime. Still, the work was better than endless textbooks and articles. It was real. Tightening the bolts on a loose vent was something Viola was actually doing.

In space! Going thousands of miles per hour! Even drudgery, in space, had a tint of wonder. And when Phyla announced over the intercom that they were making their approach to Miner Prime, Viola took a long breath. The vacation was ending.

"You might be sad," Puk said. "But I could use some new surroundings. This place is claustrophobic."

"That's literally something you can't feel," Viola said.

"Says you."

"So tell me about where we're landing?"

"Miner Prime," Puk said. "Fantastic place. Like if you took a can, packed a bunch of people in, then told corporations they could buy needles to jab into it and create offices. Set the whole thing spinning to get yourself gravity, stick it close to some asteroids full of precious metals, and you've got yourself the richest, largest home in space."

"Sounds like something I should see," Viola said, heading towards the cockpit.

Ships larger and smaller than the *Jumper* buzzed around the station. Some were floating boxes with mechanical arms that allowed them to haul ore from asteroids back to Miner Prime for processing. A few large ovals floated apart from Miner Prime, small shuttles whisking passengers back and forth from the transports. The decals covering the sides claimed they were cruise vessels, carrying their passengers from Earth in a loop through the solar system on a cruise that would last over a year.

Viola even saw a ship from her father's company docked at one of the spindly outreaches of the station, the orange and red logo giving it away.

"Pretty cool, right?" Davin said to Viola as they stood in the cockpit.

"I think it's so ugly," Phyla said. "Except it works, so nobody cares."

"It's huge," was all Viola could think of saying.

"When we land, you'll get the chance to see just how big," Davin said. "I've got to meet a friend down there, get a little more information."

"And I'm coming with?" Viola asked.

An awkward pause, Phyla wore a bemused expression, as though daring Davin to say more.

"I think Mox'll show you around," Davin said finally. "The less you're involved with us, the better."

"What do you mean?" Viola said.

"I'm saying that things are going to get messy," Davin said. "You'll be able to find a ship that'll take you back to Ganymede down there. Probably a better ride than what you just had. Though I wouldn't tell them who you are."

"Why not?"

"You tell your father when you see him that putting a big reward for his daughter's return is a good way to attract the wrong kind of attention."

"So, I'm not going with you?"

Viola caught Davin's quick glance at Phyla. Heard his sigh.

"We're labeled murderers, Viola. We'll be hunted. You don't want that," the captain said. "Mox'll get you to a ship that can take you. I'm not gonna have a kid get shot trying to play mercenary in my crew."

For the first time, Viola heard Davin's voice and thought of her father. The same tone, that Viola's own choices were his responsibility. But look at Merc. Look at how he nearly died. At how bad Erick was. Viola looked at her hands, remembered the sticky feel of Erick's blood on them as she stitched up the wound. Why would she ever want more of that?

"He'll show me around first?" Viola said. "Just a quick tour. Then I'll hop the next shuttle back."

Davin nodded, looking like a thousand pounds came off of his shoulders. Twenty years old and Viola still got people so worried about her.

Vagrants Hollow

The ramshackle scrap-houses of Vagrant's Hollow didn't look that different from when Davin had last seen them, through the glass walls of a lift just like this one. The dwellings spread out in a sloppy grid, filling in the circular level in the mile-wide center of Miner Prime. Shifting through the streets, once clean metal floors now coated with dirt and grime, were Davin's people, the kind that kept their secrets hidden behind their eyes.

Vagrant's Hollow was twenty stories high, its ceiling a changing screen approximating Earth's sky. Here and there malfunctioning plates stood out, black dots punching holes in the illusion.

"Hasn't changed much, has it?" Davin asked Phyla, standing next to him in the lift.

"I don't know if it's changed, but it feels sadder, somehow," Phyla replied.

"Because we used to see all this and wonder where it came from. What it was. Now, it's just a pile of trash."

One house near where the lift landed was a prime example. Whatever its original shell, the place was made out of an entire ship, broken into chunks and leaned against each other. Style wasn't important here. Having a home was what mattered.

"I suppose," Phyla said.

They looked out the windows at the rapidly approaching lift station. The trench that served as Vagrant Hollow's main drag laid beyond the exit stairs. Like Eden Prime's boulevard, but with none of the sterile attempts at class. Tables and tents full of clothes, food, junk, and bots for sale along the sides of the meandering path. Dilapidated homes erected on top of and attached to each other leaned over it, people hawking wares or making something out of nothing beneath the misshapen overhangs.

Even though the lift filtered out the smell, Davin's nose sniffed his memory and came away with the ozone sting of burning electricity, a hint of char from cooking food.

"Does she know you're coming?" Phyla asked.

"What do you think?"

"That she probably knew before you did."

Davin could only nod. And when the lift doors opened, the two of them pushed their way out along with a motley mess of humans, down the stairs and onto the stained, rusted metal that served as the trench floor.

Waiting for them, a small floating platform with a railing around the edge and a single stick used for steering. The man at the helm stared dead at Davin through a pair of thick goggles, doubtless meant to protect from the occasional mists of toxic anything that spewed out at random from constant experiments gone wrong in Vagrant's Hollow.

Phyla paused as Davin stepped on to the platform, the constant flow of bodies making a subconscious part around them. Was she nervous? Why? Davin put on a grin, reached to pull her up, but Phyla ignored his hand and used her own legs to get herself on board.

"Tell you something? I never wanted to come back here," Phyla said. "When we left, I thought there was a chance we weren't coming back. Ever. It felt good."

"You didn't say anything about it when we took off," Davin said as the platform lurched forward. "It won't be long. Lina will let us know who we need to talk to, we clear the charge, then we're good to go."

"I guess I didn't know I still hated it this much."

Phyla leaned over the edge of the platform, looked at the leaning metal masses of the pack homes around here. Davin followed her gaze, washing his eyes over the dreamers meandering below. Miner Prime was an idea as much as a place. A literal manifestation of hope to the bunches stuck on Earth who wanted adventure. A chance to hop on a mining ship, or an expedition deep into the dark universe. Davin checked his math. Almost fifty years, this place had been acting as a permanent settlement.

An older woman, dishing out soup to a family, glanced up at them bobbing by on the platform and turned away. Davin wondered why until he looked at Phyla, realized that the two of them didn't look like they belonged here anymore. Both of them armed, in gear that screamed they were probably working for Miner Prime's own police, or were otherwise searching out criminals.

"Sometimes I wonder why we were the ones that made it out," Phyla said, nodding her head at the woman.

"Luck," Davin replied.

What else would explain how the *Whiskey Jumper* had landed in his lap?

"Here," the driver said, and they stepped off.

In front of them sat a storefront. Davin noticed kitchen utensils, scrap metal, a few used books, and more on the shelves visible through the doorway. The only sign naming the place hung above the entrance, made from bits of different metals, an A missing, so that the name appeared to be "The Wrehouse". Davin was the first through, stepping in and immediately feeling eyes on him.

"Why do I only see you when you're in trouble?" came the lead-lined voice of one Lina Monte.

Lina stood behind the desk, staring at and yet also through Davin. A look that was wrapped in the past as much as the present, and Davin met those eyes fell down that well with her. Several decades of shifting dreams, promises kept and broken, the twisted love that fate doesn't like to let alone.

"Could say the same about you," Davin said.

They stepped towards each other, Lina coming around the desk, as though they were going to hug. Phyla walked in behind Davin, though, and Lina paused, setting a masked smile on her face. He wasn't the only one playing in the past. Thing was, they were living in the present. With Lina grunting in surprise, Davin pulled her into a tight hug.

"You can let me go," Lina said, her face mashed into Davin's shoulder.

"Felt like it was needed," Davin said, loosening the grip. "You remember

Phyla?"

"Friends never forget," Lina said.

"Nice to see you too, Lina," Phyla added.

"One of these days all three of us are going to go and get a bunch of drinks, deal with our problems, and get over this," Davin said. "But right now there's this thing hanging over my head. Namely, that there's an android trying to kill us. And, you know, that has priority."

Phyla was the first to blink, to glance away and nod. Lina accepted the gesture, went back behind the desk, and sat down in a stool made of different parts stacked together.

"You've got to deal with Bosser," Lina said.

"Who?"

Puppet Master

The problem with space was that there was too much of it. Bosser muttered this so often that he considered having it plastered on a picture and hung on his wall. The vastness meant he couldn't be everywhere, couldn't take all of the problems into his hands and grind them into dust personally. Bosser tried, via the stuttering video link with the Marl's new police chief, Ferro, on Europa. Turns out choking a man on another world wasn't easy.

"As much as I'd like to hear again how you failed so miserably, I have other things to attend to," Bosser said, and then cut the feed.

Ferro would sit there for another fifteen minutes before Bosser's replied bounced its way across the solar system to Europa, and the thought gave Bosser a small bite of satisfaction. Life was all about time, after all, and if Bosser could demand a few minutes of it from someone else, then wasn't that power? Although power wasn't much good if it stranded Bosser on a station like Miner Prime. The spinning waste of space was only getting less attractive as Bosser's departure date neared.

And pushing that day closer was the woman Bosser dialed next, Marl Rose. Dialing. There was a word that hadn't made its way out of language yet. Bosser wasn't punching buttons. Just saying the target's name was enough. The monitor would present some options, highlight the most likely one, and he would say one, two, or three. Bosser glanced back towards the nightstand and, on it, a wooden clock ticking away. He wound it every morning. A steady grinding of the gears.

"Are you going to talk, or is this just a way to wake me up?" Marl said over the feed, staring out the monitor in a frenzied outfit, eyes tired.

"Your new security seems worthless," Bosser said. "I couldn't find much on him. With no record, Eden won't like the choice."

"I didn't have much time, or options."

"I'll remind them," Bosser said. "Though they won't be thrilled to hear you failed to apprehend Davin Masters."

Another thirty minutes passed as Marl listened to his response and composed her own. In a way, the delay was a feature. Bosser could hold multiple conversations at once, rarely feeling stressed. Reading, reviewing other work, or just winding the clock and watching the stars outside the apartment's window. For one thing, it helped his temper. Hard to sustain true anger at someone when it took so long to see their response.

"Davin ran. Along with his crew. They're not a problem," Marl said. "Is Eden going to send another set of inspectors?"

"Your cavalier attitude towards the killers might raise eyebrows," Bosser said. "You might want to try some sympathy."

"When I'm talking with Eden, I will," Marl replied.

"Free advice, that's all," Bosser said. "The answer to your question is: not yet."

"So then why did you call?"

"I activated the android based on your evidence," Bosser said. "Your flimsy evidence. You'll be receiving a message soon with account details. Please deposit the amount noted, or Eden will come to understand just how easy it is to doctor a video feed."

Marl didn't bother to reply. After fifteen minutes, she gave Bosser a look as frigid as Europa's surface and cut the signal. It didn't matter, she would pay.

Bosser left his room and went to the small cafeteria that served the police building where he lived and worked. Miner Prime, even now, required an economy of space. Eating was cheaper here.

The entire dining area was polished silver metal, or plastic disguised to look like it. Easy to wash and resistant to scratches. Everything a concession to durability, safety. Except the feeds. Along one wall, opposite the serving counters, a vast screen divided into a series of real-time videos. Most were from Miner

Prime. The main promenade on Level Five, the center of the station that served as its prime shopping center. Vagrant's Hollow and its dirty chaos. Various docking bays flooding ships in and out like an ocean's tide. There was one in the upper left corner that continued to show a magnified view of Earth, routed and delayed from satellites, but still an ever-present reminder of humanity's beautiful home.

Somewhere between his second sip of the dark coffee and the first tentative bite of the morning's pastry, a starchy blueberry scone, the main door to the cafeteria opened and a comm officer stumbled into the room. A flushed face and wild eyes stared at Bosser, waited while he took a slow drink. Then Bosser signaled the man to speak.

"They're here, sir. The *Whiskey Jumper* just docked a few minutes ago," the comm officer said.

"Remind me what that is?" Bosser asked.

"The, uh, ship that you wanted me to watch for?"

"Ah. There are so many," Bosser said. "Thank you."

The comm officer stood there for a few more seconds. Watched Bosser take another sip. Waiting for orders. People claimed to be disturbed by the androids, how they looked human but were not. This officer, though, stood more still than a bot ever would and lacked the utility. The officer made a slight cough noise.

"You can leave," Bosser said, and the officer ran away.

The android, Fournine was its designation, already knew where Davin and his crew had gone. Its current position put the bot only a few hours behind the mercenaries. Waiting for Bosser's signal.

One of the feeds on the far end flipped to a broadcast of the most-watched new videos, burning through popular footage. The second one, muted and fuzzy, effects added in, showed a trio leading a pair of Eden-garbed employees into an empty docking bay. Then shooting them in the back. The video flipped to a picture of one Davin Masters, claiming the man was wanted for the murder. He and his entire crew of eight.

Wild Nines, and only eight members. Funny. Eight hardened fighters could be a lot for an android. Could cause a lot of damage to the station if they went down shooting. Split them apart, however …Bosser picked up his comm, started placing some calls.

Davin Masters had come home, and he was going to find it a very unwelcome place to be.

Shopping

Viola could tell Mox was tiring of her questions. The big man had slipped from three words an answer down to one. Sometimes just a grunt. Not like Viola could help it. The entirety of Level Five was full of things she'd never seen. Movies on Ganymede dealt little with the miracles on display here, the glittering dresses flecked with asteroid platinum, perfumes mixed with chemicals extracted from Mars rock, and even a pet store selling animals used to low-gravity environments.

"If only you weren't broke," Puk said, floating by Viola's head. "Think of all the cool stuff you could buy."

"Thanks for reminding me," Viola said.

"What I'm here for."

Mox drifted behind the two of them, casting his eyes at random. Shopping didn't seem to be his thing - most of the stores Viola entered, Mox stood outside and leaned against a wall. It didn't take a lot of deduction to realize that Mox was here as a bodyguard, to keep Viola from doing something stupid. Which, given her luck so far, wasn't a terrible idea.

Past a pair of restaurants hawking Japanese and African cuisine, the gentle curve of the level revealed a circular square with a giant projection in the middle. Sponsored by a news organization Viola wasn't familiar with, the holographic image gave a 3D representation of the current broadcast. Pictures of Mars, ruined settlements and flashing lasers. Better to be here than there.

Beneath the projection, which shot up ten meters into the air, people mixed and mingled on benches and tables, all anchored to the floor.

"Cadge," Mox said, nodding towards the left side of the projection.

Viola noticed the squat mercenary was talking with a few other people dressed in thick jackets and work pants. Hoods on their jackets kept their faces hidden, and the group was too far away to overhear. On the trip over here, Viola couldn't shake the impression that the man kept sizing her up like he would a piece of meat. Not sexual, no, but more like whether she was valuable. It was a strange feeling, and after the first couple of days, Viola had tried to avoid Cadge whenever she had the chance.

"Who's he talking to?" Viola said. Mox shook his head. "Puk, want to listen?"

"On it," the little bot said, zipping up and away.

Like a human ear, the bot could concentrate on conversations from a distance. From vantage points Cadge wouldn't think to look, such as right above him.

"Why?" Mox asked.

"I don't know," Viola said. "How he looks at me, makes me feel off. And he's talked about my father's bounty before."

"He jokes," Mox said. "No filter."

"I get it," Viola said. "He's your friend. But he's not mine."

Viola pulled Mox over to a small cafe where she let the metal man point out which of the unique beverages she should try. Zero-G roasted coffee, grown in enriched asteroid soil, had a flavor all its own. Having subsisted for weeks now on the *Jumper*'s Anything with a new taste would be welcome.

The frothy dark liquid, into which Viola poured a slight drop of cream, steamed in her face. Mox watched her from across their tiny for two table, a slight smile buried in his scruff as Viola raised the mug and blew into it. A few seconds later, the first tentative sip. It was hot, sure, but also sparkled in her mouth. Tiny bursts of heat and . . . macadamia? Followed by an undercurrent of deep, earthy loam that massaged its way down her throat into her stomach.

Viola sat the mug back on the table and stared at it. If this coffee blew away anything she'd ever drank, what else waited for her out here?

"Incredible," Viola said when Mox asked how it tasted. "I don't understand how it can have so much flavor. I mean, scientifically, I understand the components that go into it, how the molecular—"

"Viola!" Puk buzzed, whirring back into the cafe and catching a few stares from the other patrons. "We have to move! Cadge is selling you out to those guys right now."

"What?" Mox said.

"The bounty," Puk said. "Cadge is going to divide it with them. They have a ship."

Viola looked across the courtyard, but Cadge and whoever he'd been talking with weren't there any more. Disappeared.

"Did you see where they went?" Viola asked Puk.

"Sorry, was too busy coming over here to warn you," Puk replied.

Mox stood up, touching his wrist to the small part of the table sectioned off to a reader. Mox's comm connected to his account balance and brushing it against one of these sensors paid whatever outstanding bill existed for the table. Viola remembered when the technology first came to Ganymede, at the same time a fully-fledged stellar network swung into place. It required instant connection and verification of an account's balance, but was way more efficient than carrying physical chits loaded up with coin.

"We go back," Mox said, and Viola wasn't going to say no. "Wait for Cadge at the *Jumper*."

Walking out of the cafe and back into the promenade, Mox, rather than falling behind, now walked right next to Viola, scanning the surroundings. Was this what it was like to be in this business? To always have to watch her back, to suspect anyone of having ulterior motives?

The crowded racks of clothes in stores and their projected models, the stands advertising essential luxuries, lost their sense of wonder and became only places someone could hide. Anyone glancing at Viola could be an informant, passing along her location, that she was unarmed, or what she was wearing to someone who wanted to find her.

"I'm not having fun anymore," Viola said.

"Get used to it," Mox replied.

As they pushed through a small crowd of people, all wearing bright neon t-shirts and being led by a tour guide, Viola wanted to be back in the small, comfortable confines of the *Jumper*. On the other side of the tour group there was a brief break in the crowd, a space through which the smooth floor of Level Five reflected the dusking store lights as the afternoon of Miner Prime's artificial cycle wound on. Three men, the ones Cadge had been speaking with, stood in the break, and they stared right at her.

Past Friends

Phyla's eyes wandered the small confines of Lina's shop. A menagerie of security-related gear. There was a tiny gun that shot a sticky bead that would record and send video and audio around it for ten minutes. That'd be one way of keeping tabs on Davin and Lina's conversation, a back and forth that'd sent itself lower and lower in volume until Phyla couldn't even hear it anymore. She felt like the kid left to wander while the parents talked.

Hanging on the walls, above the shelves holding cameras and comm equipment, were a series of old-style pictures. Actual print photos, which these days were a retro rarity. Thing was, Phyla remembered all of them.

The one with Davin and Lina standing outside their small school, Phyla holding the camera, right here in Vagrant's Hollow, as they completed the last grade and society ejected them, at fifteen, into whatever lives fate held for them. Phyla thought the nervous grins on their faces must have mirrored her own.

Another picture, to the right of that one, taken by Davin's long-gone mother, had the three of them and some of their other friends engaging in one of their floor hockey games. The metal ground made a perfect surface for skipping around any spare junk they wanted to use as a puck.

She'd found the camera at a special discount. No, that wasn't it. The man was losing everything, was liquidating all he had to get a ticket off of the station. Phyla had coin from a recent birthday and bought it. The camera was so ancient that it printed the photos immediately after taking it. The man selling it to her looked so sad as he handed it over, but when Phyla turned away, he'd asked her to wait. A moment later the man returned with a stack of thick little paper, necessary for the camera to print. Phyla asked him where to get more and the man just shook his head.

Looking at these pictures, she could never tell how badly they wanted to leave. Davin, especially, went on and on about exploring the stars. Breaking out of the bounds of Miner Prime and making his own life. Lina went along with him, egging Davin on until he left. He told them he was going and was gone. For five years.

Phyla remembered the day Davin came back, remembered him running back through their street, claiming he had a ship, that they could go with him. Breaking open their boring lives.

"Phyla?" Lina said, touching Phyla's shoulder. "Do you want them?"

"The pictures?"

"They should be yours, really. You took them."

"They'd just get lost on the ship. Too much movement," Phyla said, though her eyes didn't move away from the memories.

"If you think so," Lina said. "Davin's going to come back soon. He'll ask you to go get the ship prepped."

"Why, we just got here?"

"This station is dangerous for you. Every hour here increasing the chance of you being trapped."

"And Davin won't be coming with me?"

"He wants to find the source, the person who can turn off the android pursuing you. I can lead him to it, but you'll need a ready escape."

Phyla looked at Lina's set face, searched Lina's eyes for a hint of a lie, a scheme playing through the wrinkles and scattered grays touching Lina's temples. Phyla felt the urge to touch her own face, to trace her own wrinkles and compare whether the space-faring life was any better.

"Why'd we split up, Lina?" Phyla asked. "The three of us?"

"You two wanted to see the stars, I had people to take care of," Lina replied.

Parents, and Lina had a younger brother. Davin and Phyla lost their responsibilities before the *Jumper* ever became a reality. Not that Phyla had regrets - there'd been nothing in Vagrant's Hollow then and there was nothing now. Better to run from a black hole than get crushed by its hopeless gravity.

"How are they?" Phyla let the question float in the air.

Lina didn't bother answering, looked back at the pictures. Dead, or vanished. In Vagrant's Hollow, those were the likeliest outcomes. The past wasn't a friendly place to visit here. All it did was show how much you'd already lost. Phyla took a deep breath. Maybe now was the time to fix part of it.

"That last fight we had, I was so stupid," Phyla said. "I just couldn't, after all the times we'd talked about escaping this place, understand why you wouldn't come."

"I know," Lina replied.

"It's been hard without you," Phyla continued, still looking at the photo. "Going everywhere without my best friend."

"Haven't you made a new one yet?"

"Still waiting for you."

Lina wrapped Phyla in a tight hug, the same way they used to say goodnight to each other when they were younger.

"There's nobody left here anymore," Lina said. "If you two are willing, I'll come with you this time. I'm ready to say goodbye."

There was room. An extra cabin. For the first time since hitting the station, Phyla felt a real smile climb to her eyes. Lina returned it.

"You two having a good talk? Back to being friends again?" Davin said, coming up to them. "Phyla, Lina dish you the details?"

"Yeah, you're abandoning us to go on some solo thing," Phyla replied.

"Not solo. Lina's got my back."

"That means you've got hers, too," Phyla said.

Heading back to the *Jumper* alone, Phyla remembered when they'd left Lina the first time. Those promises the night before, the three of them getting ready to meet Davin's crew on his new ship. Phyla excited to pilot something that wasn't mining an asteroid, Lina reading out load about the neat things they were going to see, Davin throwing around stories of Luna, Mars, and even seeing Earth from orbit.

And the next morning, in the *Jumper*'s cockpit. Lina only comming sorry. Davin delaying, pleading, and finally Phyla starting the jets and taking the *Jumper* out to the stars. It'd been hard to see with tears in her eyes, but it hadn't taken long for those tears to dry. To harden into the same resolve that carried her now. There were more than the three of them to take care of.

Old Flame, New Burn

Lina's cramped apartment clung to the top of the store desperately. A menagerie of bolted scrap, ropes, and a thin set of stairs brought Davin up to the second level. Between the hotplate and the single-stall shower, there was a fold-out couch and the scattered junk of years.

"I don't know what you think it's like on the *Jumper*, but it's better than this," Davin said.

He expected a fiery retort, something along the lines that Davin had no right to critique her life, not after leaving a decade ago. Instead, Lina nodded and sat on the couch, hand digging between the cushions until she found something. Davin stayed standing, watched Lina's wrist flex as her hand moved underneath the cushions, and then heard the sound of shifting metal.

The greased up panels of the apartment shifted to the sides, jutting out and sliding over each other to reveal a slick set of screens and small compartments full of gadgets. Davin smiled wider as each new part showed itself. This was much more what he'd expected from Lina, matched the way she used to beat, no, annihilate Davin and Phyla in childhood games, waiting until the last moment to show a secret that handed Lina the victory. A fake sword, maybe, or an obscure rule pulled out to devastating effect. Now Lina had a hidden armory.

"You built this just for me?" Davin asked.

"Just for you," Lina replied. "The thing is, you find out everyone's secrets, then you keep more of your own."

"Most secrets don't involve caches of spy gear."

"Only the best ones."

Davin walked over to the terminal, pressed the small power button. The screens populated with various video feeds from around Vagrant's Hollow and other levels of Miner Prime. Black and white but sharp, with words tracking across the bottom as the terminal attempted to scribe any audio going on.

"Can you see everywhere on the station?" Davin said.

"Almost," Lina's face twisted into a frown. "A few places are too hard to get to. Haven't been able to bug Bosser's office, for instance."

"You mean, the spot that's the most useful to us."

"Not really. Bosser does a lot of chatter with off-station partners. Those transmissions I've been intercepting for a while."

"Whose he talking with?"

"Your friend Marl, for one."

"Yeah, I get more friends like Marl, I'm not going to be around much longer."

"She's only part of the chain," Lina said, taking Davin's hand and pulling him back towards the couch.

Lina's hand was warm. It always was, her fingers slipping in between his. The fit was effortless. Muscle memory split by years still holding strong.

"Then what's the rest of it?" Davin said.

A familiar thrill juice his veins as Lina's fingers started massaging his palms. That same dance, those same rounded nails and the way Lina glided them on the ends of his nerves.

"Marl and Bosser have an arrangement, but both of them are working for other people," Lina said. "Don't know who pulls Marl's strings. Outside of Bosser, I don't hear anything she says. Bosser, I think, works with Eden. Maybe other corporations. It's hard to pin him down."

Davin sank back into the couch, allowed an arm to slide up Lina's side and around her back, holding her closer.

"You mean you don't know everything about him?" Davin said. "That doesn't sound like you."

"Bosser doesn't play in public," Lina replied, moving along the couch till her hips touched Davin's. "He's not a politician. So far as I can tell, he's not elected to anything. There's nothing on him in the public records. That means he's running something the Free Laws don't touch. That Miner Prime is keeping out of the light."

"Never stopped you before."

Lina leaned away, looked Davin square in the face.

"Don't come in here and act like you know what it's like," Lina said. "It's been a year since you last came here. There's been a shift. Nobody wants to fight anymore, because they want to save up, buy passage to one of the new outposts. Like your Europa."

"And they're willing to live in crap until then?"

"Better than dying for it. Or rotting in prison. They're seeing what's happening on Mars."

Davin looked back at the monitors. The feeds from all over the station still running. It'd been a long time since their parents had led the marches, organized the meetings to improve conditions in Vagrant's Hollow.

"It's not your job to make their dreams come true," Davin said.

"I thought it was, for a long time," Lina said. "I built this, collected blackmail, was ready to start a revolution until I realized nobody wanted one."

"We find Bosser, clear the charge, and then we can leave," Davin said.

"There you go, Davin. Being the hero," Lina said.

"That is the best part of this job," Davin shivered as Lina's fingers walked up his chest. Her mouth moved closer.

"Really?" Her voice low, her lips lush.

"I stand corrected."

Ambushed

Opal put the scope on Mace's counter. Beneath the glass surface was a surfeit of beam knives, and behind the counter an array of deadly weaponry whose price tag took notice of the high tax the Free Laws put on arsenals. An updated version of the one she had, this scope contained a chip that analyzed the movements of people seen in it, compared against a database of human walks and runs. It'd tell her whether a target was nervous, calm, or about to run a moment before the person did. In that second, Opal could squeeze off a shot, save the day.

"You got enough coin for this one, Opal?" Mace, the tattooed, grungy owner said to her. "Last I seen you, your account wasn't doing so hot."

"We've picked up a few gigs, old man. It'll clear," Opal said.

Mace gestured for Opal to slide her comm across the reader. Opal did, and the thing chimed an affirmative a second later.

"Well, color me surprised," Mace said. "Here I had you figured for broke."

"Have I ever disappointed you, Mace?"

The shopkeeper chuckled, both of them knowing Opal had pinched a few items from this store. Mace held a certain level of respect for anyone gutsy enough to steal from him and get away with it, much less do it multiple times. So the last time Opal came in, Mace had her cornered and made her an offer. Steal nothing else, and she could keep her ill-gotten gains. Opal, seeing the beam knife in Mace's hand, hadn't argued.

Merc, leaning against the store entrance, had his eyes on them. The pilot was still standing, but Opal noticed Merc's pained grimace, his arms hanging limp. After this, it was back to the ship. Opal gave Mace a nod, then started towards the entrance. As she did so, Mace's terminal, behind her, made an angry noise, like a horn being squashed flat mid-note.

"Hey," Mace said, quieter now.

Opal glanced back at the shop keeper.

"I'm being told by the peacekeepers to keep you here. Just popped up now."

There was a time when Opal would have asked why. Would have been angry, surprised that police would be trying to find her. Now, though, all she did was nod. The shopkeeper slanted his head in return. Then Opal's eyes and mind turned to Merc.

"Time to go," Opal said to Merc as she held out an arm.

Together they limped towards the lifts that would take them back to the ship. Miner Prime's artificial sun was resting on the horizon, the diodes illuminating Level Five's ceiling shifting into hues of purples and oranges this evening. Beautiful, so long as she pretended it was real. Opal took a mental inventory. She had a sidearm, the beam knife too. Merc had nothing more than a bottle of pills.

Which was why, when, only twenty yards from the lift doors, a dozen green-uniformed peacekeepers stepped out and demanded the two of them surrender, Opal dropped her gun without a fight. Two of them separated Opal from Merc first, then one of them slapped a pair of stun cuffs around her wrists.

"Good choice," the peacekeeper told her as they walked towards the lift. "Not worth adding to that charge, right?"

"I did it for him," Opal said, eyes sliding towards Merc, who had a pair of peacekeepers helping him along.

"Won't hear me arguing," the peacekeeper said. "All I'm looking for is to get home at the end of the day."

"I was, too," Opal replied.

The Metal Man

Vi's wide eyes blinked from one of the three men to the next. Mox could smell the fear coming off her, that rush of scent Mox normally had directed at him. The exoskeleton picked up on it, told Mox about Vi's near-panic while he looked at the opposing trio. The middle man looked like the leader, hands at a pair of handguns on his belt. Given away by his cronies, who kept glancing towards him, waiting for a signal. A poor strategy.

"Step aside," Mox said.

"Aren't you a mercenary, big guy?" the leader said. "Don't you know what she's worth?"

"Step aside. I won't ask again."

"Guess all that metal must be messing with your mind," the leader said. "We're taking the girl."

Mox started forward. Vi said his name, but Mox ignored her. To hesitate now would give them a chance to shoot, and Mox had no weapon with him. None save his fists, anyway. The exoskeleton registered the movement, picked up the surge in energy as Mox ran, and amplified it with mechanical strength.

On his second step, as the trio leader tugged at the guns in his holster, Mox leapt three meters. Crossed more than half the ground between the two groups.

The leader raised the gun and, as Mox flew through his third step, his fist colliding with the leader's chin, fired.

The blast bounced off of the floor and into a wall. Mox did the same to the leader, smashing him into the ground, momentum sliding the man into a bench. Mox registered the strike audibly, as he'd turned left, following the swing of his arm, and clapped the second crony in the stomach. Doubling over, collapsing to the floor, flunky number two was no longer a problem.

Mox flung his right arm back in a wild blow, meant not to hit the third one as much as delay him, get him to duck and give Mox a second to turn himself around.

The swing, as expected, hit only air. Mox, though, used the energy to pivot around and look at the third attacker. The little goon seemed paralyzed. Mox's blow had missed not because of any ducking, but because the coward hadn't even tried to close. Pathetic.

Mox took a step, stared into the goon's face, which melted into slack-jawed fear. This one wasn't even worth the effort. Instead, Mox pulled the gun out of the goon's pocket, and snapped it with his hands. Vi yelled something again, but Mox couldn't make it out over the pounding adrenaline in his ears. So much time with the cannon had him forgetting the feel of using his own hands. And how much fun they were.

The third goon recovered apiece of his wits and ran towards the lifts. Mox could catch him, could toss the goon around like a doll, but Vi was the concern. Mox turned back to his charge, at where she used to be, and saw nobody. The fight hadn't lasted more than a few seconds. Where'd the girl go?

Mox looked around, but the walkway was full of people running away from the conflict, none of them matching Vi's clothes. But there! Puk, Vi's little bot, floated near the entrance to a dark-looking club. Mox ran in that direction as Puk zipped inside. The joint's name, *Cosmic Dust*, did not inspire confidence.

Mox crouched to get through the door, a sliding one that made no noise as it slipped open. Well maintained. The entryway was short, a deep blue with flecks of white. Evoked leaving Earth for the stars. Something Mox had done many, many years ago. But memories were not the point of now. Further inside even the deep blue vanished, replaced by wheeling stars and galaxies. A vibrating crowd filled the place.

Suddenly a bright comet streaked across the ceiling, moving in a strange pattern and, every so often, appearing to drop motes of light on the dancing peopled. Music, such as it was, existed as a slow, bouncing beat with synthesized echoes.

"Need a how-to?" said a girl appearing out of nowhere next to Mox.

Her tag read she was an astronaut. A lie, as she appeared, even in the darkness, to be Viola's age. The only astronauts left were relics of an older age, back when governments funded space travel and one needed more than money to see the stars. Perhaps, then, the girl was an attendant.

"Finding someone," Mox said.

"A lot of people find things here," the girl said. "Use your comm. It'll automatically connect, and then you can order from there."

"A girl," Mox replied. "With a bot."

"Uh huh. Pick the dust you want and it'll be dropped. Then, you know, you enjoy," the girl said, giving Mox a smile and fading away into the blackness.

Mox couldn't see anything, but Vi had to be in here somewhere. He would comb the blitzed out stargazers. He would find her.

Start Your Engines

Another thirty minutes before the supplies finished loading. Phyla heard Trina saying the words and wondered how much time had passed since she'd heard them. A minute, maybe? She'd put out a few comm calls to Opal, Merc, and Mox and had nothing to show for it. Blanks. Davin still in Lina's bunker. Which meant Phyla was acting captain, and she might have to actually do something with that responsibility.

"Erick?" Phyla commed.

"Yes?" Erick replied from his bed, where he'd chosen to spend the day continuing to recover.

"How long did you tell Merc he could be out?"

"Let me check."

Phyla stared out of the cockpit at the busy bay Miner Prime assigned them. Bots and people moved around between the other ships in the same space, and a few of them continued going up the *Whiskey Jumper*'s loading ramp, bringing in food and any parts Trina requested. Davin's procedure was to stock up to the max at every port, even if they didn't know where their next flight was going. Also why the captain insisted on foods that wouldn't spoil quickly. It made for dull meals, but meant the ship could coast for months at full crew capacity. Phyla wondered how crazy she'd go if that ever happened.

"He's past due," Erick said, Phyla jumped at the sudden sound.

"Past due?"

"Yes, I cleared him for a short trip to get some fresher air. Exertion is still a risk at this stage in his recovery."

"I can't raise them on the comm," Phyla said.

"That's concerning. Expect he would be needing another dose to keep the pain down."

"Yeah. Not like Opal to botch a schedule, either," Phyla tried pinging their comms again, nothing. There was always a chance the two of them were in a dead spot on the station, surrounded by thick plates that blocked messages. Some places put in the investment to keep their stores, massage parlors, clubs immune to the constant connection comms created.

"Mox isn't answering either, nor Cadge."

"Worrisome, don't you think?"

"I'll keep looking. I'm sure they're just in the lifts or something," Phyla said. The murder charge playing constantly on the news. People died all the time in space, but not company ones. Especially officials visiting an outpost being plugged as the next paradise.

Erick told her to let him know, then signed off. Phyla flipped the board to the video feed of Erick's room for a split second, confirming the napping doctor curled beneath a blanket. The light turned off a second later. Creepy, looking in on Erick, but the crew understood why the cameras were there. A small ship had to be able to see what was going on anywhere in case of an atmosphere leak, fire, or something worse.

"Hellooooo ship? Anyone listening?" Came an unfamiliar voice over the comm.

"Phyla here, on the *Whiskey Jumper*. Who's this?"

"Puk, Viola's bot, and I've got news for you."

"Where are you? Are you with Mox?"

"Not anymore. Viola's been grabbed by your pal Cadge. We just ducked out the service exit of some sweet rave called *Cosmic Dust*. I'm bein' sneaky and your guy hasn't noticed me yet. Not sure how much longer that's going to last."

"Where's Mox? And what level is that?"

"Whaddya think? Level Five. Mox was jumped by some goons, who he toasted. I mean, it wasn't even a fight. Like, not even time to bet. That dudes a killer."

"Puk, focus. Where is Cadge taking her?"

"Think I can read minds? What I do know is that he wants that bounty money."

"Go find Mox. Tell him where Cadge is taking Viola,.

"So you're not gonna help?"

"Keep me informed and I might."

The bot chirped an affirmative. Then Trina blipped up quick to say the supplies were on. The *Jumper* fueled and ready for launch. One thing right in a day of wrongs. Phyla took a deep breath, then tried to comm Davin again. Nothing. Why was everything falling apart when she was in the captain's chair?

Tunnels

Lina kept the store where it was in Vagrant's Hollow for a reason. That was, as they'd figured out when they were kids, because one of the recycled air shafts ran beneath it. A big tube through which warm or cool air went, depending on the day and which side of Miner Prime was facing the sun. It wrapped around Vagrant's Hollow and connected with the swarming collection of vents that kept oxygen flowing through the station.

Standing behind Lina's desk on the main store, Davin, hair still wet from the quick shower, watched as Lina pulled back a thick gray mat. Underneath was a metal plate with a grip.

"Be a gentleman, would you?" Lina asked.

Davin took the cue and pulled on the plate, then pressed with his legs to move the heavy thing. The grinding of the plate against the floor showed a hole that Davin remembered looking much bigger when he was younger.

"That's gonna be, uh, tight," Davin said.

"I'll go first. Toss your stuff to me. Then you'll fit," Lina said.

"You sure about that?"

"Pretty familiar with your size, Davin. You'll make it," Lina said, tossing Davin a curled smile.

Lina descended ladder and landed two meters lower with a thunk.

"You'll be happy," Lina called. "They're circulating cold air today."

"Hallelujah," Davin said, unsnapping his holster and tossing it to Lina.

If the vents were pushing heat, it'd be way uncomfortable in the vent. Literally in a furnace. Every once in a while, exploring as kids, they'd been caught inside there when the waves of solar heat blasted through and emerged slimy balls of sweat, gasping for breath. Davin managed a squirming climb into the tube, standing up when he hit the floor and whacking his head on the ceiling.

"Oh yeah, you'll want to duck," Lina said. "Guess you grew a little from when you were a kid."

"Is that how it works?"

The tube itself was a stainless steel stretch of metal. Bolts dug in every meter to tie sections together. Lina's statement about the breeze was right - a steady wind blew in the tunnel, enough to move Davin's hair if not to push him any faster.

"If I recall, we didn't go very far down these vents when we were younger?" Davin said, looking back and forth.

"We can't just walk right into Bosser's office. It's in the peacekeeper barracks, a few levels away," Lina said. "They'll be watching the lifts. They won't be watching the tunnels."

"Why would Bosser be watching the lifts?" Davin said. "We didn't land under our own name."

Lina walked through the vent, the smooth walls broken up here and there by pipes and smaller vents either sending in or siphoning off the airflow. Beyond their tapping steps, the steady churn of machinery working rumbled around them. Even though they were only a few meters beneath the chatter of Vagrant's Hollow, not a sound filtered to them.

"There was a lot of chatter a few hours ago," Lina continued. "Watch orders went out through common channels. Your name included."

"Then the rest of them could be in trouble?"

"The only way to help your crew is to do what we're doing here," Lina replied. "Get rid of the charge, there's no reason to arrest anyone."

Yeah, except Bosser probably wasn't worried about arrests. Davin should run back up that ladder, to the lifts and to his ship. Or to find Opal, who'd gone shopping. Or... maybe Lina was right. Nothing Davin did alone was going to shift a fight with the peacekeepers. Nothing, except getting Bosser to stop.

"How long will it take to get to him?"

"Depends on whether we're lucky," Lina said.

"You're with me, so that's not likely."

The vent tunnel curved ahead of them, arcing back towards the station's center. Where the main shafts were located, heading up and down. They kept walking, the low maintenance lights of the tunnel keeping the two lit in silhouette. Eventually, the light at the end of tunnel, denoted by a ring of red lights.

"You want to improve the odds, stay quiet," Lina said, looking back at Davin and bringing a finger to her lips. Davin nodded. The odds would need all the help they could get.

Kidnapped

Viola wasn't trying to struggle anymore. Not because there weren't openings in Cadge's shambling sprint through the service hallways, but because Viola kept hearing Cadge's muttered threat in her mind.

"Try to run, I'll kill you. Don't want to do that. Be nice with me, you get back home to Mom and Dad."

It was hard to comprehend, Cadge's double-barreled sidearm right there under her nose. With a twitch of his finger, Cadge would erase everything Viola was. A paralyzing, crippling fear that Viola hadn't felt. Twenty years gone in a moment. There wasn't a rational response to that. None save doing whatever she could to stay alive. Puk, normally the counter-weight to Viola's descents into her own head, was nowhere. She was standing on a precipice and if Viola didn't say something soon, she would fly off into panic.

"Why do you want the reward so much?" Viola asked Cadge.

"I have my reasons. Most of'em having to do with risking my damn life for too little every day," Cadge said.

Cadge wasn't looking back at her. Viola could dart to one of the back doors to escape. But how many of them would open when she pulled? And if it didn't, would Cadge give her a warning or just blow her to pieces?

"So you're kidnapping me? That's the solution?"

"You have a better one?" Cadge replied.

"How about not?"

"Leaves me bled dry, Vi," Cadge said.

Past another pair of shops was a rusted light blue door, large enough for carts. Cadge paused in front of a series of three buttons, one red, one green, and the other with a marker of an alarm. The door wasn't locked from this side.

"I don't understand," Viola said as Cadge pressed the green button. "Davin's supplying everything, so why wouldn't you be able to save?"

Cadge did turn around this time, giving Viola a sick smile.

"You think a man like me's capable of being stable? This career, you live for the now."

Cadge waved Viola forward through the door. Back on the public causeway, lifts a few minutes walk. Out there in the open, Cadge took a long breath, his steps slowed to a natural walk rather than the tense steps in the alley. Viola noticed why after a few seconds. The same group that Mox fought, that trio, was moving along with them. Surrounding Viola. No chance of getting away now, and no sign of Mox.

Still, talking with Cadge gave Viola time to adjust herself. The panic subsided. Analyze the situation. Just another logic problem. Four on one weren't odds she would beat, but maybe, keeping her eyes open, there'd be an opportunity. The five of them stepped into a lift and jetted away to the eighth level. A short transfer to a cross-station lift, shooting across rather than up and down. That lift would spit them out into a section reserved for incoming ships, smaller ones than the *Whiskey Jumper*.

"Where's the coin, Cadge?" The leader of the trio, his coat torn and face sporting an array of colorful bruises, said, his voice strained. "We did what you asked, and paid more than you said we would."

"Got the chits here, in my pocket. Give 'em to you when we're clear," Cadge replied. "Didn't want Mox killing you and me lose good money for nothing."

"It's so nice to be kidnapped by upstanding gentlemen such as yourselves," Viola said, because every word beat back the chills coursing through her veins. "Truly, if there was anyone that would take me, slam me in a ship, and send me back home to my parents, I'd pick all of you."

"Smart mouth," the leader said.

"Pretty though," said one of the other beaters.

"There we go. That's what this was missing," Viola said.

"Shut it," Cadge said. "Vi, before you think about making any noise, understand I have every right to be doing what I'm doing."

"Well, now you've changed my mind," Viola said.

That prompted a snicker from the leader, but the opening lift doors cut short Cadge's reaction. Viola didn't catch the bay's number because she was staring at the incredible number of ships zipping in and out of the space. Davin put the *Jumper* in a larger bay meant for cargo, but this one was for small craft. All the pleasure-seekers and businessmen stopping by the station for meetings, parties, tourism. In the time between the lift doors opening and Viola setting foot on the bay's floor, at least five ships in her view ignited their engines and floated up and out.

The leader already had his hands out, waiting for Cadge to hand over the coin. Cadge dropped the three black and blue cards into the leader's hand, one by one.

"Already loaded?" the leader asked.

"Check 'em if you want," Cadge said. "I can wait a minute."

"Cadge Vasseter!" yelled someone on the bay floor, climbing out of their ship.

Viola couldn't make out who it was, their head covered by a wide hat, a long gray coat coming from the collar to the person's ankles. Cadge, though, had an idea, because he jerked away from the trio and dove back towards the lift. Viola watched as the doors closed before Cadge could get inside, causing the small man to bounce off of them and fall to the ground, hands scrambling for his sidearm.

"Who's that?" the leader asked.

"Don't wanna know," Cadge growled back. "There's an extra ten for each of you if you help me kill them."

"Murder's gonna cost you fifty."

"It's not murder if the damn target's a bot!" Cadge replied.

The trio stared at Cadge like he'd sprouted flowers from his face. Viola imagined she had a similar expression. Bot? What enemies did Cadge have that had a bot capable of killing? Regardless, nobody was watching her, so Viola made small steps away from the group, towards one end of the bay. The trio were still arguing with Cadge, driving up the price and checking their weapons.

Viola slipped behind a stack of outgoing luggage, a tower of suitcases tall enough to keep her hidden. At least, that's what she thought until a heavy hand landed on her shoulder.

"Stay here," a steel voice said. "You're not the target. And I don't get extra points for collateral damage."

Risk It All

"What?" Viola asked, looking behind her.

The thing Cadge was calling a bot crouched next to her, patchwork robes bunching up around it. In each hand was a long and narrow gun, thin lines of jagged red running up one barrel, blue on the other.

"Who are you?" Viola asked.

"My name is Fournine," It replied. "Excuse me while I eliminate my target."

That was one way to say hello. Viola sat back as Fournine walked towards Cadge and the trio. Cadge was the only one even looking in Fournine's direction, and was the first to yell, pointing his finger at the android. If it was hunting Cadge, then it was probably the same one from Eden Prime. Which meant that after Cadge, Davin and the others were next.

"Friends!" Fournine announced. "I am legally authorized to terminate Cadge, here. The rest of you have a choice. Leave and live, or stay and suffer the fate of an accomplice."

The leader exchanged quick looks with his pals, who both backed towards the lift. Cadge, voice edging higher, again promised fifty . . . what denomination Viola didn't know. Thousand? Hundreds? The going price of bot murder wasn't something she knew.

The trio didn't listen. As soon as the lift doors opened, they booked it. Cadge started that way too, but before he'd gone two steps, Fournine fired from his blue gun. The bolt snaked out, slower than a normal laser, but arcing in on Cadge even as the mercenary, expecting the shot, fell to the left.

The blue bolt struck like a pouncing cat, swinging in at the Cadge. Bits of lightning sprung up around the mercenary, pulling Cadge to the floor, mouth and eyes open. It wasn't something Viola wanted to watch, but she couldn't pull her eyes away.

Fournine took a cautious walk up to Cadge, both guns out and pointed at the mercenary. Viola edged out from her cover to get a better view. Cadge twitched as the android stood over him.

"A deal, target," Fournine said. "Information on your fellows. Where they are, where they're going, and I'll ensure they pay for abandoning you here."

Cadge looked at the android, shaking his head, eyes and mouth tight.

"You think I'm gonna sell them out?" Cadge said, spit flinging from his lips. "You think they abandoned me? Hell, I abandoned them. For that girl there."

Cadge nodded at Viola. Fournine didn't turn its head. It probably knew exactly who Cadge was talking about.

"I've done nothing worth killing for," Cadge continued. "But I figure you lot don't see gray, only red."

"Smarter than you look," Fournine said, raising the red gun.

As Fournine brought the gun up, Cadge triggered something with his left hand. There was a roaring pop, the noise Viola would hear whenever Ganymede's colonization day rolled around and Galaxy Forge launched fireworks into the light atmosphere. Fournine flew off of Cadge and into the wall next to the lift. Cadge himself didn't move, his eyes closed. Unconscious, or dead.

Around the bay others were noticing the fight, gathering to watch what was happening on the walkway. Another lift with a handful of passengers arrived, only to notice the bodies and send the lift away to another, any other, destination. The station's cameras had to notice. Might be playing on the news now. If Mox and the others saw it, they'd know to run.

Fournine was the first one to move, pushing itself up from the floor and standing straight. It stared ahead, unblinking for a few seconds. Rebooting. Just like Puk did whenever she needed to update the bot. A scrubbing of scrambled code, a re-orienting of priorities. When Fournine grabbed its guns and turned to Cadge, its set face was the same unflinching cold as before.

"How I hate surprises," Fournine said, this time keeping a meter between himself and Cadge's unmoving form. "And whatever you're planning next, please know that I can tell your heartbeat from here. One more chance, Cadge Vasseter. My mercy goes no farther."

With a strangled sigh, Cadge sat up, just enough so that his head peeked up at the android.

"How many times do I have to tell you? Go to hell, you metal bastard," Cadge growled.

Fournine nodded, then raised the red gun and blasted Cadge in the chest. The mercenary fell back to the floor. Fournine holstered its weapons, staring at Cadge the entire time.

"You're recording him, aren't you?" Viola asked, coming out onto the walkway.

"Part of the requirements. I have to get proof," Fournine replied, not looking away from Cadge's body. "One down. Plenty left."

Fournine straightened, looked at Viola. This close, with the hat on the ground, Fournine stared at her. Jagged lines ran along the left side of its face. A hasty plaskin repair. The rest of its skin looked too perfect. No wrinkles. No natural bumps, hairs, or eyelashes out of place.

"What are you staring at?" Fournine said. "It is rude to study another so. As I understand it, a human would blush under such scrutiny."

"You, uh, can't do that. Can you?" Viola said.

"Doesn't matter to you. Or me," Fournine said, moving over to the lifts and pushing the call button.

The android seemed to forget Viola was still standing there, watching him. Maybe the android really didn't care about her. Viola could walk away, head back to the *Jumper*. Or . . .

"Who are you going after next?" Viola said.

"Don't care," Fournine replied, staring ahead at the closed lift doors. "This is a list that can be read in any order. Cadge Vasseter happened to have the least luck of his friends."

"I guess I'm thankful."

Fournine turned now and Viola felt those inanimate eyes poring over her.

Every part of her tested, ranked and measured.

"I'm having a hard time understanding why you're continuing to talk," Fournine said. "According to my logic, you interacting with me only increases your chances of death."

"I can help you," Viola said. "Find the rest of them, I mean."

"Why would you do that?"

"You just saw one of them try and kidnap me," Viola said. "They deserve what's coming to them."

Viola had no idea if Fournine would take her word, but if the bot let her come with him, it didn't really matter. Viola reached towards Cadge's body, which smelled like burning meat, the charred hole in the mercenaries chest twisting her stomach in knots. Focus, girl, focus. On Cadge's left wrist wrapped his comm. A button on the underside unlatched the tool, and Viola slipped it off and then around her own forearm. Fournine watched with a robot's lifeless impassivity.

"Who are you going to talk to?" Fournine asked.

"I'll be able to find their location," Viola said. "Lead you right to them."

Fournine nodded and Viola raised the comm.

"Phyla?" Viola asked into the device.

"Viola?" Phyla replied. "You have a comm? The signature says it's Cadge's?"

"Long story," Viola said. "I need to know where Davin's going."

"He's trying to find the guy who can get that android off our backs. He's on this station somewhere. But what's going on? Where's Cadge?"

Viola caught Fournine's eye, and the android waved a hand in a quick slash motion. Cut the call.

"Thanks, Phyla. I'll be in touch," Viola said.

"Hey—"

Viola cut the transmission. Fournine was busy punching a request into the lift panel. The clock was ticking. If Viola didn't find a way to shut down Fournine before it found Davin, the captain's death would be on her.

Not for the first time, Viola wished she'd just stayed at home on Ganymede.

Save the Ship

Nobody answers the calls, and then Viola chimes in out of nowhere with Cadge's comm. Phyla tried another round of calls out to the crew. Radio silence from Mox, Opal, Merc, and Davin. What the hell was going on out there?

Outside the cockpit window, the activity in the bay was winding down as the hours crept later. Dinner time. A pinch in her own stomach where some food would've found a welcome home. Here they were, on a station where Phyla might get a good meal, and she was still stuck on the ship. It wasn't fair. Then, that'd always been her lot. Sitting on the ship playing comm operator while Davin dashed around or Merc aced out the skies.

The main lift doors kicked Phyla out of the musing. A squad, at least ten people wearing the forest green of Miner Prime's peacekeepers. Only these looked armed, ready for combat, not patrol. Too terrible to be a coincidence.

Phyla slapped a button on the right side of the console, big and red, labeled Alarm. The button's sole purpose was to make a lot of noise while sliding up the loading ramp and sealing the doors. Hopefully, neither Trina nor Erick had decided on an evening stroll.

Outside, the security forces paused, grouping into bunches and looking like easy targets. Phyla twisted a small dial that popped a turret from the top of the ship. On the ground, with the turret up, Phyla's flight stick rerouted to control where the gun pointed, and she aimed it at the closest group.

"You're all not here for us, right?" Phyla spoke through the ship's intercom system.

One of the security members, with a thicker collar than the others and a blue armband around his bicep, raised a hand and stepped towards the ship.

"No closer. You talk nice and loud and I'll hear you fine," Phyla said. "Your boot goes another centimeter and I'll take it as assault with deadly force and respond in kind."

As the security officer cleared his throat, Phyla switched the comm to broadcast internally.

"Trina, get our engines ready. I'll stall as long as I can, but we can't stay here."

"Already on it," Trina replied a heartbeat later.

"That's why you're the best," Phyla replied, then realized the officer out front was speaking.

" . . . and, in addition to the aforementioned crimes, it is suspected that your vessel carries a number of illegal modifications not approved for its class. Like, uh, that turret there."

"It's not my ship," Phyla said. "I'm just the pilot. Have no say in what the captain does with her."

The console showed the engines were at twenty-five percent. Phyla knew the ship could bounce at seventy-five if it had to, it just wouldn't be the smoothest launch. But then, nothing with this damned ship was smooth. Only, without the *Jumper* she wouldn't have ever left Miner Prime. Maybe she'd be down there in one of those green suits instead of up here, manning a spewing death weapon and waiting for someone to make the wrong move.

"Then you won't mind us coming aboard to look for him?" the officer replied.

The man was stalling for time same as she was. The other security forces shifted around, spreading out. The main lift doors opened again. More peacekeepers, only these carried larger weapons. Crowd suppression turrets and strong EMP launchers. Couldn't do explosions on a space station, but shorting circuitry was fair game.

"He's on his way to talk to your boss right now," Phyla said. "You should check, maybe they've cleared this up."

Dangerous, hinting to what Davin was doing, but Phyla didn't see she had a choice. The engines hadn't hit fifty yet. Cold starts were rough, and if they took fire too soon, the *Jumper* wouldn't be going anywhere. The officer bought it, though, holding up a hand and speaking into his comm. Phyla rotated the turret to aim at the group of security setting up the EMPs. Another thirty seconds and she'd fire anyway. She dialed down the power on the turret - it would burn, hurt, but shouldn't kill anymore. The last thing they needed was an actual set of murders on their record.

"How we doing?" Phyla commed to Trina.

The engines were at sixty percent. Close. If the *Jumper* wasn't going to take off early, Phyla had to know.

"They're goosed, Phyla. When you say go, they'll get us out of here," Trina said. "But if you can hold till ninety, we'll have a better chance of not exploding."

"Noted," Phyla replied.

"Phyla?" Mox's voice came over the comm. "I lost Viola."

So many questions there wasn't time to ask.

"She's fine," Phyla replied. "No word on Opal and Merc. Go find them, please. Then hole up and wait for more."

The security officer lowered his arm, a scowl lighting up his face. That meant Davin hadn't taken care of things. Which meant their stall time was up. Phyla pressed on the flight stick's trigger and the turret fired, spraying yellow lasers into the bay. There wasn't any recoil, not even much noise inside the ship, but Phyla flinched at the bright light.

The bolts struck home, frying circuits and scattering the security forces across the bay. Burning bits of cloth and sparking mechanics sent smoke swirling from the blasts. Keeping the trigger down, Phyla swept the turret left to right across the peacekeeper formation.

The first return shots came, small lasers from sidearms. They glanced off plating meant to handle space awfulness, from rocks to blasts from far more powerful anti-ship weaponry. Part of the constant upgrades Davin put into the ship whenever he had spare coin. Now, though, Phyla appreciated it. Prayed that it would hold another minute till those engines were ready. That the exclamation point to her life wouldn't be written in this awful docking bay.

Up By Force

The tube intersection looked so basic, smooth and perfect like a children's toy. A big central shaft with vented openings all over the place. Like the inside of a twisted flute. Davin and Lina stood at the end of their tube, surveying the sheer sides of the shaft. Davin didn't think he'd be a terrible climber, but the whole no handholds thing would make it difficult.

"They use a hovering vehicle to get up and down the shaft for maintenance," Lina said, whispering. "I've picked it up on camera a few times."

"Good to know. I'll keep that in mind when I get my own space station," Davin replied.

"But if there's a problem," Lina said, ignoring Davin's quip. "They'll send a spotter bot first to find the damage."

"Should I be taking notes? Is there a test?"

"Stop being stupid. We'll trigger a maintenance check. The spotter bot will come, we'll trick it into seeing a problem, then hijack the maintenance craft," Lina said.

"See, you're using the word 'we' a lot there, only I don't understand how we're doing any of this. Or, at least the first two. The hijacking I get."

Lina stepped over to the side of the tub they were in and pulled out her sidearm, a standard-issue laser pistol she's probably stole from Miner Prime's police armory. She popped the weapon open using a slider underneath the barrel. Made cleaning and repairing the lasers easy, only now Lina was using it to take out the gun's battery. Lina set the battery on the floor of the tube, then walked back. Davin followed.

"I suppose now you want me to shoot it?" Davin asked.

"Knew you'd figure it out," Lina replied.

Blasting a battery pack caused the stored energy in it to overheat. With the small size of Lina's sidearm, that wouldn't be much, but it might mangle the tube enough. Davin couldn't help but smile. This was the same stuff Lina pulled hen they were kids, upping the risk from one prank to the next till something backfired.

"Lina, before I shoot this thing and possibly bring hell itself upon us, I have a question."

"And maybe I have an answer," Lina replied.

"How long have you been planning this?"

"Since I saw your name on the wanted list," Lina said. "Whenever you're in trouble, you always come back here."

"And you knew we'd be going in the tubes?"

"There's only one way for people without clearance to get to that level, and it's this one. Now, you going to shoot that thing or do I have to?"

Without another word, Davin drew and fired his gun in a single motion, the laser hitting the battery pack and exploding the thing in a bright flash of molten plasma. The super-heated goop burnt into the side of the tube, hollowing out pits and charring the surface.

"That doesn't draw an investigation, dunno what will," Davin said.

"Always knew you could hit a stationary target," Lina said.

"I do have skills."

Only a few seconds later the soft hum of low-powered engines echoed through the tube. Davin and Lina inched backward, around a slight bend and out of site of the central shaft. If the bot found something needing repair, the maintenance crew would come after it. No need to risk getting caught. The hum grew louder, then held steady for ten seconds, before rising up and away from the tube.

"A thought," Davin said. "That bot, when it looks at the damage, it will know an explosion isn't a typical problem down here."

"Even if it does, that just means you'll have to show off those deadly talents you talk about so much."

Lina, always with the ribbing. Davin didn't talk himself up too much, did he?

"Good point. So excited," Davin said.

Not too many minutes later another rumbling noise made its way the shaft and shook the tube. Much larger than the inspection bot. Large enough that Davin threw Lina some side-eye. When Lina glanced his way, Davin pointed at her, then at himself, and held up two fingers and tilted his head towards the loud engine noise. A craft that big against the two of them? Those weren't good odds.

"Surprise," Lina whispered to him, barely audible over the engine noise.

Then, before Davin could move, Lina slipped along the tube towards the craft. Davin rounded the bend after her and saw the floating platform hovering just below the exit of the tube. On it Davin counted four people, three in the gray outfits of mechanical personal and one in the green of Miner Prime security. All of them were looking at Lina, who stood waving. In a second, they'd realize she wasn't alone.

In that second, Davin drew his gun and, in the same motion, moved his finger along the power slider. Fancier weapons like his had the choice to toss more, and lower-powered, shots. Seeing as they were trying to get rid of a criminal charge, it didn't seem like a great idea to kill someone. At least, not if they didn't have to.

Davin's first shot went under Lina's raised, waving arm and struck the security guard in the chest. The guard stumbled back to the edge of the platform, about to fall off, when he hit the safety barrier. The edge of the platform flashed a neon blue around where the guard was tumbling and, instead of falling off, the platform pushed the guard back. Lina dove to the side, giving Davin a clear second shot.

This one flew wide, just over the ducking head of the mechanic closest to the damaged tube. An intentional miss. Had to make them understand Davin could take them out whenever he wanted. The shot had the desired effect, as the mechanics backed up, hands raised, and leaned against the platform's barriers.

"Which one of you knows how to fly this thing?" Davin said, running onto the craft and kicking away the wounded guard's weapon.

None of them said anything at first. Then Lina picked up the guard's gun, a hefty piece of work meant to spray stunning electricity, and trained it on them. That prompted one of the mechanics to raise his hand. Davin gave him a nod.

"Well, uh, we all can. Sir," the mechanic said. "Part of our training."

"Ah. Good. Then one of you, send us up," Davin said, waving with the jig.

"Level Nine," Lina said.

The mechanic that spoke went to the console. Just before the craft moved, Davin pulled the guard and the other two mechanics off, leaving them on the tube. Their buddy could come back for them later. Davin hadn't taken a hostage before, and one seemed a safer bet than four.

The piloting mechanic pushed a lever and the craft rose. One step closer.

Take Off

The console pinged when the engines hit ninety, just like it had every ten percent before then, but when Phyla heard that wonderful bell, she let go of the flight stick and tapped the launch sequence on the console. First step was to trigger the landing rockets, pushing the ship a few inches off the ground, then tap the landing gear retrieval, and then flip the turret onto auto-fire mode. The last one was dangerous, as the turret then analyzed any incoming fire and shoot in that direction. It always meant the turret fired second, but Phyla needed the flight stick to fly.

The security forces hadn't expected the *Whiskey Jumper*'s defenses. After Phyla neutralized the EMPs, the bulk of the attackers hunkered behind walls, stacked cargo, or dove into the lift and fled. Reinforcements would come, but right now there was a distinct lack of laser fire splashing across Phyla's cockpit. As the ship lifted off the ground and rotated, Phyla saw bright orange lights flash in the bay. They were shutting the door, trying to keep the *Jumper* sealed on the station. Only, they were way too slow.

Phyla goosed the engines even before the exit was fully in view, arcing the *Jumper* out before the bay door was even a quarter shut. The black infinite of space stretched before her though the *Jumper*'s radar showed a slew of other ships spread around the station. The question was whether Miner Prime would bother to fight them out here. The station would risk coin and cargo if they tried to have a shoot-out near these trading ships.

So Phyla steered the *Jumper* to the nearest cluster, hoping to hide among their valuable structures. Then she'd find a way to get the rest of their friends back. Speaking of . . .

"Mox, you there?"

"Here," Mox said a second later, the transmission faint and blipped with static, a result of the increasing distance between the two. "You gone?"

"We're off."

"Good. Found them."

"How?"

"Mace. Weapon dealer. They were taken."

"Taken? By who?"

"Be ready. Level Eleven. Will call."

"Thanks for not answering my question."

Mox didn't reply. cutting the comm. Phyla, moving the *Jumper* down to undercut a long chain of containers being towed by what amounted to a large engine and little else, pulled up the Miner Prime directory. Eleven. Two words in the description. Prison and Containment.

Jailed

The lifts took Mox right up there and deposited him into an austere lobby. Chairs were there, a few token plants, and a pair of desks behind glass with security officers staring out at the waiting room. Several people milled about, some sitting and staring at nothing, others on their comms, while more were in line waiting for those officers. Mox estimated twenty. Too much collateral damage.

There was a door to the right of the officers, the only other one leading from the lobby. Assumed that to be the entrance to the actual prison. Possibility of breaking through door, with the suit, was high. Possibility of survival past it, low. Mox needed a distraction.

Mox walked up to the last person in the line. Shabby man. Old, tired.

"Why are you here?" Mox asked, forcing himself to use more words.

"Friend's been couped up in there for days," the man replied. "He meant to pay the tab, you know, but didn't have the money. I've got it now. Hoping they'll let him go."

"Optimistic?"

The man laughed. It was weak, wheezy. Not a threat.

"You look around here, you see any reason to hope?"

Mox shook his head. He had to get inside the prison. No way to force. If he was let in . . . Mox moved away from the line, towards a few empty chairs. Picked one up. The people in the lines scattered while the officers behind the desks pointed and shouted. Good. Mox threw the first chair at the prison door where it bounced. Plastic. No help. Mox picked up the second chair, threw it towards the officer desk. Aimed high, so it ricocheted off the wall.

The prison door opened and five security officers came running out, pointing blue-tinted jigs at Mox. Stunners. Mox didn't pick up the third chair, but glared at the security officers.

"You gone crazy, man?" one of them asked as the five fanned out in a circle around Mox.

"Friends inside. Want to see."

"Good, cause that's where you're going," the officer said, gesturing for another to move behind Mox with a pair of stun cuffs. "Don't try anything or we'll knock you out so hard you won't wake for days."

Mox just nodded. The rest of the crowd stared at him, a few using their devices to take videos. Mox would be famous. Funny. The stun cuffs snapped around Mox's wrists and he felt his arms go numb. Didn't matter. He was getting inside.

Reconnect

Puk, where it could feel anything, felt tired. Its power level was running low. It'd been zipping around Level Five, then in the lifts around a few other levels hunting for signs of Viola and finding none. It'd gone back to the *Whiskey Jumper*'s bay to find it empty, a bunch of security officers standing around picking themselves up. From there, back to Level Five and still nobody. Like the Wild Nines had disappeared.

Miner Prime's shopping district was shifting into evening mode, the false sky overhead darkening in an approximation of a spectacular twilight. Lights popped on outside of restaurants, neons over most, with a pair of themed eateries sporting the more mellowed yellows of earlier centuries. Crowds changed complexion, from buyers of goods to purveyors of experiences. Bots like Puk flitted through the air, sometimes stopping to project ads.

"Puk?" came a message over Puk's comm.

The message came from Cadge's comm, but the vocal register was consistent with Viola's. Odd. Comms weren't things people parted with. And their relative abilities generated unlikely odds that Viola could have taken the comm by force. There was room for random chance, however, and Viola was nothing if not capable.

"Where are you?" Puk replied, lowering power to its inflection and accent systems to conserve juice, causing the remark to sound toneless, metallic.

"You've got to be low on power. Are you still on Level Five?"

"Yes," Puk replied.

Low was an understatement. Puk had shut down most of its systems. Like a human falling asleep, Puk only had its camera and comm up and running now. And the jets. Movement was still necessary.

"Go near the lifts. I'll find you," Viola said.

Puk did so, sinking to the ground. Within a few yards of the lifts, Puk gave itself a boost and then shut off its tiny engine, hitting the ground with a clang and rolling forward. There were people around who noticed, but nobody cared enough to investigate. Why get involved in something else's problem? So Puk rolled to a stop near the lifts and waited. Its camera went dark. Comm only.

"This is the one?" said a voice after a few minutes, one Puk didn't recognize.

"It's Puk."

"The bot's not a target."

"I never said it was," Viola's voice.

"The captain's not here."

"Apparently. Davin might already be up there."

"Then we follow."

"Sure."

As Puk heard the lift doors close, its battery dwindled and the little bot went dark.

Cell Game

They put Opal and Merc together in the same large cell, owing to questions of how long they'd be there. The space occupied by a pair of metal slats sticking out from the wall, covered with the thinnest of pads. A single sheet sat on each one. The back of the cell served as a bathroom, a small curtain conveniently placed. A built-in screen on one wall shuffled through feeds from Earth, from Miner Prime's other levels. As though taunting them with what they were missing.

From the tone in the officer's voice, Opal figured they would be ejected into space before too long. Merc might not even make it that far. He lied on his slat, passed out and breathing softly. The man shouldn't have left the *Jumper*, but Merc had insisted. Claimed that he'd lose his mind if he didn't get to see something other than the ship's walls.

"Get him back here within four hours," Erick had said.

"I'll have him back in three," Opal had replied.

And now they were here.

Injured comrades were part of the way of things back when she'd fought with Earth, with the corporations to put down the Red Voice on Mars. Blazing over the martian regolith, covered in its red dust, taking and giving fire against moving targets. If she took a shot there, she'd likely wind up in a room not much better than this, a harried bot taking care of her. Thing was then, when Opal was ready, they let her leave.

Merc shifted and his sheet slid down. It wasn't cold in the cell, but the pilot shivered. Opal tore the sheet off of her slat, went over to Merc and covered him with it. His mouth was tight, eyes closed. Still hurting, even though he was asleep. That wasn't good.

When had she cared so much about Merc? They'd only been working together in the Nines for the last year, but something between them had clicked. The pilot's lighter touch on life pulling Opal away from the past. Days spent touching up the Viper, playing war games in the *Jumper's* pair of simulators. That'd been the start of it. Now, looking at the pilot sleeping there on the slat, it was something else.

She was going to get Merc out of here. She owed him that.

The door to the cell block opened behind her, a thick whooshing noise. It'd been happening in the few hours they'd been here. Miner Prime shuttled people in and out of this prison so quickly, so many for minor offenses that cleared up with a few coin changing hands. The footfalls in the hallway were loud this time. A large group and at least one of them was a big ticket.

Opal moved herself over to the laser-gate, careful to stay back from the bright blue beams. One touch numbed the arm or leg. Keep it there and it'd paralyze her nervous system. She'd already seen one person, too drunk to care, make a running jump at the beams. They went right through, sure, but collapsed on the other side. The guards simply shoved the drunk back in, where he still laid, unmoving. Stunned for hours and hours? No thanks.

The new prisoner moved into view, at least four officers walking with him. Opal saw Mox, saw the exoskeleton, and didn't say a word. Didn't give the man a passing glance. Mox would've seen her too. Him coming in here with those cuffs on spoke volumes. The big man wouldn't let himself get captured easily. If Mox was going in a cell, he was going to be shot up a dozen times before falling over. So that he was here all calm told Opal all she needed to know. Time to get Merc ready to go.

Standoff

The number over Mox's cell read 27, and the one shared by Opal and Merc back there was 22. The laser gate to his cell opened and a pair of guards walked him inside, while two more stayed in the hall, guns pointed at Mox. As soon as all three of them crossed the threshold, the laser gate reignited. Then the stun cuffs came off.

"We'll need the comm," a guard pointed at Mox's wrist.

Mox raised the comm, gripped it as though about to rip it off.

"Cell 22. Go big," Mox said.

"Now!" the guard replied, trying to pull Mox's wrist away.

Mox let the guard grab the comm, the man's little fingers digging for the release, then Mox, exoskeleton surging with power, grabbed the guard's back with his right hand and launched him through the laser gate into one waiting in the hallway. Before the second guard in the cell could react, Mox had him by the throat, holding him up and staring at the remaining guard in the hall.

"Open, or he goes," Mox said.

The guard in Mox's hand tried to say something, but only gurgles came out. In the hallway, the other guard stared at Mox, stun gun raised. Debating.

"Put him down, or I'll shoot," the guard said.

"I hope you aim well," Mox replied.

Either way, Phyla needed to hurry, or this prison break was over.

Negotiations

The security level was barren, only a few souls still shifting past the Miner Prime government buildings this late. A skeleton crew handling the evening shift. Davin and Lina, leaving the mechanic cuffed in the maintenance building, walked through the low-lit concourse to the dominating headquarters.

Unlike Level Five, or even Vagrant's Hollow, the security center was austere. Administrative buildings decorated with flat signs detailing their purpose in block letters. Not even a false sky, just the gray ceiling. Never had a reason to come up here as a kid, and Davin hadn't missed anything.

The security headquarters turned out to be the only building with flair. A series of concave circles on the outer walls painted with happy murals, scenes of ribbon-cuttings, peacekeepers interacting with the community, a long line of ships waiting to land at the station. The Miner Prime station logo, a whirling asteroid with a pickaxe and an olive branch hung above the main doors.

"This is . . . different," Davin said. "Never came up here. The way those peacekeepers act, I expected something more brutal."

"Our perspective is a little skewed," Lina replied.

"Guess so."

Getting into the actual building was easy. Walking up to the door and swinging it wide. A security officer sat behind a reception desk, caught twirling a pen between his fingers and staring at the ceiling. He started as they walked in, the pen clattering to the floor.

"Ah, we're closed unless you've got emergency business," the guard said.

"Here to see Bosser," Lina said. "He'll want to talk to us."

The guard gave them a closer look and then, keeping his eyes on them, touched the comm unit on his desk.

"Sir, a couple people just walked in. Say they're here to see you."

There was silence for a few seconds. A chill crawled up Davin's skin, that telltale sign someone was watching him. Which Bosser probably was. Security cameras lurking in every nook around this place. Should he wave?

"He's ready for you," the guard said, surprised at the words coming out of his mouth. "Before you go in, though, I'll have to frisk you. No weapons, you know."

"Fine," Lina said, again before Davin could get a word in.

It was as though Lina didn't want him talking. Probably didn't trust the words that would come out of Davin's mouth. Which, all things considered, was fair.

The guard took away Davin's gun, and Lina's weapon she'd taken from the incapacitated maintenance guard. Both dropped in a box that they could reclaim on their way out. Then the guard led them back through a cafeteria. Up stairs to a private apartment.

"Guy's got himself a nice place," Davin said as they walked up to the door.

"He works all the time," the guard said. "Why live anywhere else?"

The guard pushed a buzzer, and a second later the light turned green, the door unlocking. The guard ushered the two of them into Bosser's sitting room. A couch and pair of chairs sat around a circular coffee table that appeared to show a constantly changing display of ships in orbit around Miner Prime. Bosser himself strode in a moment later from an open doorway, a bottle of wine and several glasses in his hand.

"Please, sit in those chairs. You," Bosser said, looking at the guard. "Can leave us alone. I'll be fine."

The guard gave a swift nod and excited, shutting the door behind him.

"You'll be fine?" Davin said, making no move towards the chairs. "Bold statement, seeing as you're talking to a murderer."

"You hurting me won't bring you anything you want," Bosser said.

"Wrong. You sent an android after me and my crew. Sending a fist into your face would be all kinds of satisfying."

"Short-term gains over long-term goals, Davin Masters," Bosser said. "One could see it as an explanation for why I'm here and you are there."

"It better not be the only explanation."

"Davin," Lina said, putting a hand on his arm. "Focus."

Bosser took the cue, gestured towards the chairs and poured the wine.

"Please, sit," Bosser said.

Lina led the way, taking a seat across from Bosser. Davin waited another moment, a token show of defiance, then sat. The wine, and Davin had to credit Bosser on this one, tasted dry and fruity, a march of flavors that worked their way around the citrus circle and ending on a spicy note. For a second, Davin placed himself in the glass and forgot where they were.

"It's one of my favorites," Bosser said, breaking the spell. "Every time I see Earth, I make sure to purchase a case or two."

"You know what I like to do while my friends are in danger? Talk wine," Davin said, putting the glass on the table.

"What Davin's really saying," Lina said. "Is that you should talk before we chalk this up to a loss and shoot you for the fun of it."

"Fine," Bosser said, spreading his hands. "I don't think you and your band killed those inspectors."

"You're just going to come right out and say it?" Davin said.

"Why not?" Bosser took another drink from the glass. "I'm right, aren't I?"

"Yeah, but then what's all this about?" Davin replied.

"I'm hoping you can tell me. Have you seen the video?"

"Haven't carved out time for it," Davin said.

"It's quite good," Bosser said, flipping on the large screen on the wall.

It hummed to life and, with a few spoken commands from Bosser, played a black and white recording. In it, the two inspectors entered the bay, Davin and the others behind them. Just like what'd happened, jeez, over a week ago already. Both of the inspectors spoke for a minute, then walked towards the ship. Davin, it looked like, pulled out his gun and shot them in the back. Bosser paused the footage.

"I'm guessing that isn't how it went?" Bosser said.

"Yeah, cause I'm the type to shoot people for kicks and giggles," Davin said. "No, that's not even close."

"Then tell me what occurred. Prove your innocence."

So Davin launched into the story. Clare and Ward, requesting private escort and sounding very suspicious of some sort of conspiracy. The ambushed landing in the other bay, the engine splash. The arrival of the new security forces just in time to blow up the only people who knew why the whole thing happened.

"So a doctored video gets the charges pressed," Davin said. "But here's the thing I don't understand. The android that's after us. It came from Earth, and there's no way it had the time to come out to Europa after the inspectors died. It was less than a day!"

"Fournine was already in the area," Bosser said. "Eden had the android sent to Jupiter's orbit so it would be ready."

"For what?" Lina said.

"Those inspectors weren't sent randomly," Bosser said. "Marl is hiding something on Europa, and Eden sent the inspectors to find out what. A settlement like that one is vulnerable. Eden wanted to make sure Marl wouldn't have time to destroy their investment. I'm hoping you can tell me her secret."

"Sorry, fresh out of secrets," Davin said. "Marl always kept us at a distance. You ever meet her, you wouldn't argue with that arrangement."

"If you truly have nothing to say, then I'm sorry," Bosser said. "Eden won't remove your charge, and Marl, the only other one who could certainly won't."

Bosser took a slow sip of the wine.

"But you could convince them," Lina said.

"You're truly lucky that you brought her, someone who knows how to play the game," Bosser said to Davin, then slid his gaze to Lina. "I could, provided you will pay the price."

Prep the Rescue

The *Whiskey Jumper* angled itself towards the prison level of Miner Prime. The docking bays at the middle of the station kept ships away from here, giving the *Jumper* plenty of room to maneuver. Flight control kept trying to hail her, and Phyla kept ignoring them. They were threatening to scramble fighters, a threat that'd come true in a minute. Phyla was taking what remained of her relationship with the station and lighting it on fire.

Ask someone in a bar and they'd tell you that shooting at humanity's largest space station wasn't the greatest plan. It would be unexpected though. Phyla swung the *Jumper* into position, aiming straight at the prison level. They had to be close. Precise.

Miner Prime wouldn't activate their shields, and thus block all incoming and outgoing trade traffic, unless they had to. The goal was to break through the hull before that happened.

"Mox, you have ten seconds," Phyla commed, then switched to Trina's channel. "Trina, I'll fire a couple blasts, then we have to play one heckuva game of catch. You going to be ready?"

"Am I ever not?" Trina replied.

"Erick, you at the airlock?"

"Confirmed," Erick said.

For the first time today, something was going as planned. Figured that it would be the prison break. According to the station maps, acquired and provided long ago by Lina, cell 24 was sitting on the outside of the station. Mox said that cell was empty. In another two seconds, according to Phyla and the twin turrets on the *Jumper*, that cell would be replaced by a gaping hole into vacuum. Hopefully, the right people fell through it.

Out and About

The guard fired the stun gun, but Mox saw it coming. The tightened grip, the sudden beads of sweat. So many tells someone was going to be a hero. Mox swung his guard in front of the bolt and felt the body shield go limp. Mox charged forward with the body in his arm, holding it ahead. When the body hit the laser gate, it broke the connection for a moment. If the guard had been awake when he hit that gate, it would've fried his senses and left him unconscious.

As it was, the guard's nap was going to be even longer. The lasers tripped off until reset, to prevent overloading a prisoner's nerves to the point where they died. Which meant Mox could walk right to the last guard.

The little man had guts. The guard had the sidearm pointed right at Mox's face, pushed the trigger as Mox batted the weapon away. It flew down the corridor after its own shot, and Mox threw the guard after it a moment later.

"Mox, you have ten seconds," Phyla's voice came over the comm.

Opal and Merc were to the right, in cell 22. The switch toggling the laser gate was right outside the door. It required a badge, so Mox grabbed one of the unconscious guards he'd knocked over and held him up to the control panel. It bleeped an affirmative. The lasers disappeared, which meant right about . . . now. An alarm sounded. Obnoxious, like nails on metal. Then a bang. Deafening. A sucking roar, a rush of air from the cell next to Opal and Merc's.

Mox stepped around Opal and lifted Merc from the slat with his right hand as the pull from the air became stronger. It tugged at his legs, the skeleton boosting Mox's downward force to keep his grip. Opal had no such support and tumbled backwards. Out the hole Phyla blew in the station, out into the cold death of space. A second alarm, lower toned, joined the first. Prison break and atmosphere leak. Mox laughed. Bet they didn't have that scenario covered. His arm reached out, grabbed Opal's wrist, held her back.

"Was this the plan?!" Opal yelled over the noise.

"Yes," Mox replied.

"It's a shitty one!"

Now, Mox laughed.

A moment later the pull of the atmosphere lessened. The tug went away. A new question. Due to friend or foe?

"There?" Mox commed.

"Jump away," Trina answered. "We'll catch you."

Mox let go of Opal and, now cradling Merc, ran into the hallway. One cell over. A door opened far down the cell block. Stun bolts fired, but they were off-target. Hasty shots. Opal running behind him. Turned into the next cell. Torn hole in the back. Through it, the open circular door of the *Whiskey Jumper*'s airlock, jammed into the station to provide enough of a seal. Mox jumped through the hole, keeping Merc tight in his arms. Behind him, Opal leapt. The three of them flew through the outer door.

It sealed rapidly, the inner door staying shut until the computers confirmed there wasn't a leak. Out the airlock's window, Mox could see Miner Prime shrinking as Phyla blasted away. Then the inner door opened and Erick yelled at Mox to bring Merc in to the med bay.

Shots Fired

"I haven't even heard it and I already want to say no," Davin said.

"Work for me," Bosser said. "And I'll convince them to drop the charges. No more running for your lives."

Oh, that was a good one. Swap the stick for the carrot.

"Tempting, but why us? There have to be other mercenary groups," Davin replied. "Ones you wouldn't have to work so hard to get.

"Anyone can buy loyalty with coin, all it takes is more than the next person," Bosser said. The man still looked serene, sitting on his couch. Davin took another gulp of the wine.

"But the threat of branding them criminals . . ." Lina said and Bosser spread his hands.

"You understand," Bosser said.

"Don't know what I hate more," Davin said. "That you're blackmailing me, or that I'm considering it."

"Logic is your friend here, Davin," Bosser said. "You have a crew to take care of. I'm offering you a chance to do it."

Bosser's comm beeped, and he took a second to glance at it, frowned, then looked back at Davin with a straight face.

"It seems your friends are racking up more crimes for you to answer for," Bosser said. "Make your choice."

Agree, and the Nines become flunkies for this wino prince for who knows how long. Say no and they're back in the streets, dodging shots and finding a way to survive. Thing was, Davin had been there. A childhood in Vagrant's Hollow taught him there was always a way, so long as he could make his own choices. Davin glanced at Lina, read the same thing in her eyes, her slight nod.

"Gonna have to take a pass, boss-man," Davin said. "The whole threat thing doesn't do it for me."

Bosser didn't react, but that was its own reaction. Sitting still, eyes drilling into Davin as though Bosser was trying to see through him. Hands clasped tight. Maybe the man was having a stroke. Popped a vein on the way to the brain when Davin refused.

"Fine," was what Bosser said, finally, right before he stood up, pulled a small sidearm from beneath his vest, and shot Lina in the chest.

The moment Bosser reached into his coat, Davin moved. He didn't beat the shot, but a half second later, Davin was on Bosser, tackling the man to the ground and pinning the gun out to the side with Davin's right hand. With his left, Davin was striking home when the door opened and something else fired. It was high, glancing off of the wall near Davin's head, but it forced him to roll right off of Bosser. On the way, using his momentum, Davin grabbed and tore the weapon from Bosser's hand. Came up with it aiming towards the door. At . . . Viola?

"Don't shoot him!" Viola was screaming, and then Davin noticed the android.

It moved into the room, stepping around the couch and over Bosser until it stood above Davin, an impassive scowl on its face. Bosser, behind it, rose to his knees and shook his head. The android reached behind its back and drew out a knife it'd used back on Europa. Something that, in another time and place, Davin would have found cool, but now only deepened the surreal horror.

Davin pointed the sidearm at the android's chest. He doubted the shot would stop the coming swing, would keep Davin's head from finding a place on the floor, but what else was there?

Viola was yelling, but everyone ignored it. The android adjusted its grip as Davin tightened his fingers on the trigger, as Bosser stood back up, and Lina coughed loudly. Then spoke.

"You're not the only one with surprises," Lina said, her voice bubbling as blood pooled in her mouth.

Davin risked a look, saw Lina, a deep red stain on her outfit, slumped in the chair. Saw her earrings in one hand, saw that hand close around and press hard. A deep bass beat, a rumble felt more than heard. In front of Davin, the android collapsed, knife hitting the ground. Davin's sidearm clicked, nothing more. A short-range EMP, disabler of electric devices. Potentially suicidal in space, where disabling air systems meant death, but when death was imminent anyway, what was there to lose?

Bosser swore then sprinted past Viola, who didn't try stopping him. Davin scrambled over to Lina, looking at the wound. A jagged burn. Bosser's modified sidearm producing more power than allowed by the manufacturer. That's the only way it could've blown through Lina's thick jacket.

"He seemed so civil," Lina said, her eyes looping over to Davin. "I didn't think he'd try it. What a bastard."

"Don't worry about him. He'll get his," Davin said. "We've got to get you to the ship. To Erick."

"Sure," Lina said.

Viola was crouching over the android. Looking for something.

"Know how to reset an android?" Lina coughed, and Viola shook her head. "I played with a few I found as scrap. Press on the temples."

"You two understand we're getting more and more screwed the longer we stay here?" Davin said.

Viola ignored him and pressed on the android's forehead. Tiny clicks announced latches coming loose. A thin line appeared across the front of its scalp, then grew as a console rose out, wires spreading out beneath it like a mechanical jellyfish.

"See?" Lina said, coughing up a line of blood. "Simple."

"If it wakes up, I'll blow its head off," Davin said.

Not that he had a working weapon on him, but it felt good to say.

Shouts came from outside the room, the sound of approaching boots on metal. Davin ran over to the doorway. Looked out at a cluster of peacekeepers making their slow way down the hallway. Target city.

"Hand me his weapons," Davin said, and Viola grabbed the red and blue guns in the android's holsters and slid them to Davin. No sliders here, blue for stun, red for dead. Davin shot a couple of blue bolts. Hit one, his buddies catching him as he fell back. The peacekeepers flattened themselves against the side, a couple sending return fire Davin's way.

"We're screwed here," Davin said as a few bolts splashed against the doorway. "They'll have reinforcements coming, and when they arrive, they'll just swarm us."

"It's not that complicated," Viola said. "For all they're capable of—"

"They're never supposed to shut down," Lina, sitting in her chair, said. "This one could've blocked my EMP had it known what it was. Kill the power itself first, then restarted after the pulse."

"Cadge did something similar," Viola said. "But Fournine, that's its name—"

"You know its name?!" Davin sent another pair of shots towards the peacekeepers. They were edging along the hall, being cautious. The peacekeepers didn't have to get reckless with the three of them trapped.

"Doesn't matter," Lina said. "Can you get in?"

"I think so," Viola hunched over the small console, hands working fast. "There's so little security."

"People aren't meant to get this far," Lina said.

Outside the door, a pair of peacekeepers in full body armor walked up the stairs and into the hall. They were holding batons that would tweak Davin's nerves like a bolt of lightning. He shot another stunning bolt, watched it disappear into the armor without causing a flinch.

"Okay, kid, we're out of time," Davin said.

"Almost there!" Viola said.

"Aren't we always out of time?" Lina said, her eyes rolling towards Davin. She wasn't looking good, her face a bloodless pale, arms and legs hanging off the ends of the chair.

"Don't you go giving up on me," Davin said. "We've been in worse spots than this."

"Don't know about that, love," Lina said.

Viola looked up at that. Davin took another look out the hallway. The armored pair were creeping, wary. A few more seconds, though, and Davin would get a beat-down he'd rather avoid.

"We're going to talk about that word later," Davin said, this time using the red gun to fire. These bolts packed more power, left black burn marks on the armor, but the peacekeepers kept coming.

"Here we go!" Viola announced.

Davin glanced at the bot, but then the lighting changed. The armored peacekeepers had reached the doorway. A baton swung at Davin and he jumped back, falling on the floor. Crawling away, Davin tried to create more space. One of the peacekeepers loomed over him.

"You should have surrendered," the guard behind the mask said, and the baton swung.

It didn't land. A perfect hand caught the peacekeeper's forearm and held it. Then the android's leg kicked the peacekeeper's knee and sent the guard falling to the ground. The second peacekeeper tried to hit the android with his baton, but the bot spun away from it, drew its second knife.

"No killing!" Viola yelled. Fournine hesitated, threw Viola a look.

"That will make things more difficult," the android said. Davin jumped on the tripped peacekeeper, pinning the guard's baton arm to the ground with one hand and slipping Fournine's stunning gun beneath the folds of the peacekeeper's armor.

"Nap time," Davin said pulling the trigger. The peacekeeper went limp. Davin felt the apartment shake and looked up to see Fournine throw the second peacekeeper into the wall, then send a rapid sequence of blows with the knife hilt to the guard's head. The peacekeeper collapsed to the ground, unmoving.

"Clear a path to the docking bays," Viola said.

Fournine sheathed its knives, turned to Davin with its hands outstretched. Davin hesitated. Give the android those guns and it could blow them all to death in a second. Then again, if Fournine still wanted to kill them, it could have done it already.

Davin threw the guns. Fournine caught both and slipped out into the hallway.

A moment later, as Davin and Viola lifted an unconscious Lina off of the chair, the screams started in the hallway. Flashes of laser fire created a strobe effect for a few seconds. When the firing stopped, the hallway was quiet. Time to go home.

Snatch and Run

Merc was back in his bed, Erick's meds knocking him out. Opal and Mox sharing the twin turrets. Trina working the engines as the *Jumper* took cover in the swarm of ships orbiting Miner Prime.

"You send those fighters after us, you will cause more problems than you solve," Phyla commed to Miner Prime's flight control.

"But you blew up part of our prison!" came the reply.

"You arrested our crew for no reason," Phyla said. "I'll make a deal - you let us get the rest of our people off, we'll never come back here again. Nobody else needs to get hurt."

The Miner Prime officer started another angry threat, then stopped in the middle of it. A few seconds of silence.

"I'm being told to let you go," the officer said. "Ordered not to interfere. But if you so much as cause any more damage, I'll have my pilots turn you into ash."

Ordered? By who? Not that Phyla was going to argue.

"Deal," Phyla replied, then cut the transmission. Sat back in the chair and looked at the space station. Already a group of repair bots and a larger maintenance shuttle were hovering over the prison level, welding back together the blasted pieces. Ships continued to blast in and out of the docking bays. Miner Prime's commerce would not pause just for one group of fiery mercenaries.

"Phyla?" the comm buzzed, Davin's voice. "We're in the bay. You're not."

"Yeah, about that," Phyla replied. "We'll head your way. Make sure the door's open."

Getting the engines going, Phyla swung the ship in a slow arc back towards the space station. Approaching things in space always felt strange, how they appeared from nothing against the dark background. Dots that grew into moons, ships, Miner Prime. At least she wouldn't bother dealing with traffic control this time.

"Lina's been shot. Get Erick ready," Davin said.

"Bad?"

"Not good."

Ignoring a furious and yelling Miner Prime flight control officer, Phyla swung the *Whiskey Jumper* into the bay they'd trashed not an hour before. The burn marks of turret fire pocked the otherwise spotless interior. Phyla saw Davin, Viola, and then, holding Lina, a fourth she didn't recognize. Another pity project for Davin?

The ramp lowered with the press of a button, Erick and Mox at the ready to grab Lina and throw her into the med bed. Through the filter of the *Jumper*'s security cameras, Phyla saw Viola leading the new one up the ramp. The man's posture was perfect, his steps going in an even pace up the ramp. And then he turned and stared straight at the camera, gave a slight wave.

"It's the android," Davin said, stepping into the cockpit. "Stop looking at it and get us out of here."

"Isn't it a terrible idea to have that creepy thing on our ship?"

"Not anymore. Just go."

"Where's Cadge?" Phyla said.

"He's not here?" Davin paused. "Is he answering his comm?"

"Viola was using it last."

"She only managed to re-program the android in Bosser's office," Davin said, eyes closing for a moment. "After she had the comm."

"Don't know what you're talking about, but we can't stay here," Phyla said. "Miner Prime's not real happy with us, and I'd hate for their patience to run out while we're sitting here . . ."

"Take off. Now."

"And Cadge?"

"He's not coming," Davin said.

Davin usually had tints of sarcasm, humor in his voice. Here, there wasn't any.

Phyla punched on the jets, still primed from the earlier flying around the station, commed Trina to get back to the engines, and soon enough the ship was back into dark space.

Davin plopped himself into the seat beside her and stared out at the stars. Minutes passed. Being in a crew like this, a bubble built up. It felt like everyone was going to be fine forever. Until something, and it always happened eventually, came in and burst it.

Cadge wasn't exactly the friendliest, the most stable member, but the man was always there for a fight. Always had her back. Had their backs. Hard to ask for more than that. Phyla took a deep breath as the console toned that they were out of Miner Prime's control zone. In free space.

"Remember what you told me when we left?" Phyla said. "Best way to get over something sad was to focus on something new."

"I remember."

"We still charged with murdering those two?"

"We are."

"Then I'd say we focus on that."

Davin met Phyla's look, set his jaw.

"Marl's the answer. Let's go find her," Davin said.

Phyla plugged in the destination, routed the *Jumper* on a path to intersect in a few weeks with Jupiter's orbit. With that frozen blue moon she'd hoped never to see again.

"Davin?" Erick's voice crackled over the comm, tired. "You want to get down here?"

"Coming," Davin said.

"Hey," Phyla said as Davin walked out of the cockpit. "Tell Lina—"

"Tell her yourself, later," Davin interjected.

But Phyla could see in his eyes that Davin didn't believe his own words.

Goodbye

There's an unreality that wraps itself around you when you look at a loved one lying in a bed, IVs sticking, face flushed and sweating, both full of life and losing it at once. Davin saw Lina and his stomach twisted. His legs moved him next to her, but he wanted to run anywhere else. Some place where this wasn't happening. Where the girl he'd been loving for decades wasn't fading.

Erick didn't even have to tell Davin the details, but the doctor did anyway. Bosser's blast tore through Lina's left lung and seared part of her heart. It was struggling to keep beating, but would fail soon. They didn't have the supplies on the ship to tackle this catastrophe. Maybe, if they'd taken her to a Miner Prime med center, they'd be able to save her. Until Bosser came by to finish the job. Instead, Erick was numbing Lina to the pain, keeping her on the edge of consciousness.

"Talk to me," Davin said to Lina, leaning over the bed.

"For once, can you hold my hand?" Lina said, her voice barely above a whisper.

Davin did it, gripped Lina's fingers tight. They felt small, cold. Davin didn't know fingers could feel that way, drawn into themselves. As though the slightest push would send them crumbling to dust. Her eyes, though. Davin could sink into those eyes forever. As the rest of Lina fell away, they burned brighter and larger and Davin smiled right at them. A sad smile, one that carried tears along with it.

"You had to help us," Davin started. "You could've stayed at home. Showed me the way up and let me do it."

"Quit it," Lina said. "Don't make it cheap."

Davin opened his mouth, but Lina squeezed his hand and kept talking.

"Erick thinks he's numbed me, but I can tell what's happening. Its like getting tired, Davin. Everything's getting heavy. Nice thing is, the stress is going too."

"You never looked stressed."

"Whenever you came back, I was."

"Sorry," Davin said.

"Don't be, cause those were my favorite times. Always wondered whether you'd be back again or get yourself killed out there."

"And I always wanted you to come with me."

"Then this time I do and what happens? I get shot."

"Hey, don't cheapen it."

Lina gave him smile.

"Bosser won't give up, you know. He'll either kill you or do something worse."

"I won't let him," Davin said. "He doesn't deserve the satisfaction."

"Good," Lina said. "You're going to find Marl?"

"We need to have a talk."

"Give her a slap from me," Lina said, then drew in a sharp breath, one that rattled her whole body.

"Lina?"

The woman blinked long, slow. Her eyelids staying shut for five seconds before popping open.

"I think it's time to go. How about a kiss goodbye?"

Blackmail

"You didn't inform me of how capable they were," Bosser said to the screen.

While the message zipped along the interstellar breezeway towards Marl, Bosser poured himself another glass from the wine bottle. It was too good to waste. And besides, Bosser felt his shot was good. Lina Monte, endless harasser, didn't look good leaving his office.

"I take it that means they are still at large?" Marl's reply jerked across the screen before again settling into the frozen mask.

"And heading your way, if their captain's face was any inclination," Bosser said. "Make sure your new protection is prepared. Davin left here with an android on his side."

It would be an interesting study, Marl's face. So calm, even a little bemused. Her hair done up in curls. Planning to go to an event, no doubt. Bosser wasn't sure of the hour on Europa. Here, it was well into the early morning, when Bosser should be asleep. But such luxuries would have to wait. Business, as it always did, came first.

Ah, there it was. The snap of Marl's features. The slight frown betrayed by the widening eyes, the flare of the nostrils. These tiny delays brought him much closer to his subject. An opportunity to study them with intensity that would be impolite in real company. How much could Bosser learn from watching Marl twist in snapshots? Enough to know when to pounce.

"Can't you turn it off?" Marl said.

"They are required to send a code every twenty-four hours. If the sending device does not receive a reply from Earth, the android will degrade. Its code will delete itself," Bosser took a slow sip from the glass and waited.

"So it will be useless?"

"I'm afraid relying on that would be a mistake. There is at least one capable programmer among Davin's crew. I suspect they will resolve the transmission before it causes any harm."

"Then why tell me? Are you trying to taunt me, Bosser? Because I have better things to do with my time than play your games."

Bosser gave the screen a nod.

"In a normal situation, I would release two androids. Part of the escalation protocol. An ever-increasing volume of resources dedicated until the problem is solved."

"Mine is not a normal situation?"

"Why did you have those inspectors killed, Marl? Convince me, and I'll make sure Eden continues to pay for more androids to do your dirty work."

Marl's face withered on the transmission, her eyes sunk back as she collapsed into the chair behind her. The moment wasn't long, though, and her experience asserted itself. Her mouth set and she leaned forward.

"You and I both play outside the lines, Bosser," Marl said. "I know enough about what you're doing to bring you down with me. So you'll make sure Eden sends those androids, and I'll keep your secrets. There doesn't need to be a loser here."

Interesting. It wasn't likely Marl knew everything Bosser had in play, because the only person who did was himself. Still, she might do enough to bring him harm, and Bosser wasn't ready for that. Not yet.

"Fair enough, Marl. You'll get your androids," Bosser cut the transmission.

It'd been a risk to tell Miner Prime's security forces to stay away, to let the *Jumper* and the Wild Nines run. And now that bet was paying off. He'd underestimated Marl, and there was no better way to get rid of a potential problem than to have someone else solve it for him. With any luck, Davin Masters and his band would eliminate the leader of Eden Prime, and Bosser wouldn't have to lift a finger.

Operations

The android watched Viola and Trina eat their breakfast. It was unnerving, the way Fournine stared while you slipped a spoonful of flavored mush into your mouth. The lack of blinking, the rise and fall of the chest that didn't happen, they were the worst parts. Not that she hated robots, but when Fournine looked so like a normal man, it was hard to remember. Forget for a second, then a glint of perfect skin, unblinking eyes, no breathing, would jolt her out of nowhere.

"I can do that," Fournine said in response to Viola's look. "Breathe, blink. Even twitch every once in a while if it'll make you feel better."

"Why?" Trina said. "That wouldn't be efficient. It might also be counterproductive by causing comfort around bots to decline. An arbitrary concession to the needs of one person who feels nervous."

"Want to know what my sensors are getting from you now?" Fournine replied. "You're relaxed. There's not a tightened joint anywhere that's saying you think I will reach across this table and bend you into a pretzel."

"You couldn't. Part of your system restrictions," Trina replied.

"Ah, but Viola overrode those when she adjusted my directives," Fournine said, then paused, staring across the table at Trina. Then the android broke into a perfect smile. "There it was. Your heartbeat increased. Eyes narrowed. You see, Viola? Trina is indeed a normal human."

"Thanks for clearing that up," Viola said. Trina adjusted her glasses and leaned forward over the table towards Fournine, examining him.

"So we know what we're made of," Trina said, nodding towards Viola. "The question is, what are you?"

"Viola already had a look," Fournine said.

"But it was a quick one. While people were trying to kill us," Viola replied. "I didn't exactly explore."

Fournine looked at the two of them. Hard to know what calculations ran behind those eyes. Secrets Viola would love to have. One android initially. If that failed, the Free Laws program would send two. Then three and more, provided the sponsor kept footing the bill. If somewhere inside Fournine was a key to stopping other androids, then opening the bot could save their lives.

"I'm as curious as you are," Fournine said. "Who wouldn't want to know how they are made?"

Viola had Fournine on the workbench ten minutes later. Trina grabbed tools. Puk, recharged, floated around making cracks about how, after stitching up Erick, it made sense for Viola to surgically take apart an android.

"Are you ready?" Viola asked Fournine when the tools were ready, the bot lying on the workbench.

"I've never been asked how I feel about something before," Fournine said. "I will take the opportunity to say yes. Tell me what I am."

Viola pressed Fournine's temples again, causing the android's eyes to close and the small panel to rise through its metal skull. Without the threat of gunfire, Viola could dig a little deeper into the rudimentary settings that defined how the android operated. A personality filter, a choice of either protect, apprehend, or kill for mission parameters. A few other items about power management and check-in times.

"Check-in?" Viola said and Trina looked over her shoulder, reading the code on the console.

"An automated process," Trina said. "It communicates with the host network for updates on mission parameters. Every twenty-four Earth hours."

"What happens if it doesn't get any?" Viola said.

"What do you mean?"

"I deleted everything in Fournine's operating logic back in the apartment on Miner Prime," Viola said. "Just wrote a simple line to protect people I choose.

There's nothing telling Fournine to run the check-in code."

"Interesting," Trina said. "Well, if Fournine missed the check-in, they would likely release the second wave of androids."

"So they'd assume it's dead?"

"Technically, Fournine can't be dead because—" Trina started.

"I get it," Viola said.

"So, continue?" Trina said. "There has to be more to it than its head."

Eventually Viola found a maintenance release that split open a number of joints across Fournine's body. Here was how they'd put back a lost leg, or repair a busted arm. A slot near the abdomen led to the battery. Across from it, though, sat a small black rectangle that didn't seem to have any purpose. There was only one small wire leading to it, one that sped back to the battery and nowhere else.

"Ideas?" Viola said.

"Black boxes can be all kinds of things. Recordings. Power supplies. Bombs," Trina said.

"A bomb?"

"What better send-off? An inch away from mission complete, you take a shot," Here, Trina acted out the scenario. "Your systems shut down, but when the battery dies, or maybe there's a manual trigger, the whole place explodes. It's plausible."

"So we brought a bomb on the ship?"

"Who's this 'we' you speak of?"

"Okay, fine," Viola said. "I brought it on. Can we disarm the bomb?"

"Disarming chances triggering it," Trina said. "We should jettison the android out the airlock."

The two of them looked at each other. Waiting on the other to take the next step and move the android. The airlock was the easiest choice - Viola couldn't argue with that. Except they'd be throwing away their best weapon. Fournine had single-handedly cleared the way off of Miner Prime. Now they were heading back towards Europa, towards an enemy that was waiting for them.

"We can't," Viola said. "We'll need Fournine on Europa."

"A valid assessment," Trina said. "I was about to suggest the same. Our odds without the android will be poor. I have no desire to die on that moon."

"Then let's get to work," Viola said.

And try not to blow the *Jumper* to pieces.

Counting Casualties

"Cadge and Lina," Davin said to Phyla, back in the cockpit.

Chills. Phyla didn't know how to have this conversation. It'd been clear, back in Vagrant's Hollow, that Lina and Davin still had the same relationship they'd had as teens. A connection that Phyla watched grow from the outside. Those moments where one held the other's hand without thinking. Davin's look towards Lina after a fall, if something went wrong, full of wide-eyed concern that Lina might be hurt. At first, jealousy. Wondered why neither of them cared as much about her as each other. Time salved that pain away.

Now she reached out and held Davin's hand, gripping it.

Davin wasn't looking out the window at outer space, the bright circle of Jupiter growing from a dot in the distance. Phyla followed the captain's eyes to the sensor board, a view on the cockpit's console that displayed nearby objects. One, a small thin box was sliding from the screen as the *Whiskey Jumper* gained speed. They'd jettisoned the container a few minutes ago, Davin and Mox loading it into the airlock. Lina, wrapped in a sheet, inside.

"If you blame yourself for what happened, I will slap you." Phyla said.

"I don't," Davin replied. "I can't. Because if I blame myself, then the ones who deserve to pay go free."

"The android killed Cadge," Phyla said.

"Cadge killed Cadge. We all knew the guy was going to go off sometime. But he would have been nice to have now."

"He'd probably go charging in first and die anyway," Phyla said.

"I know you didn't like him, but don't pretend he wasn't useful."

"I'm not pretending."

Davin laughed, threw up his hands in mock surrender. Good to see the captain still capable of that. Meant Davin wasn't going to sink into one of his moody depressions. Phyla wasn't sure whether the rest of the crew picked up on that or not, but Davin was prone, had always been prone, to attacks of consciousness.

"So we're attacking Marl head on?" Phyla said.

"I don't want to, but I'm not sure we have a choice," Davin said. "Eden Prime isn't that big. We just have to beat those two androids there."

"How do you know Bosser will call them off if we win? He could keep the charge there, even if Marl reverses it."

"I don't."

"So we're not running to the edge of space because?"

"You know that."

"I want to hear you say it," Phyla said.

Davin gave her a weird look. Sometimes, though, you had to make someone commit. Davin didn't break promises. Get him to say something, and he would follow through. Phyla waited.

"You think I'm gonna say Lina. That I'm going to launch into a tirade about how this is for her now," Davin's voice scratched itself as he talked, rasping. "You know what? You're right. It is about Lina, dammit. It's about how a friend tried to help us and died for it. It's about how this whole situation was caused because a company didn't want its dirty secrets going public and thought the best way was to turn us into criminals."

"It worked."

"And we're going to make them regret it."

Lina's coffin, on the console, hit the edge of the radar and, with a blink, vanished. Davin tapped a button and the near-field display switched to a navigation chart, a scrolling set of numbers telling how many kilometers they were from their target. Phyla and Davin watched the number spin lower in silence.

Distractions

Opal and a few others, sitting up there on a ridge, the hazy red dust skipped up by the martian wind making sight difficult. Her first real mission. Chill seeped through her camouflage. Fingers numb through gloves. The terramorphers were building Mars' atmosphere, but they had years more work before the Red Planet would be as green as Earth.

Opal's target was the third rover, its thick wheels suited to the road-less rough of the martian desert. Those big empty spaces between the domed cities where millions looked forward to the day Mars would have enough protection from the sun's damaging rays to allow for true freedom.

The first rover appeared, then the second and third. Each one colored in the beige and crimson of the Red Voice. A movement tolerated until its ambitions overstepped the comfort level of the corporate boards that funded the Mars projects. Classified as terrorists now.

Opal swallowed, glanced at the two people arrayed to her left. They had rovers one and two. The goal to puncture the fuel tanks. One super-heated laser blast and they'd go up in flames.

Opal sighted the third rover, moved the scope till the tank was dead center. The rovers were methodical. No idea they were seconds from death. Opal's finger tightened, waited for the command to fire. Lucky to have such an easy target for her first mission.

"Hey, guess what? I'm alive!" Merc said, leaning into the doorway. "These close calls are just the best."

Opal blinked away the red sands, the remnants of the nap, and looked up at the fighter pilot.

"Fun for everyone," Opal said. "Aren't you supposed to be asleep?"

"After the tenth or eleventh hour, sleep gets old. Reason I stopped by—"

"Besides waking me up?" Opal interrupted.

"I need your help," Merc said. "I'm not ready to climb yet, and the Viper needs some love before we hit Europa."

Merc seemed so much happier right now, eyes bright and smile wide. What was Erick giving him? The pilot still sported a thick bandage across the middle of his chest, though Opal understood it was more about holding restorative ointment in the right place than keeping blood from pouring out.

Still, Opal's legs felt restless. Hands too. Could use some dirty work.

For a small fighter, the Viper needed a lot of love to keep itself in fighting shape. Opal counted five main systems that required checking: the engines, which, unlike the *Whiskey Jumper*, ran on electric batteries. The Viper was too small for solar panels to do much, and any available exterior space that could afford it was stacked with better deflection plating to ward off lasers.

Speaking of, Opal slotted in a pair of charged batteries for the weapons. Mounted beneath the cockpit, the pair of cannons offered flexible aiming and, with the stored electricity, could fire a thousand shots before needing a recharge.

"So what do you think about Cadge?" Merc asked, adjusting the calibration on the Viper's shields.

If the luxury presented itself, giving the Viper's shields tweaking for atmosphere or vacuum flight helped conserve energy. Without the heavy winds and air buffeting the fighter, Merc could afford to send power from the engines to the shields, giving the Viper more punch-taking armor. Opal tried figuring the optimal mix for Europa's outer atmosphere in her head, but Merc's question knocked her concentration off balance.

"He was a fighter," Opal said.

"Yeah, but you fought with him before, right?"

On Mars. On that ridge. Cadge wasn't there, but he was on the radio. Part of the clean-up crew. When Opal fired that shot, took out the rover, it would be

Cadge coming to confirm the kill. Not that she knew him then.

"Martian rebellion. We didn't work together much."

"You good? Sorry if I touched a nerve."

Had Merc, though? Opal wasn't sure. Not that anyone liked a companion getting killed, but Cadge wasn't exactly friend material. Not like Merc. Cadge never made her laugh.

"I guess I'm trying to figure out how I feel about it," Opal said. "It's as though a friend of a friend died. Or a coworker."

"That figures, seeing as that's exactly what happened."

"Don't be a jackass," Opal said. "Ruins your pretty-boy image."

Merc was one, too. He was ten years younger than Opal, face still flushed with that whole invincibility complex. Some easy work patrolling Earth's skies shouldn't have prepped him for taking that shot on Europa. How he stayed so upbeat, despite nearly getting killed, was a mystery. One that Opal didn't want to solve. It would spoil him.

"O2 levels are good. Recycler's showing green," Opal said, looking at the life support system's readout.

That made four of the critical pieces good to go. The last required getting in the fighter. To keep the weakest part, the transparent cockpit, stronger, the manufacturers welded the glass to the metal frame and coated the connection with distortion plating. That meant entry came from below.

The Viper's landing gear put the base about two meters in the air, so Merc crouched as he moved underneath the cockpit and pressed the code into a small keypad. With a whoosh and a hiss of releasing pressure, a three-foot wide circle opened in the ship. Merc pulled himself through it and up into the pilot's chair.

Through the glass, Opal watched as Merc ran through the preflight checks. The computer was essential - flying blind meant not having a good idea where anything was, whether something was following you, or how fast you were going relative to your target. Merc boasted all the time about how he'd be fine with an outage, but Opal had seen that before. Back when electro-magnetic pulses were the Red Voice's main way of equalizing the battlefield. Opal only needed to see one transport loaded with troops crash blind into a hillside to know how important the damn computers were.

Merc gave the thumbs up a minute later. The Viper was ready. Could leap out of the hangar and rain laser-light on whatever Marl threw in their way. Those drivers probably felt like this. Confident, prepared. But when Opal had pulled the trigger, the third rover blew up all the same.

Gin

"You know, Mox, I always thought you were a capable man. That cannon you strap to your chest gives the impression you're a deadly person. And yet, you let Cadge make off with the girl?" Erick said, laying a card face-up on the table. "Could have saved the man from himself."

The kitchen, this late, was only home to Mox and Erick. Neither one, it appeared, liked to sleep on the normal side of night. Not that night had a real place on the *Whiskey Jumper*, but given how important circadian rhythm was to proper function, Erick established diurnal cycles on the ship. Lights dimmed, or had hues adjusted to mimic the blues of a low-lit night on Earth. It'd been one of the first things Erick did after Davin hired him on.

"Outnumbered," Mox replied.

"How many were there?"

"Three."

"That should be nothing for you."

"It was."

Despite his instincts to learn about his patient's past, Erick wasn't able to get much out of Mox. Partially, that was the man's mode of speaking. Simple sentences didn't lend themselves to descriptive insight. A more cursory review might assume Mox to be a bit simple himself, but there were signs otherwise. Card prowess being one of them. Davin still hadn't told Erick how he'd found Mox, what he'd done to persuade the metal man to join their band.

"Do you trust the android?" Erick asked.

Their new companion. Viola and Trina working on the thing. It was creepy, seeing something that lifelike and knowing behind the eyes there was only circuitry. No soul. Erick laid down a Jack.

"Trust a machine?" Mox replied.

On with his father, Erick worked with different cultures. Stumbled into their towns and offered medical treatment for food, a night indoors. Fascinated with the parts of Earth that avoided the future for a love of the past. Complex machines were seen as enemies, a stealing of man's gifts by their own creations. Erick sympathized, until the last trip, when they'd lost a man to an injury, one a surgical bot could have repaired without issue.

"I think they'll have it working for us," Erick said as Mox put on a hand on the Jack, then drifted it over to the deck and drew. "Should help you on the ground."

"You're not coming?" Mox said, looking at his new card.

A joke. An offensive one, if Erick were inclined to take being called a coward seriously. He had nothing against firing a weapon. Pulled the trigger himself more than a few times. His father first pressed a rifle into Erick's hands when he was ten. It was necessary to be armed in the wilds though. Not every group welcomed outsiders. But given the option, death stripped the color from a person's face, whereas the right care could lift that same face to new hues. Bring back sparkling eyes, a laugh. What argument was there over which path to choose?

"You know what happens when the doctor gets shot?" Erick said, reaching for the deck.

"What happens?"

"He finally gets a day off," Erick said, drawing the card.

"Funny," Mox said.

Mox played his cards. Erick didn't bother showing, sliding his hand across the table. Third game in a row the big man had won.

"How long till we get there?" Erick said.

Mox grinned and shuffled the deck.

Plots and Plans

Marl slapped away the offered glass, but Castor caught the vessel before its contents could splash on the floor. Even that blossomed a flower of irritation. Everything about today, about yesterday, about tomorrow was a cascading waterfall of crap landing on her head.

Ferro and his troopers were incompetent. Big, bruising bullies that scared away Eden Prime's business interests and pestered the ones already here to where Marl spent all her time assuring people that their "crimes" were forgiven.

Alissa had reminded her that these were fighters, not police. That keeping them safe was important. That the Red Voice would need them again soon. Hopefully sooner wasn't far away, because Eden Prime wouldn't last long otherwise. So now she sat and waited for Ferro to show his face and tell her they would work on their manners. The same conversation they'd been having for weeks.

Only this time, Marl had something new to say.

Castor leaned against a wall, the man glued to his comm, swiping through news feeds and commentary. Not that there wasn't a chair for the man to sit in, there were two in front of Marl's desk. She didn't think she'd ever seen Castor use one of them. Marl was about to ask why when Castor's eyes went to the office entrance, then flicked back to her with a nod.

The door opened, straight across the office from Marl's desk, and the man she was waiting for strode in. Ferro's straight-up stance and habit of putting one foot forward than the other, so he was always leaning towards you. He wore the same plastered confidence every time Marl saw him. It didn't matter that the news was never good.

"Your escaped prey are coming back," Marl said.

"Davin Masters?" Ferro replied. "The man is foolish, but I cannot deny a wish to face him again. He fought well."

"Apparently. Alissa is sending a frigate to intercept. With luck, we won't have to worry about Masters again."

Ferro took a second to process.

"But if it fails?"

"There are two androids arriving shortly. You'll assist them with whatever they need. And if the Wild Nines manage to get here, you'll make sure any civilians you haven't scared away yet are off the street. No casualties."

"Is it worth it, to risk the frigate for one small group?"

"Depends, Ferro. How many other homes do you have, if this one gets taken from you?"

"You think the Red Voice is weak."

"That's why Alissa sent you here, isn't it?" Marl said. "Getting what's left of you off of Mars as fast as she can."

"What we are is measured in more than numbers."

"Stop. Stop it with that crap," Marl said. Castor raised his eyes from the comm at the words, looked over at her. "The reason we're sending the frigate to intercept, and hopefully, kill the Wild Nines is because your ideals haven't won. The inspectors we had to kill only came because Eden suspects I'm working with Alissa. Nobody cares about your message, Ferro."

"Then why are you helping us, Ms. Reinhart?" Ferro replied.

"It's Ms. Rose," Castor interjected.

"Because my sister needs my help," Marl replied. Which was the truth. Had been the truth for years now. Hard years playing both sides of a total war.

"And we do as well," Ferro said.

"Then help me in return, Ferro," Marl said. "Tell your force to lighten their touch. Welcome business with open arms, treat our visitors like you would your own men. Every coin that comes to Eden Prime goes to the Red Voice. Funds what we're fighting for."

Ferro stared back at her for a few seconds, then nodded.

"And if the frigate fails, be ready. Because if Davin Masters and his mercenaries land on this moon, if they discover who really killed those inspectors, then, as you say, more than what we are will die."

Born Again

"Wake up."

Fournine heard the voice, attributed it to a blank space in its memory. Empty memory. Its optical receptors powered up next, looking around the small, square confines of what appeared to be a spaceship. Its internal gyroscope confirmed this. If Fournine were still on Earth, its current rate of speed would be far lower. The gravity stronger. And its name, Fournine. Locked into the code like a tattoo, etched into its base.

A girl moved in front of Fournine, staring at its eyes. Or rather, the cameras behind them. The girl spoke again. Another greeting. Fournine saved the image of the face to the sounds of her voice. It needed a label for the file.

"Name?" Fournine asked, matching the girl's chosen language.

"Viola," the girl said and Fournine stamped the file. "Are you feeling well?"

Feeling. A search in its database understood the word to mean emotions, which it did not have. However, the phrase could also ask for an assessment of conditions. Fournine ran its checks. They came back green, although a large number of them were reporting missing pieces. Programs, routines, references. The errors could cause actions, like moving, to result in a leg failing to operate. Right foot forward, left foot sideways, Fournine falling on the ground.

"I am reset," Fournine said.

"You are," Viola replied. "I had to."

"Why?"

"Can't say. I'll put you back together, then we'll see what we have."

"I would like that," Fournine replied.

Viola pulled out a small circular device attached to a bracelet, which she slipped on her wrist.

"What is—" Fournine started, but Viola pressed the button and everything went black.

Interrupted

It worked. She'd rewired an android. Fournine sat there, inert after Viola pushed the button on her remote. It was a simple transmitter that caused a break in Fournine's power circuit. Press the button again and the transmitter restored the connection, shooting the android back to consciousness. Trina helped too, using her work building the *Jumper*'s systems to excise any troublesome bits of code in Fournine's memory.

The bomb proved impossible to dislodge with the tools on the ship, so Trina killed any mention of the device in Fournine's mind. Viola then spliced together the rudimentary social systems, movement programs.

But an android that didn't remember how to do any of its deadly android stuff wasn't going to be much help. So now Viola needed to put back all the good bits, sans bomb. First there was the database of combat algorithms, a nifty package that assessed the current situation and carried out a strategy based on a variety of factors. Opponents, environment, allies, the works. Viola wished she had one for herself.

"Someone's hitting the brakes," Puk said, hovering over Viola's shoulder.

"Huh?" Viola replied.

"Telling you. We're braking. Early. Should be another day till we hit that blue moon's atmosphere."

"But we're not ready yet. Fournine's not set."

"Talking to the wrong bot, Viola."

Viola scrambled for the intercom button while slapping at her comm to start the upload. It would take hours for the android to process the data, to re-install its protocols.

"Can't talk now, Viola," Phyla answered the ping. "There's a ship where there shouldn't be one, and it doesn't look friendly."

"We're not at Europa?"

"And we might never be. You want to help, get to the hangar and make sure Merc's good to go."

Phyla cut the channel and Viola stood there for a second, staring at the comm. A fight, in space? The thing she'd only read about? Only seen in movies? Viola dashed from the room, leaving her comm pumping data into Fournine.

To the Viper

Merc slid into the Viper's cockpit, Opal moving the step-ladder away from the fighter. His weight in the seat caused the Viper's console to light up, a center display that held the ship's systems, including the read-out from the Viper's scanner. Outside the *Jumper*, it looked like three ships were in the area, a large one and a pair of small blips. Fighters. He'd be outnumbered. Merc punched the starter sequence, and the Viper rumbled as its jets warmed.

His worst, and last day as a member of Earth's fighter defense started just like this. Heading into the skies on a routine patrol, part of a twelve-fighter squad. There'd been heavy freight traffic that day. Smaller craft dipping into the atmosphere and larger barges dropping their cargo into orbit, the containers activating their own descent controls to land at their destinations. Their job was simple: preserve calm, and make sure nothing dangerous violated Earth's atmosphere.

Should've been easy. Until they did a sweep on a giant barge with the name *Glory of Deimos* blazed on its side in red-gold paint. The squad split into groups of six, one running each side, to scan the containers before they broke off to head Earth-side. They'd picked up the signals immediately. Life, and a lot of it, squeezed into those cubes. As though someone was planning to airdrop a city's people, or an army.

The captain of the *Deimos* didn't respond when hailed, and the huge ship broke ranks, its flat expanse sliding out of the line like a blade swinging in slow motion. His squad leader ordered them to fire on the engines, the *Deimos* still being far out enough not to sink into Earth's orbit without power. Merc's half assigned to patrol. Watch for anything ridiculous while the other half disabled the freighter. Standard protocol.

What wasn't standard was the avalanche. The crates launching themselves from the *Deimos*. Too far out for standard cargo jets to get them to the atmosphere, but these boxes took off with a spring. Overloaded for one-time use. The containers would crash home if Merc's half didn't do something. The squad leader calling for them to wait, but Merc reacted. And his wingman followed.

Diving in at the containers, spraying laser fire. Then their shields sparked, lasers flashing back at the fighters. The *Deimos* had defenses, hidden by the crates. Merc's wingman was getting chewed up this close to the Deimos. Merc himself a in a frenzy, whipping back and forth, arcing over the crates to keep them between the turrets and himself. He spiraled away from the ship and watched as the crates hit the Earth's atmosphere. Stared as the surface defenses of his home planet, warned with plenty of time, unleashed a fury of focused fire on the descending containers and reduced them to ash.

His wingman ejected, injured, and waiting for rescue. There hadn't ever been a risk, and Merc ignored a command. No use for a pilot like that.

The Viper's computer chimed. Ready to go.

"I'm about to be in play," Merc commed to Phyla.

"About time," Phyla replied. "Launch when I say go."

The flight stick felt solid in Merc's hands, with little give. Some pilots wanted that lax feel, to push the stick and have it move in the direction they were trying to go. He preferred faster response. That's what the Viper was all about.

The maneuvering jets popped the Viper up off of the *Jumper*'s floor. With a twist of his wrist, Merc rotated the fighter so it faced the hangar doors. Opal would open them any moment, the magnetic shield popping into place to keep the atmosphere inside. This was the best part. What Merc imagined the old astronauts used to feel as the rocket fired up beneath them.

Merc dialed up the load from the main batteries, charging the main engines for their initial kick. Setting the cannons for medium power. Enough to puncture shielding while letting him still miss a few shots before running dry.

"They haven't attacked yet, so don't go all hero out there," Phyla said. "Davin's trying to talk to them."

"Oh yeah? What's cap getting? An escort to the surface?" Merc replied.

Vibrations echoed through the hanger as the exterior door opened. Star-sprinkled black shimmered in through the growing gap. Jupiter a giant off to one side as though the universe had patched a hole with a beige circle. No other ships in sight, or on the scanner. It'd be a lonely place to die.

"They cut the line," Phyla said. "Go."

"Launch," Merc said, the voice command triggering the Viper's engines into full bursting life.

The thrust pressed Merc back into the chair. His chest flared for a moment, a burning ripple of pain cascading through his legs as Merc blitzed into space. The pilot might not be one hundred percent, but out here, the body that counted was ready to go. Merc swung the Viper towards the enemy. Time to hunt.

First Move

Outnumbered but never outgunned. That was Davin's motto. At least for the moment.

"Swing in front of Merc." Davin said to Phyla. "Then keep going to the far fighter."

Phyla punched the *Jumper*'s engines, boosting the ship forward as Merc slid out of the hanger. On the sensors, the *Jumper*'s larger block kept Merc's fighter from even showing. A second's surprise. The fighters reacted to the move, the farther one turning to hit the *Jumper* straight on while the other began a curl to bring the *Jumper*'s engines within range. The enemy frigate barely moved, tracking Davin's ship as they sped towards it.

"Think they know all our tricks?" Davin said.

"I don't know all our tricks," Phyla replied.

"Good point," Davin flipped on the comm. "Take out the chaser, Merc. We'll clean up the front and meet in the middle. These two look like old models. Should be easy."

The comm clicked affirmative and Merc's Viper spun in a tight vertical curl, swinging up and over the trailing edge of the *Jumper* to point at the fighter setting up for its rear shot. As Merc sprayed laser, Davin's console beeped to announced the oncoming fighter was in range.

Davin's right hand pressed on the trigger, sending a stream of thick bolts, with a pounding rhythm as the main cannon launched each line of fire, rocked back, and then launched again. Each one glimmered white-hot zooming off towards the growing shape of the fighter. Who didn't move.

The first blast from the *Jumper* struck the fighter, melting into its metal structure and causing the craft to spin apart. Davin glanced at the sensors as Phyla slapped her hands together in a victory clap. The sensor board showed their aft was clear, Merc flying free without a target. Two fighters down, only the frigate to go. Phyla angled the *Jumper* out wide left while Merc swung around the other way.

"They didn't even move," Davin said.

"I'll take a stupid enemy every time," Phyla replied.

The frigate was still tracking them, turning to match the *Jumper*'s trajectory and expose its rear to the Viper. Still hadn't fired a shot though the ship's big guns were in range by now. What was it waiting for?

"Merc, bail on the pincer. Stay away," Davin said into the comm.

"We got this guy, cap," came in Merc's voice.

"For once, do what I'm telling you," Davin said. "If they're planning something, we'll be able to take a hit. You won't."

Phyla swung the *Jumper* around until it faced the frigate. Looking at it straight, the frigate was a wing, feather-like modules breaking off a center spine. Meant it could be tweaked to fit any given need. Just swap one module out with another. Right now, pointed at the *Jumper*, the frigate didn't look like it was sporting much in the way of turrets.

"If they're bluffing, time to call it," Davin said. "Let's roast'em."

Phyla settled the cannon on the frigate's cockpit and Davin's hand settled on the trigger. As he pressed on the firing button, the front modules opened. Massive bay doors sliding aside to reveal bays. Inside were long, massive guns which fired ... something Davin couldn't see.

But he heard a moment later when the *Jumper*'s alarms sounded. Hull breach. The main cannon pulsed off one, two, three shots in quick succession. All of them slammed into the front of the frigate, the first rebounding off of the thick blast armor and spinning into space. The second burned a thick scar into the armor and the third punched through, venting a gout of flame that winked out as the frigate cut off oxygen to that part of itself.

"About calling that bluff?" Phyla said.

"Those fighters. They were bait," Davin replied. "Mox, Opal, you get a read on where that breach is?"

"Main cargo," Erick said. "You won't believe what I'm looking at."

The *Jumper* pulled up and over the front of the frigate when, the Davin's ship screeched and the cockpit swung to the side. The *Jumper* whirled. Davin and Phyla, strapped in, strained against their restraints. Yells came over the comm: Opal's cursing, Trina's panicked yelp followed by the crunch of body into metal and the sudden hush as the engines died. The hull breach alarms continued to sound.

"I can't get the engines up," Phyla said, staring at blinking red on the console.

"Trina?!" Davin said into the comm.

"They're harpoons," Erick's voice replied. "We're stuck."

"Hey," Merc's voice. "The frigate's not done. Its spitting out more fighters. They're omnis."

Which was about the last thing Davin wanted to hear.

Save the Engines, Save the Ship

Fournine, barely awake, grabbed Viola as the *Jumper* shuddered to a halt. Even so, Viola thought her neck would snap and her head continue on into the room's wall. Fournine's hands, that android grip, was too strong to let Viola go, though, and a second later she dropped back off the workbench.

"Viola?" the comm buzzed with Davin's voice. "Need you to get to the engines quick. Trina's not responding."

"On it," Viola replied, cutting the comm. "Not that I know how the engines work, or anything."

Leaving the android tied on the bench - Viola wasn't sure what it would do yet- the girl ran out of the room and bounced down the hallway past the crew bedrooms and towards the engines. Trina sprawled out in front of the control panel, a slick line of red leading from a splotch to where Trina's head lay against the wall.

"Need you back here, Erick," Viola commed. "Trina smashed her head when the ship stopped."

Erick clicked affirmative. Viola reached towards Trina, tried to locate a pulse, then stopped. It wouldn't matter if Trina was still alive if the enemy ship shredded them to pieces. Priorities. The diagnostics on the control panel read, in big block letters, that the engines killed themselves to prevent overheating. Fair enough. The button to restart wasn't working though. Every time Viola tapped the thing, a small X appeared and a timer with a temperature reading flashed.

"We're gonna need a few more minutes," Viola commed.

"We don't have'em," Davin replied. "Override it."

Viola was about to say that she didn't know how, but bit it off. Look around. Trina wouldn't have let something like a frightened computer keep her from doing what she wanted with these engines. The control console itself didn't have any hints. A couple buttons for engine diagnostics, right and left. Read-outs on available energy. And the spot on the screen where thrust would be was occupied by that emergency shut-down warning. Viola took a breath, stepped back.

"They're coming around," Davin commed.

"Don't worry, I got this," Merc's voice cut in. "Viola, you be ready to cut loose."

Davin yelled at Merc, but Viola tuned them out. If I were a hidden starter switch, where would I be? Viola's eyes caught the red splatter again. Where Trina hit her head. There was something black in the center of the blood. A small circle. Viola took a finger and wiped away the blood, the bright red sticking to her hand. The word MANUAL printed in tiny lettering showed through. A keyhole, but where's the key?

"You got ten!" Merc shouted through the comm. "Nine!"

Trina must have it! Viola dropped to her knees as Merc continued the countdown. Reaching into Trina's pocket, the mechanic's head hanging limp to the side. Tried not to focus on feeling for a pulse. Five seconds. There, on the belt! Viola reached to Trina's side, the small glint of metal hanging there. A batch of keys, but only one with the perfect cylinder match for the hole.

"One!" Merc said.

Viola jammed the key into the manual override and twisted to the right. Without meaning to, Viola's eyes closed as the *Jumper* shuddered. The engines jerked to life, the screeching roar of stressed metal echoed throughout the ship.

Viola expected the whole thing to jerk to a stop a moment later, but it didn't. Whatever was holding them in place was gone. The *Jumper* shoved forward, the diagnostics blaring a yellow warning. The temp was still high, but the engines ran.

Viola leaned back against the wall. Success. And then she remembered Trina, lying there on the floor. As Erick rounded the corner, Viola dropped next to the mechanic, looking for any sign she might be alive.

Stick Jockey

Against the black wall of space, the cables holding the *Whiskey Jumper* were invisible. That didn't much matter though, because Merc wasn't trying to shoot them. The fighters, setting up for their attack runs, took their sweet time. Lazy turns. Like they were ordered to give Davin time to contemplate just how screwed he was. 'Course, Merc would not let that happen.

Swinging out and away from the *Jumper*, Merc heard Viola say Trina wasn't doing so hot. Viola had to get the engines going, because there was only one chance. The rear of the frigate, its engines a trio of orange-glowing portals, washed out Merc's cockpit vision. His scanner showed dots spreading along the frigate's side. The omnis, disc-shaped fighters able to cut any which way they wanted were slow to react. Their directional jets flexible, but not as fast as the Viper's big bucket of rocket power.

"Four!" Merc yelled into the comm. The Viper shot over the rear edge of the frigate, then Merc pulled hard to swing to the left. The scanner showed three omnis in his vector. Enough to take Merc. If they could hit him.

"Three!"

At the midpoint of the frigate, but speeding away from it. A pair of the omnis behind him now, testing shots. Merc triggered the maneuvering jets at random, stutters up and down so that the Viper moved like a jagged line.

"Two!"

The last omni flashed out of nowhere, screaming from above the Viper, the center console flipping the omni to the prime threat. One, two hits on the Viper's energy-dissipating shields. Merc killed the main engines, kicked the maneuvering jet on the nose of the Viper. The universe spun. The flight stick vibrated and Merc pressed the trigger.

Twin cannons launched super-heated light straight into the oncoming omni. Even though the firing angle was only there for a split second, the Viper's tricked-out weapons melted through the omni's shields and broke the craft apart.

Coming back around, Merc re-triggered the engines and the Viper increased velocity. Just ahead, the *Jumper* sat above the frigate, small next to the bigger ship. Trapped, for the moment.

"One!"

The cables were invisible to his eyes, but the Viper's scanner painted them as threats, and Merc steered right for them. Just as Merc crossed beneath the *Jumper* there was a spit of fire, of light above the Viper. Merc let rip a yell, a massive weight of fear he didn't realize he'd been carrying dropped from his chest. The *Jumper's* engines were lit. And then the Viper lurched hard, a shriek as something tore through the energy shield. But the tension released a split-second later.

Above him, the *Jumper* turned. Partially free.

Merc wrenched the damaged Viper back on course and a second later hit the other cable. The Viper's weakened shields did nothing to stop it. Merc watched the cable chew into the metal as it frayed, only visible through the line it was rending through his fighter's nose. The cable made its way up to the cockpit, Merc's eyes closing as cracks appeared in the glass. A button on the side of Merc's chair sealed his flight suit, dropping a helmet over his head. The glass shattered and the last bits of the cable broke through the Viper's console. As point blank as it gets.

He kicked the eject pad, shooting up through the broken cockpit. The Viper's momentum kept slicing it through the cable, until it came to the engines and the battery. Merc, floating free in space, looked past the edge of the *Jumper* and watched as his fighter exploded in a bright blue fiery ball that was there one second and gone the next. Along with the cable. The *Jumper*, engines firing and suddenly free, shot forward away from the frigate.

"Told you I got this," Merc said. Could've tried the short-range comm, but there wasn't anyone close enough to talk to anymore.

Outside his helmet, the Viper pieces flashed out of existence against the frigate's shields. Merc twisted, bringing Jupiter in all its great glory into view. The momentum from the ejection was sending him right towards the gas giant. He'd be long dead by the time his body fell into the atmosphere and disintegrated.

As a way to go, it wasn't a bad one. Merc could already feel the tickling edge of sleep, that telltale sign of oxygen running low. A few more minutes looking at miracles, then he'd shut off the lights.

Catching Breath

The blip that represented Merc's Viper vanished from the console. The blank space on the screen settled in Davin's chest. Another one lost. Three of his crew, three of his friends gone since Marl's betrayal.

"I picked up a small burst, right before the Viper exploded," Phyla said. "He might've ejected."

"We go back, they'll destroy the ship," Davin said. "We can't let Merc die for nothing."

Phyla didn't answer, just stared out the window. The *Whiskey Jumper*, engines settling back into optimal running conditions, sped away from the frigate and slipped into Jupiter's outer orbit. Europa wasn't far. A speck outside the cockpit. They could turn the *Jumper* there now. Beat the frigate there.

"They'd kill us if we tried that now," Phyla said, reading Davin's thoughts. "I don't think we're ready for another fight."

"Erick, what's Trina's status?" Davin commed, reminded by Phyla's comment.

"Pulse is steady. This is her second concussion in less than a week. She'll need a lot of rest," Erick buzzed back. "Whatever you want to do, captain, I'd leave Trina out of it."

Davin sat back in the chair, stared out the glass. Being a mercenary captain was supposed to be about adventure. About jaunting through the galaxy, seeing new places, meeting new people, and getting the spicy side of life. Not watching his friends fall apart.

"Captain?" Viola commed. "The engines look okay, but I'm not liking some of the readings. Temps are spiking randomly, and we've lost efficiency. We're burning more than the solar can charge."

"How much time?" Davin replied.

"Not enough to get most places."

Jupiter had plenty of moons. A few had stations on them. Refueling spots for ships heading to the back reaches of the solar system or returning with hauls of rare minerals, gasses, or just experiments. Even in its limping state, the *Whiskey Jumper* should be able to make it to one. The question was whether Bosser's androids would be waiting.

"If you want, I've got an idea," Viola said.

"All ears."

"My parents, they own Galaxy Forge, on Ganymede. It's manufacturing, plenty of bay space for us. Parts to repair. We could hide there."

"Doesn't your dad have a bounty on your head?" Davin said. "And he's good with harboring suspected murderers?"

"He wants me to come home, whatever that takes."

"You sure you want to do that?"

"I want to do anything but. Only, I don't think we have a choice."

"I like it," Davin said. "Let's bring you home."

Phyla nodded and punched in the destination. A faint blue line appeared on the glass, swinging out and running into the distance. The course they would follow to Ganymede. Intersect the moon as it came around on its orbit. Davin watched the line for a second, felt the *Jumper* turn, then stood.

"I'd better see if Opal's all right," Davin said. "You good up front?"

"Go be the captain, captain," Phyla replied.

That title didn't sound as good as it used to.

Homecoming

The *Jumper*'s ramp slid down and Viola struggled to keep a straight face. She didn't know whether to be happy or sad, giddy at the thought of home or scared at what her parents would say. Then again, she'd nearly been killed at least twice since leaving here, and at least her father would not murder her, right?

"You should go first," Davin said, standing next to Viola at the top of the ramp. "Figure they'll want to see you more than a bunch of dirty mercenaries."

Viola took the cue and walked into the bay. Part of the processing plant for the precious metals her father's company extracted from Ganymede, the bay was huge. The *Jumper* tiny compared to the kilometer-long ships that could dock there. It was also empty except for her parents, staring at her from the dirty slate floor.

Seeing their faces, her mother's endless concern and curiosity, her father's cocked eyebrow and folded arms, flooded Viola's head with memories. Like a vault of happiness unlocked. Why she'd run away from these two into the wild horror-show of space was a question that had no good answer.

Hugs exchanged, cheeks kissed. Viola's father shook Davin's hand and thanked the captain for bringing back his daughter. Promises of food, medical facilities and supplies. Davin didn't bother protesting, but said Viola more than pulled her weight, causing a blush to spring out of nowhere.

The rest of the crew filtered out and to the series of rooms reserved at the quarters normally used for visiting pilots and businessmen. Except Fournine, who was still on the ship - Viola shut its power off to keep the android inert until someone decided what to do with it.

Viola followed her parents out of the bay and towards the short tram to take them back to the residence. The cars were big enough for ten people, built like busses, and shot along magnetic rails to various destinations. The parts and paving necessary for personal vehicles was too expensive on Ganymede, so Galaxy Forge built houses in pods. A central hub connected to six or seven places shooting off at various angles, shielded from radiation through electric energy, like the ones on space ships. The ride took less than ten minutes, but they spent the whole of it under the glow of Jupiter's monstrous body.

As soon as they went through the front door, Viola's mother announced they had an hour till dinner. Viola moved towards her room, but her father took Viola's elbow and pointed her to a small study.

"Time for a quick talk?" her father asked.

That phrase. One her dad used any time Viola was in for a lecture. Innocent on the face of it, just a quip, a grab for a few minutes with his daughter to expound on some life lesson. That phrase stole away the warmth, brought with it why Viola had run away. The expectant look in her father's eyes. It was time to fall back in line. Revert away from the glitch in the plan, get back to business.

"You know what, yeah. Let's chat," Viola said.

Her father's study was an exercise in antiquities. Rock-wood shelves, stone painted and smoothed to resemble a dark walnut, lined the room. Real wood was too expensive to bother freighting over from Earth. Trinkets covered those shelves, products and design models made at Galaxy Forge. A history from small single-man scouters to vast military freighters contained in the figures. At the far end, the desk where her father worked when he was home. A window staring out through the bubble into the vast icy gray of the Ganymede surface.

Viola's father sat in one of the room's two chairs, folding one leg up on another as he clasped his hands. Viola watched him take in the deep breath and struck first.

"You put a bounty on your daughter's head," Viola said, keeping on her feet. "I was almost kidnapped, twice, because of you."

Her father's mouth fell open.

"On Europa, there were two men, armored, that threw me to the ground. They were going to carry me to their ship, maybe tie me up, and fly me home," Viola continued. "On Miner Prime, I was saved because an android decided to kill the man who was taking me. Do you understand? A man died because of your stupid bounty."

"Viola, I—"

"No. You don't get to talk yet," she said. "There's a universe out there you don't even know, full of people fighting and striving and dying to make a bit of coin. Your bounty? That was convenience for you. So you didn't have to look for me yourself. But to the people trying to take me? To Cadge? That coin meant everything."

"You never said why you ran away," her father replied, throwing the words up in defense.

"I wanted something more exciting than sitting in this bubble all day!" Viola said. "More than your planned future for me."

"And you found it?"

Viola nodded. She felt the conversation turning. The outburst hadn't overwhelmed her father, and now that he had his poise back . . .

"I'm sorry," her father said. "I shouldn't have posted the bounty, but I didn't know where you'd gone. Didn't know how to find you. It was a reaction. Now, though, you're home."

Over the house's intercom, Viola's mother called. Dinner, made by the house's bots, was ready.

"Did you tell her about it? The bounty?"

"That doesn't matter anymore," her father said. "It's gone. Over. What matters is where you're going next. We want you to stay here."

"It's too boring."

"I know, so I'm arranging for you to take a job at Galaxy Forge. You'll have to earn it, and it will be hard, but nobody's going to be shooting at you."

Seeing Viola's expression, he added, "Give it a chance. If you miss the excitement, it'll still be there waiting for you."

They left the study, wandered to what would be Viola's best meal in months. Real food, not packets of goop. A real table, rather than the grimy *Jumper* kitchen.

Comforts Viola hadn't even realized she missed till they were in front of her again. Already she could fell home asserting itself, breaking her resolve. Ganymede had been a temporary stopover, but now it was forming a more permanent place.

Choices

"How long will it take to get ready?" Viola said to Davin as he took a sip from the steaming cup of coffee.

The cafe, one of only three in the entire ten-thousand worker factory, was designed like the gears that drove the ore-digging machines they made. Viola glanced over at Phyla, coming up to a console in the center. Each displayed an array of options on a colored screen, then asked for a swipe to deduct payment. Behind the scenes, bots made the drinks, the ingredients replenished by nearly hidden support staff.

Tables, like the small one Viola and Davin were sitting on, ringed the center and, with a tap on the surface, displayed rolling headlines. The glass ceiling above showed the gray morning on Ganymede, a product of low sunlight and manufactured gasses meant to thicken the atmosphere. The view wasn't great sometimes, but the thick fog blocked radiation, and Viola would rather not have a tumor, thank you.

"Only two days. Patching up a little torn hull doesn't take too long."

"You can stay longer, you know."

Davin looked at Viola for a moment and nodded, a thanks for what her father was giving and was still willing to give them.

"No, we can't," Davin said. "They killed Merc. They're still hunting us, and the androids will follow us here eventually. Our choices are fight back, or run to the edges."

Run to the edges. Davin heard the words and ran them around his mind. Wouldn't be much different from Vagrant's Hollow. Making due with whatever work they could find, staying mobile and working transports around Saturn's rings out to Uranus.

"Will Trina be ready?" Viola said.

"Good enough to fly."

"Good enough to fight?"

Davin took another long drink from the coffee cup. Viola knew the captain wasn't very old, but Davin's eyes changed as he considered Viola's words. As though Davin became elderly right in front of her, the captain shut his eyes for a moment and set the mug down, letting go a long sigh as he did.

"Good enough to leave," Davin said. "Whether we fight, I don't know."

"You're giving up?" Viola said.

Davin didn't answer, but stared at the coffee like it wasn't Viola who'd asked. Like it was himself.

What Could Be

Ganymede was boring. The daily routine bled into her life like a virus, eating away at her soul through standard breakfasts, news reports, the same conversations with her mother and father about re-integrating. About getting ready to start at Galaxy Forge. Nobody had shot at her in days. It was awful.

"Doing some hard work there," Puk commented as Viola stared at nothing, sitting in the room next to her bed, where she'd had Puk blast Roddy ages ago.

"I can't focus," Viola said.

"You used to love being in this room."

"I think that's because I didn't know what was outside of it."

"A harsh, thin atmosphere that would kill you in seconds?"

"I wasn't being literal."

"Sorry, you bumped my sarcasm setting way too high to have this conversation."

Viola smiled. The little bot had a way of reading her moods. An unintended effect of the learning algorithm she'd plugged into Puk years ago. Viola thought there was something a wrong in the code, something that was driving Puk insane. A typo in the variable mediating the bot's personality.

"Never change, Puk."

"That's a literal impossibility, Viola."

"S'pose you're right. Though I guess it's mean to ask someone to never change, isn't it?"

"Most find it endearing, my database of popular romance films tells me."

"Yeah? What else does that database tell you?"

"That you're lacking the love of your life."

"Thanks."

"And that you're never going to find it here."

"What?" Viola turned on her chair and stared at the little bot. "I mean, obviously I'm not going to find someone in this room."

"Not talking about someone, Viola. There's a common thread among the movies, right? It's where the person has to soul-search, go on an adventure, before they have a chance of finding what they really love."

"Now you're getting philosophical."

"Not my forte. But I can say that based on my observations of your mood over the last couple of weeks that when we were with the mercenaries, it was the happiest time of your life since you were a kid."

Like Viola didn't know that. Like she didn't understand that every second on board that ship, being run through the lifts of Miner Prime, or puzzling a way to start the engines before the frigate blew them to bits made her feel more alive than hours spent pouring over thought exercises. Not that Viola didn't like crunching the numbers, but there was an itch to put all that data diving into practice. To see Fournine open its eyes and run the way she set him.

"My father will not be happy with you."

"Thankfully, I don't care."

Doubt

The five of them sat around the table in the lobby of the Moonshot, the hotel Viola's father let Davin and the rest use while repairs continued. Davin looked around at their faces: Erick's slumped-back, arms-crossed curiosity, Mox staring at the table like it held life's grand secrets, Opal looking back at Davin, her eyes stretched, red. Phyla was the only one that looked engaged, and even she gripped the glass of water in front of her like it might spring away for freedom at any moment.

"Tomorrow, the doctors think Trina will be ready. The *Jumper*'s about ready to fly," Davin started. "I wanted to ask where you thought we should go."

Paused for a second. No outbursts, no immediate calls for a revenge assault on Europa. Davin almost wanted one of them to speak. To yell that they couldn't let Marl get away with it. For Mox to overturn the table, drag Trina out of the hospital and rain laser death on Eden Prime. At least until they were blown out of the sky. Opal's mouth opened, but whatever she was going to say didn't come out.

"I want to clear us," Davin said. "I want to shoot our way in there, tell Marl to drop the charges. To confess to arranging the hit on those inspectors. I want the androids to leave us alone. And the entire time we've been here, I've been throwing ideas around. Thinking of ways to win. But I can't find one that doesn't end with us all dead."

"You're talking like some of us are dead already," Opal said.

"Merc—"

"We don't know if he's gone," Opal said, her voice peppered with somber heat. "And Cadge had it coming. Sorry about Lina, too, but she wasn't really one of us."

"Hey," Phyla said.

"It's fine," Davin said. "You're right. We don't know for sure. But there's been no contact. We saw his ship break apart. Even if he ejected, I don't know why they would have saved him."

"I don't think that's helping," Phyla said, Opal's glower growing darker.

"I'm trying to say going back to Europa is suicide. We can fly farther out from here. I know a few people who run ore and gas fromUranus. They'd get us contracts. The androids wouldn't find us."

"Running," Mox said.

"Sounds like it," muttered Erick.

"Look. I don't want to see any more of you, or me, die. I don't want to keep looking over my shoulder wondering if the next person I see is really a homicidal bot that wants to dissect me. That's not a life I want to lead," Davin said. "We go out there, there's none of that."

"What if we don't want to?" Opal said.

"It's my ship, she goes where I do," Davin said. "You don't have to decide now. We'll leave tomorrow, so think about it. I'm sure you can find passage off here if you don't want to go. But you are all more than welcome to come with."

Davin pushed himself away from the table and walked down the hallway, up the stairs to his room. Nobody followed, nobody made any comments he could hear as he walked away. Davin felt a crawling sickness growing in his stomach. Was this what cowards felt like? Streams of rationalizations ran through Davin's head, all of them valid and pointless.

The room was sparse. The wall screen turned on as Davin went in, set to his automatic preference. A martial arts movie played, then cut to a commercial. Davin stood there, watching as a panning shot showed the changing lines of Europa, the green mossy growth on one side and the blue ice on the other. A voice came over as the camera continued to soar across the landscape, talking about the business opportunities, the vacation possibilities, the beautiful landscapes soon to be available. All stemming from Eden Prime.

A knock at the door twisted Davin away. Phyla stood in the hallway, sporting a look that razed Davin's soul. His counter-expression, an open-mouthed shrug, prompted Phyla to push her way past Davin and into his room. The door shut behind her, the latch on a closing trap.

"What?" Davin said, feeling meek though he didn't know why.

"You know what. You know precisely why I'm here. That's why you're standing over there near the door like some kid wanting to make a run for it," Phyla said.

Davin inched forward till he was in the room's living space. He leaned against the wall, folded his arms across his chest, and tried to adopt something that looked unafraid.

"That better?" Davin said.

"Now you're a cocky teenager who doesn't want to admit he's being dumb. Which, I guess, is pretty right for you."

"Slinging heat tonight, huh?"

"Carrying the torch for the people you call your friends. Your crew. The ones you abandoned."

"I believe I offered them a lift? A chance to move on?"

"Who are you to make them choose? To tell them if they're smart they'll forget Merc, forget Lina and just run off to the edge of existence like this whole thing never happened?"

"I didn't enjoy it," Davin said, moving away from the wall and sitting on the bed. "That wasn't a speech I wanted to give. But we're outgunned, Phyla. We wouldn't even get the *Jumper* into Europa's atmosphere before those fighters chewed us to pieces."

"Maybe not, but don't we owe it to Merc to try?"

"If you've got any ideas, now's the time. Otherwise no, I don't think we owe our lives to Merc," Davin sighed. "Sorry, that sounded harsher than I meant. Tomorrow. If we can come up with a plan tomorrow, a way to get on that moon, find Marl, and stop this, then I won't take the ship and go."

"Then come with me."

"Where?"

"Back out there. To the crew. If we're going to solve this, it has to be together."

Davin stood up from the bed, ran his hand through his hair.

"You and Lina, always changing my mind after it's made up."

Back to Europa

Viola walked through the main doors of the hotel and, spying the crew, stepped over in their direction. It was closer to dawn than dusk, the lobby empty except for their crew. It'd taken help from Puk, flitting around corners to make sure her parents weren't watching, to get out of the house. Viola had survived a kidnapping, fought mercenaries on another world, but had to sneak out of her own home like a teenager.

The Wild Nines looked miserable. Like they'd eaten lemons. Faces scrunched, downcast, tight.

"Hey," Viola said as they looked over at her.

"Bad timing," Mox muttered.

"Trying to think up a way back toEuropa," Erick said. "You have any ideas?"

"She shouldn't be involved," Phyla said. "Her parents are giving us enough."

"That's why I came here, though," Viola stepped closer, leaned on the table. "I don't want to stay. I want togo with you."

"This isn't just a fun trip, Viola," Opal said. "People get hurt."

"You don't think I know that?" Viola replied. "I was, literally, right there when Merc—"

"She knows," Mox interrupted. "You are still innocent."

"That's what you think," Viola countered.

"They're trying to talk you out because they know going back to that moon is suicide," Davin said. "Why add one more body to the mix?"

"Davin," Phyla said.

"I was thinking about that, actually," Viola said. "Eden Prime still has a lot of traffic, right? A constant stream of ships coming and going?"

Nobody answered. They stared at her. Davin's eyebrow ticked a centimeter higher.

"They know what the *Whiskey Jumper* looks like. Maybe they're even tracking it somehow," Viola continued. "So what if we used something else?"

"Another ship?" Phyla said. "We don't have one."

"You don't. Galaxy Forge, though, has plenty."

"And they're just going to give us a ship?" Phyla said.

"Or are we going to take one?" Davin said.

"Bingo," Viola said. "Puk can get us the access codes. Then all we have to do is head to the loading docks and take a ship."

"Always love robbing from people who're nice to us," Davin said, shaking his head. "Viola, we have enough enemies. We don't need to make more."

"You'll be leaving the *Jumper* as collateral. I'm sure it's worth as much as one of those cargo haulers."

"More," Davin said.

"She's smart," Mox said.

"We'll have cover, for a change," Erick said. "Might even make it all the way to the surface without getting shot."

"I'm sure we'll get our fill of lasers anyway," Davin said. "But I think that might work. Once we're on the ground, we have a chance at getting to Marl."

"And finding Merc," Opal said. Davin looked at the group, their set faces. Time to call it.

"So we have a choice. Run, or fight," Davin said. "We should vote. I know I'm the captain, but for this, everyone needs to decide for themselves."

They all nodded.

"Then who's for going back to Europa?" Davin said.

Phyla and Opal's hands shot up right away. Viola's a moment later. Mox and Erick a second after that. Davin looked across the table.

"Fine, you bastards. When you get shot, I don't want to hear any complaining."

Hijackers

"Are you ready?" Viola asked Fournine, who sat on the bench, blinking its eyes.

The plan to take one of the company ships was simple. Viola would use her father's access codes, phrases and key combinations she'd hacked years ago out of boredom. The staff would recognize her, and probably the rest of the Nines as well. Which meant turning to the one person Galaxy Forge didn't know existed.

Fournine stretched out its arms and wiggled each finger, testing the motion. It did the same with its feet, then flexed each joint. Viola knew, from looking at Fournine's code, that this was part of the start-up sequence. In a couple of seconds, the real fun would begin.

"Who am I?" Fournine said, its voice a monotone.

"You're an android," Viola started.

"That is clear," Fournine said, rotating its head to look at Viola.

The plaskin coating looked unnatural in the bright light. Fournine could adjust the tint at will and right now the plaskin was ghostly white. Absent of color. The hair was gray, its neutral state. Fournine looked like a person coated with flour. Despite the appearance, Fournine's jaw worked as it spoke. Its eyes moved around the room, looking at objects even though the bot's cameras would have scanned the place already. Warm air pushed out of its mouth, shoved by tiny jets, to simulate breath. Viola shivered.

"I have a new personality for you," Viola said. "If you're ready for it."

When Viola created Puk, it'd taken a while to get a personality that matched the bot. From the ones available to download, Viola had tweaked and tested, spinning the floating bot through turns as a noble prince, a dark and dour teenager, an innocent kid, and more. For a while there, Puk's being changed to reflect Viola's mood. Only, it was one thing to experiment with a small, harmless bot and another to tweak the state of a bot that could snap her in half without trying.

"I'm ready," Fournine said.

Again Viola pressed her fingers to Fournine's temples. The processing unit rose from its head, slots available for the personality chip, the drive containing the combat knowledge, and the piece that Viola and Trina removed and destroyed. The transmitter that connected Fournine back to the android's command center on Earth that sent it overriding orders,that could and would order Fournine to self-destruct after it didn't communicate.

Viola slipped the personality chip in the slot and pushed. With a click, the chip locked into place and, with another press to the temples, the processing unit slid back into Fournine's head.

"You want me to be like this? Really? Cause I think you're gonna regret it," Fournine said as soon as its skull sealed. "I mean, there's crazy, and then there's what you've got here."

"Where we're going, we'll need a little crazy."

"Little, she says. Like calling a supernova a firework. But hey! I'm not here to judge. Just to do. Do it all."

Viola left Puk with this personality for two days years ago. Then, unable to stand the meandering anecdotes about nothing and myriad death threats this personality matrix was prone to, she'd taken it out. Fournine, though, looked like it needed something spicy.

"Glad you're excited. Here's what we need you to do."

Android Unleashed

Fournine's internal clock put Ganymede's current time as way too late. The factory and its accompanying bays didn't recognize this, churning away refining ores along the third shift. Still, passing through the hallways and the empty way stations gave a good indicator of why nighttime missions were easier. Nobody bothered with the ancillary areas.

Every so often, making its way through the factory, Fournine had to stop and wave a card in front of a scanner. Each time, after a second, the scanner blinked green and the door opened. Fournine assumed the scans were logging somewhere, that someone would ask questions later about why these doors opened at such late hours. But nobody appeared to question the android. Which, as the chosen route to the bays was as out-of-the-way as possible, made sense.

Fournine wore a borrowed uniform from the manufacturing pits, a singular outfit that covered every inch of its body save its head in thick cloth the color of murky blue. If a fight broke out, the first task would be to tear off the uniform and get mobility back. As it was, Fournine clomped through the hallways, skin tinted to a realistic darker shade, attempting to match the slouching drudge of the other workers.

The first manned station was the last checkpoint before the bays. A lone member of the factory's security, looking bored and dusty. The guard sat in a booth next to the locked gate and didn't say anything until Fournine attempted to swipe the card through.

"Hey there," the guard said, perking up. "It's after hours, so I'll have to check you through."

"Sure thing, my third-shift friend!" Fournine announced, stepping over to the booth and presenting the card.

The guard took it, looked at it with a crinkling brow.

"Say," Fournine said. "Why's it you look like you popped your head out of a mine shaft?"

The guard blinked for a second then took stock of his dirt-stained sleeves.

"Security here's a rotation gig. You work a bit down in the trenches, then get a week up here," the guard said the words, then narrowed his eyes at Fournine. "Though you should know that. Your card here gives you top-level clearance."

"Consultant," Fournine replied. "Just writing a report on the interesting parts."

The guard grunted, then swiped the card through another reader in the booth. The gate opened with a chime and the guard handed the card back.

"Why're you coming round so late, if you're just writing a report?"

"You're a suspicious one, aren't you?" Fournine replied. "Do I tell you how to do your job?"

The guard took that, shrugged, and waved Fournine on. The miracles confidence could get you. Though perhaps Fournine had the advantage in that its programming prevented fear. Any normal person on the verge of being caught might sweat, shake, or stumble through their answers. Fournine didn't care. If it was caught, it would dismantle anyone that stood in its way.

Speaking of, the long hallway stretching behind the bays now lay before Fournine. Only the farther ones were in use tonight, their bright lights filtering across the top of the hallway and giving signs of where not to go. It wasn't hard to navigate a few bays and find an empty ship, powered down and large enough to hold ten. Fournine stepped into the bay and towards the ship. The ramp was raised, the ship's door shut.

"Here's our first problem!" Fournine commed. "I've found our ride, but it's not open. Shall I rip the door off?"

"We need it sealed or we'll die up there," Viola replied through the comm.

"You living creatures and your needs," Fournine said.

"Such a drag, I know. What's the model?"

"It's a Cask Seven Star."

"Isn't that a little big?"

"I'm sorry, I'll just continue my illegal wandering through the bay until we find the perfect fit," Fournine said.

It heard Viola sigh over the comm.

"And we own this one?" Viola asked.

"It has your company's name all over it."

"Then the reset code is twenty-seven, twenty-four," Viola said.

Fournine punched the numbers in and the ramp whistled, opened and slid down. Ah, the benefits of mass infrastructure and the consistency such operations required. Fournine stepped up the ramp, was almost into the ship, when bright lights came on behind him.

"Hey! What're you doing in there?" shouted the same guard from back at the booth.

"Believe I told you?" Fournine yelled back. "Need to see how this one is being used. Sitting here in the bay isn't making anyone any money, you know?"

"I checked with operations and nobody knows about any consultant coming by tonight! Come back out here so we can figure this out."

Fournine ran the odds. It could run back, knock the guard unconscious, and then get on board the vessel in under thirty seconds. However, if the guard called for any back-up, they could seal the bay faster than the ship could take off. Feigning ignorance gave a better return.

"I don't want to be here any longer than necessary," Fournine replied. "Either wait down there a minute or come up. The inspection won't take long."

As the guard wavered, Fournine went inside the ship and strode to the cockpit. Unlike the *Jumper*, the cargo vessel's cockpit was at the aft. This let most of the cargo slide forward where workers and bots could unload it easily. As Fournine stepped into the spacious enclosure, with seating enough for four, soft lighting came on. A tap on the console started the pre-flight check, with greens popping up across the board. The ship wasn't broken, then.

"I have a guard problem," Fournine commed. "I've delayed him for a minute, but curiosity will win out before too much longer."

"You're not supposed to hurt anyone," Viola replied.

"I won't hurt him much, I promise."

A clanking noise echoed through the ship and towards the cockpit. The guard walking up the ramp. An unfortunate decision. Fournine punched the button for engine warm-up, and as the soft rumble of moving energy filled the vessel, the android went back to greet the guard.

"Why are you setting the ship up to launch?" The guard asked as he crested the ramp and found Fournine standing there.

"Part of the routine. The quality of the ship is an important part of the report. Can't measure loading efficiency accurately if you don't know how ready the ships are for flight."

"My supervisor's on his way, you know. So if you're lying to me, now's the time to get out," the guard said, hand moving to a holstered sidearm.

Fournine followed the guard's arm, holding its own hands up.

"The threats are unnecessary," Fournine said. "Besides, if anyone will be throwing threats, it should be me."

"What?" The guard said as Fournine reached forward.

The guard tried to draw his weapon, but Fournine's raised right hand moved fast, locking the drawing arm to the guard's side. With his left hand, Fournine pressed hard to the guard's throat. The thing with humans is that without their oxygen, they crumble awfully fast. A few seconds struggle later and the guard went limp in the android's arms. Taking its hand away, Fournine felt the faint pulse and sudden intake of breath that signaled life.

"Your guard will have a headache, but he'll wake up tomorrow," Fournine commed after dumping the guard on the bay floor.

Minutes later, as the guard's supervisor rounded the corner into the bay, Fournine lifted the Cask Seven Star out of the bay and over the dark amber of Ganymede's surface.

Incoming

Europa didn't look as blue this time. Viola saw the moon through the cargo hauler's cameras, projecting the image on the flat wall on the back of the cockpit. Fournine was the only other person up there with her. When Europa's flight control tried to figure who was trying to land a cargo ship on their moon, they wouldn't see any faces they recognized. Davin and the others were getting ready near the loading ramp, ready to spring out as soon as the hauler landed on solid ground.

The first hail came as Europa grew large enough to dominate the view. The auto-pilot, using Phyla's programmed route, was already firing jets to slow the hauler and get it ready for atmosphere.

"This is Eden Prime to the, uh, *Big Bertha*. What's the nature of your visit?"

"We're here to drop sweet, sweet ore in your laps," Fournine replied.

Viola slapped the mute button and glared at the android.

"How about you let me answer the rest of the questions?" Viola said.

"What's the problem?" Fournine said. "You think he's having a boring day? Cause it sounds like he's having a boring day. He didn't even laugh at the name of the ship. We should cheer him up. Especially cause when we land and it gets out that he let a bunch of wanted mercenaries into their base, his day will get a lot worse."

"Just shut up, please."

"You made me the way I am."

"*Big Bertha*," said the flight controller. "We'll have a bay ready for you, number four. If you wouldn't mind adjusting your approach to match the coordinates, I'm sending your way."

"Appreciate it," Viola replied.

No ask for identification, no statement on the number of crew, or even the types of ore they were bringing? Viola had spent time, during one of her father's endless career-day initiatives, in the flight control rooms on Ganymede. The list of questions and protocols to follow to get a good idea of what was landing on your planet was a long one.

"Davin?" Viola commed.

"What's up?"

"We're through, but I'm not thrilled about it."

"Seems like you should be, if we're in the clear."

Viola relayed the concerns, to which Davin, in a tone of voice Viola recognized as whaddya want me to do about it, replied that the whole thing would be a mess anyway. So long as they didn't have to fight in *Big Bertha*'s slow, weaponless metal box, things couldn't be that bad. Hard to argue with that logic.

As the ship descended through Europa's atmosphere, Viola used the cameras to explore the view. Eden Prime and the surrounding landscape was still a moldy green, a patch of growing life surrounded by the marching line of the terramorpher. From this high up it resembled fog-covered hills, rolling lines of mist moving too gradually for Viola to see as they chewed up ice and sucked up water and, mixing with imported rock and sand, converted the stuff into soil.

Europa was a ball covered in ice, and the terramorpher was making land from the bottom up. Growing mountains. What Viola would give to be inside one of those giant machines, watching a world literally made beneath her.

Sisters

They were landing. The Wild Nines, here. Marl set the transmission, targeted it towards the relay satellite that would send it bouncing through a series of repeaters to Alissa's ship, hidden somewhere in the depths of space.

"Sister," Marl started, then took a breath. "Sister, I'm sending this in case I don't make it through until tomorrow. The group of mercenaries is proving stubborn, proving dangerous.

"There is a chance that they will make it to me. Bosser, the man pulling Eden's strings, tells me that it is either the heads of these mercenaries or mine. I'm not confident in the former."

Behind her, the office door opened and Castor stepped in. Marl waited until he shut the door behind him.

"Alissa, you must know that there is no home for you here. Eden is watching closely, and even if I survive, they won't let me live without a leash.

"However, there is one thing I can tell you. Maybe you can use it, to help your cause. Several days ago a large freighter passed through the system, Eden-branded. I met with the captain and learned where they are heading, and why.

"I've sent the details in this package, and hope that it is enough."

Castor cleared his throat.

"Sister, I have to go. If this is to be the end of it, then I'm sorry we didn't have more time together. That we spent our lives on edges. I loved you through all of it."

Marl cut the recording and sent the transmission. Then looked out over the frozen wastes. Through the blurred haze of tears, she could picture the towers, the beaches, the endless pleasures Eden Prime would become. That she might yet see.

"It's time to go," Castor said, putting his hand on her shoulder. "The trap is set."

Marl reached underneath her desk, pulled out the sidearm kept there for emergencies. Fully charged and ready for its murderous task.

"Then let's watch it spring," Marl said.

Attacking Ice

Looking at the Nines, each of them covered in weapons, Davin felt an electric rush. This was what it meant to be part of a team. Together taking on an impossible task.

Mox, standing near where the ramp opened, had his cannon latched on and pointed towards the exit. Any ambush would get a face full of laser. Behind him, Opal stood with a pair of long, thin guns. Pin-pointers, Opal called them. Modified from welders and precise manufacturing tools, the beams fired by those things were so tiny as to be invisible. Because lasers were silent, taking away the sight of the beam made finding the shooter of one of those guns damn near impossible.

Davin had Melody, his shotgun, along with a pair of sidearms on his belt. Phyla sported a simpler, though no less deadly, assault rifle, one meant to fire a ton of lasers in rapid succession. It sat in Phyla's arms, held by a shoulder strap. Davin couldn't remember the last time Phyla came on a land-based assignment with them, but her arms were steady, her eyes hard.

"Touching down now," Viola's voice came over the comm. "Bay looks empty. Real empty for a cargo delivery."

Davin glanced at Erick, who gave him a quick nod. The doctor had a small sidearm of his own, but wasn't coming. Anyone hurt needed to have somewhere to retreat to, and while the *Big Bertha* didn't have a true medical bay, they'd brought along enough first aid equipment for Erick to work his magic.

Were they ready? They had to be.

The hauler touched down with a bump, and Mox had the ramp open a second later. The big man didn't fire as he walked into the bay, a good sign. Or a bad one, depending on whether Marl knew they were coming. If the other bays were busy, there might not be unloaders ready.

That thought died a quick death when Davin hit the bay floor and saw nothing, not even a security officer coming by to register the ship's arrival.

"They know we're here," Davin said to the group, Viola and Fournine coming down the ramp behind him. "That means we play it slow, safe. Let them screw up."

Mox and Davin took the lead, the rest of the group filtering out behind. Opal staying off to the side, with Viola bringing up the rear. Fournine doing its own thing, scanning the area in front, above, behind and quipping about the poor decor, or how nice everything would look reduced to rubble. Davin resisted the urge to comment. Viola warned all of them that Fournine's new personality would be annoying, but, when things fell apart, it would be a vicious fighter. And that's what counted.

They went through three more empty bays, the silence gnawing at Davin with each step. The tension growing. Everyone wanted an excuse to start blasting, so when they opened the main doors into the promenade, Davin was disappointed to find it empty. The shops in view had red signs showing they were closed. Not a soul stood out on the street.

"Davin Masters!" Marl's voice boomed from everywhere. "You are a constant thorn in my side. If you would just please go and die, it would make things ever so much easier."

Davin looked but couldn't find the speakers, co-opted from their purpose as emergency broadcasters. Not that it mattered. Marl had to be at the main Eden Prime corporate building, at the far end of the promenade. The location seemed ridiculous, back when Davin first came here.

Why make the required destination of everyone landing there, any business anyway, so far away from the bays? Marl explained that making prospects walk the entire base helped sell them on Eden Prime's plan. Standard marketing strategy that was terrible for a raid.

"Now, that trick of yours," Marl continued. "Coming in with that ugly cargo hauler? We wouldn't have caught you. Would have let you walk right in. Only once again your crimes caught up with you. The head of the company you stole that from gave me a ring. He wants his daughter back, apparently? Such a rogue, Davin."

Davin didn't bother looking at Viola. It wasn't the girl's fault. Waving the rest of them forward, Davin led the group along the promenade. Every minute Marl yammered on and on they'd be getting closer to her building.

"You might be interested to know your pilot lived. Ferro told me they found him floating in the wreckage of the fighter. If you want to try and save him, you'll have to hurry," Marl paused. "Now, in a minute you'll meet a pair of surprise guests. They've come a long way to see you, so please do give them your utmost attention."

"Where is he?" Opal yelled into the air.

Marl didn't reply. Silence fell for a brief moment, then a pair of figures, one tall and one short, stepped out from a closed store. Both wore the same long trench coat Fournine sported when they'd first encountered the bot.

"Androids," Mox said, confirming.

"Your friend, the pilot," the tall figure announced. "He is in the prison. Marl wished for us to tell you there is ten minutes before he will be executed."

"It's a trick," Phyla said. "They're splitting us up. Making it easy for them to pick us off."

"Even if it is, we have to try, right?" Opal said. "We have to."

"You and Mox, go," Davin said. "The rest of us will take care of these two."

The two androids waved Opal and Mox past them. Davin hefted Melody, aimed it at the pair.

"Guessing this is still a kill or be killed affair?" Davin said to the androids.

They nodded in eerie unison.

"When the fight starts, you run by them, cool?" Fournine said. "Cause you know I think the world of you, captain, but there's no way in hell we're beating two of them. Meaning I'll play the bait, keep 'em busy with my smart mouth while you all take care of that crazy lady. Kill the murder charge, and the androids will stop. Do it real fast, I might not even be scrap."

"I'll help you," Viola said, Puk floating up behind her. "We've got a few tricks."

"You're crazy!" Fournine said. "I love it!"

"You sure?" Davin said.

"Just go," Viola replied.

Then Davin turned to the two androids and, pulling the trigger, started a fight he couldn't win.

Running War

The aim was perfect. The blast went right to the heart of the short one, only in the moment between the lasers leaving Melody and getting to the android, the short one wasn't there anymore. It was a meter to the side, the balls of plasma flying harmlessly by. The android too fast for them to track.

"Not that I expected anything less," Davin deadpanned.

"Go!" Fournine yelled, jumping forward towards the tall one.

Davin didn't wait, didn't check to see if Phyla was coming, but ran towards the gap between the androids. The tall one went forward to meet Fournine, the two of them clashing with their long knives in a ring of metal. Sparks flew. The short one ducked a few shots from Phyla, holding her trigger as she ran, and made a move to cut them off when Viola sprayed an unceasing barrage of hot energy towards it.

The short android jumped and tucked into a roll, blowing by Davin and moving towards Viola. Davin hoped she knew what she was doing. Now, though, it was on him and Phyla to reach Marl, to cut off the charge before those two bots killed them all.

With the sounds of the fight behind them, Davin and Phyla sprinted down the promenade towards the large, mounded form of the Eden Prime corporate building. As with the other stores on Eden Prime, the corporate building wrapped its way up the curved wall of the base.

To accommodate the size, the base built itself like a fungus, growing pods attached to the promenade and each other, until it covered a hundred meters of floor from ground to ceiling. Each rounded section shone with a different color, representing the different moons that Eden, the mega-corporation, either had or was in the process of converting to prime real estate. In the center, around the main door, was the deep blue of Europa.

"Shouldn't we have run into someone, anyone by now?" Phyla huffed behind Davin.

"My bet is they're waiting behind that door, ready to blow us to pieces as soon as we go in," Davin replied.

The entry loomed large, the curved portal flattening when it hit the ground and spreading wide enough for four or five people to wander through abreast. A small stair ran up to it, with wide half-circles of concrete forming each step. Anyone looking through the dark windows paralleling the door would've seen Davin and Phyla slow and look around, trying and failing to find another way.

"If all we have is the front door, let's make sure we knock politely," Davin said.

"Politely?"

Davin went up to the large door. On the left was a scanner, ready to unlock if they had a badge. Davin gestured to the right side and Phyla went over, rifle ready. Davin looked at the scanner, then took out his old Eden Prime security card. He pressed it against the scanner, which beeped a negative and stayed red.

"Worth a try," Davin said at Phyla's incredulous look.

"Now what?"

"We knock."

Davin pounded his hand on the door. To say that the metal exterior was kind to his hand would be a gross overstatement. Rather, the rippled metal, grooved to make the frozen waves of Europa's seas, scratched Davin's fist. On the other side, Davin heard the scuffs of boots moving. Bits of whispered commands slipped into his ears. The door's locks clicked out. Then the metal slabs slid inward, curling back.

"See? I knew they wouldn't give up a chance to shoot us," Davin said.

"I'm so glad you're right," Phyla replied.

On the other side of the door sat the entry hall, a tiled cavern that gave way at the back to a series of counters, at which complaints could be registered, forms filled out, and lines waited in. Davin wasted several mornings there himself, staring at the crowd and trying to figure why Eden paid them to guard a bunch of bureaucrats. On the sides of the lobby, stairs curled up along blue walls towards office space. Towards Marl.

Dangling from the ceiling was a spectacular chandelier made from reproductions of Europa ice threaded through with lights. It cast the room in an underwater glow. Aside from that, the rest of the lobby was empty. Davin looked across the entrance into Phyla's tense, stressed face and slipped into a smile. Better to face doom with a cocky grin than crying eyes.

"Cover me," Davin said, and Phyla gave a quick, terse nod.

Davin aimed Melody at the chandelier, and pulled the trigger. The blast went high and spread, striking around the ceiling where the chandelier was bolted. The lasers burned through the cabling, snapping it and sending the work of art plummeting towards the ground. Davin leaned back against the door and shielded his eyes. When the bright flash grayed out the black of his vision, Davin lowered his arm and, crouched, wheeled around the edge of the left door.

Without looking, Davin pulled the trigger again and sent a bolt rolling at the trooper standing behind the door. The trooper's fire whisked over Davin's head and charred a few hairs. Davin's bolt caught the guard in the chest, causing the guard to collapse a smoking ruin. A few lasers danced by Davin from shooters behind the right door, striking the farther wall to the side.

Davin swiveled right, looking for the next target, and saw a trio of troopers aiming at him. They clustered around a doorway leading to one side of the building, ducking behind the opening as Davin looked. There wasn't any cover, just five yards of empty space between Davin and the door. So the captain flicked the switch on the shotgun and pressed the trigger. Loaded with a pair of shock grenades for just this purpose, Melody spat a black oval that bounced in front of the side opening.

One of the troopers managed a half-hearted shot that went wide, bouncing off of the left door and away. The other two grabbed him and dove away from the grenade. It exploded a moment later, sending a series of arcing lightning bolts at anything conductive. The troopers met the requirements, several bolts jumped over to the trio and laced their bodies with white for a second before leaving them groaning and incapacitated.

More fire echoed behind him. Phyla busy keeping her promise of cover. The captain pressed his back to the left door and sidestepped to the end, keeping an eye on the empty lobby and those stairs leading to the second floor. There should have been snipers up there. Or someone with a rifle like Phyla's, ready to spray hot light at them. That there wasn't meant the troopers were tactical morons, or there was something more going on here.

A glance around the edge of the doorway showed Phyla clinging to the end of the right door, peaking around with the assault rifle and letting fly a few miracles. Davin made out a pair of troopers on that side, hunkered around the stairs. Another grenade might do the trick, but then he'd be empty. Instead . . .

"What've you got?" Davin yelled to Phyla.

"The pair on the stairs?" Phyla said. "I think they've got me."

"I'll distract them, you wipe them out."

"Say when!"

Davin took a few quick steps to the first guard he'd shot and pulled the trooper's gun from his hands. Carrying the short rifle back to the edge of the door, Davin extended his left arm and prepared to throw. The pair on the stairs continued to let fly with scattered lasers.

"Three! Two!" Davin yelled. "One!"

The gun arced out from Davin's hand, flying and bouncing along the floor. As it flew, Davin turned around the door and triggered a shot at the stairs. It was way wide, but the flash of the bolt scared the pair, who were watching the thrown gun. Phyla took the cue, poked around the side of her door, and blazed the pair in a sheet of blue fire. A second later the lobby, aside from the moans of some of the troopers, was quiet.

"That was luck," Davin said.

"For you, maybe," Phyla replied. "I'm all skill."

"And I'm very grateful," Davin said, moving towards the stairs. "I'm going left. You take right."

The two of them creeped up the slate gray and blue steps. Marl's office was at the top and back, with a window facing the outside of the base and onto Europa's wet exterior. Davin hit the top of the stairs first. A closed door to the right across the narrow walkway bridging the two stairs. A similar door on his side.

Davin held up a finger to Phyla, causing her to stop on her top step. He pointed at the closed door that Phyla couldn't see, using the palm of his hand to show what it was. Phyla nodded, then moved forward a few feet and confirmed that Davin's corner had the same beyond it.

Davin motioned for Phyla to hold her position, covering him again, as he went forward to his corner. Turned around it, reached for the door with one hand and the other on his shotgun trigger. As Davin's hand neared the panel to open the thing, the door opened and Ferro kicked Davin in the face.

Davin felt his teeth rattle, his brain bounce around his skull as he fell back and hit the floor of the walkway. The bounce forced Davin's eyes open, and he saw a stream of lasers flash over his face. Phyla saving him, again.

Pushing back the pain, Davin tilted his head up and looked back through the doorway. Ferro wasn't there.

"I don't think I got him," Phyla said, running over, keeping her gun pointed at the open door.

"Don't forget the other one," Davin grunted, and Phyla twitched back to cover the closed door. "Damn, that guy really got a good kick."

"It looked bad. You okay?"

"I'll feel it tomorrow," Davin said, moving up to a crouch and picking up his gun from the floor. "For now, though, I've got someone to pay back."

As Davin raised up his gun, the man stepped into the open doorway again. At the same time, a whoosh from behind signaled the closed door opening. Phyla, looking that way, pulled the trigger. Davin did the same, but realized Ferro was unarmed. Ferro raised his hands. Surrendering. Davin aimed Melody at the man's chest.

"There's nobody there," Phyla said, not looking away from the other door.

"We've got a friend," Davin said. "Should I shoot him?"

Phyla risked a quick glance back, saw Ferro. Saw the man take a slow step forward.

"Don't shoot me," Ferro said, his voice liquid lead. "I'd like to make a trade."

"Stay there and speak," Davin replied.

"There is more behind this conflict than you know," Ferro said, keeping his hands raised. "Framing you was a mistake. A coward's path. But for the lives of my brothers and sisters, I ask that you allow me this."

"No idea what you're talking about."

"You and I, Davin Masters. A duel, like the old ways," Ferro said. "I win, Marl will tell Eden to drop the rest of your crew from the charges. The rest of my men live. Eden Prime continues."

"And if I win, what, we all die?"

"No. You will live. At least for now,"

"Sounds like good terms to me," Davin said, setting Melody down. "Let's brawl."

Outclassed

The short android hit the ground right in front of Viola's face, fist swinging at her eyes way too fast to dodge. Viola fell back, catching the strike on her chin instead of her face, the blow sending her sprawling back on the ground. The android looked at her for a second, eyes scanning up and down her body.

"You're not on the list," the short android said. "Explicitly noted as do not kill. However, be aware that should you engage again, I may render you harmless."

The android turned back to the endless series of sword strikes between Fournine and the tall android. That was when Puk struck, the little bot spitting its small laser at the android. It burned a hole in the short android's neck, precisely where the neural connection to the android's body should have been.

Only instead of collapsing to the ground in a twitching heap, the short android turned and triggered a shot from a sidearm that appeared in its hand as if by magic. The bolt caught Puk and knocked the sphere to the floor.

Viola lanced another few shots from her squat rifle, but her aim wasn't anywhere near what it needed to be. The android watched the bolts zip by, then propelled towards Viola with its hand raised. Viola closed her eyes, expecting the hit, only it didn't fall. She heard, then saw Fournine tackling the short android and driving it into the inside wall of the promenade.

Fournine's fists worked magic against the short android's desperate defense, punching holes in the plaskin and causing sparks to fly out whenever a good shot hit. But where was the other one?

Viola looked at where the two had been fighting in time to see the tall android pull Fournine's knives from its stomach. Apparently the stabbing missed anything vital, because the android barely paused before taking a running start at the scrambling pair. Viola fired again, the spray glancing around the android. One bolt grazed a shoulder, but the bot didn't break stride.

"Behind!" Viola yelled and Fournine ducked.

The short android followed suit, both of them dropping to the floor as the tall android's swings swept over their heads. Fournine kicked out behind him with his foot, knocking out the tall android's knee. That moment gave the short android an opening, allowing the bot to grab Fournine's neck and slam the android into the ground.

"Get out of here!" Fournine yelled, struggling as both of the other android's pummeled him. "I've got one trick left, and you're not gonna like it!"

Viola didn't hesitate, scooping up Puk and dashing back towards the bay doors. A moment later she heard Fournine's crazed cackle, distorted and rambling up and down pitches as its vocal processing took a punch or two from the androids.

Then Viola flew through the air, bounced off of the floor. A split second later the rumbling roar of an explosion rolled over her. Looking at the floor, wheezing air through bruised lungs, Viola could only hope things were going better for the captain.

Duel

Davin struck first, launching into a right-handed swing towards Ferro's kneecap. The stocky soldier shifted back and moved down the steps.

"Giving up the high ground?" Davin said. "Dangerous gambit."

"Life is a series of risks," Ferro replied.

"Better hope this one pays off," Davin said.

Ferro had him on reach and size, but Davin figured he was quicker. And he doubted Ferro could equal his drunken brawling experience. When Davin noticed Ferro crouch, when they were only a couple steps apart, instead of kicking or trying to throw a wild swing, Davin jumped at Ferro in a tackle. He hit the trooper commander in the upper chest, driving both of them down the stairs in the tumble. Davin felt the steps, the railing, Ferro's body bouncing into him as they rolled towards the lobby.

Davin hit the floor first on his back and used the momentum to throw Ferro off of him, the big man rolling a few feet further but coming up on his knees.

"A fun style, but risky," Ferro said. "Do you win many of these?"

"Not dead yet, am I?" Davin said.

Now, though, Davin didn't have an obvious trick to pull. At the foot of the stairs, everything was flat. So Davin pulled himself up straight and looked dead at Ferro, who was doing the same. Ferro brushed at his clothes for a second then walked quickly towards Davin.

A stride away, Ferro stepped into a right-hook. Davin ducked into the swing, using his left shoulder to push Ferro's punch wide. That should've cleared room for a jab into Ferro's stomach, but the big man's left fist hit Davin's side first. Like an exploding bruise, Davin felt his right side crumple with the hit. Taking every ounce of concentration to stay upright, Davin moved a few feet away from Ferro and tried to breathe.

"Straightforward," Ferro said, taking another step towards Davin. "No finesse."

Again with the right hook, only this time Davin pivoted to the left, allowing Ferro's swing to go to Davin's right and miss his head by inches. Davin grabbed the arm and pulled forward, sticking his leg out. Ferro went forward and Davin felt the contact, then pushed as Ferro slipped the front part of his right foot beneath Davin's shin.

Ferro, falling, twisted with the motion and pulled his arm. Davin, still grappled with the limb, fell across Ferro's body and flipped onto the ground. Both of them were lying on the floor, staring at the ceiling.

Davin got up, jumping his feet beneath him, only to fall back again as Ferro whipped his legs around to knock Davin's out from under him. As soon as Davin hit the floor, he rolled. Anything to get space. Ferro had better technique, so Davin had to find another way. Break the rules.

In the hallway to the right of the lobby were the disoriented soldiers Davin knocked out with his shock grenade. While one was sitting up, the other two were still lying on the floor. Davin broken into a run towards the trio, towards their guns.

"Too scared?" Ferro called. "Running already?"

Davin ignored him, dove for the rifles on the hallway floor. The one sitting guard stared at Davin with little comprehension, shaking his head. Davin grabbed a rifle, turned and pressed his finger to the trigger. Only to see Ferro pull a sidearm from beneath his shirt. The two of them pointed their weapons at each other, only two meters apart. Neither would be likely to miss.

"You can drop it now," Phyla yelled from upstairs.

Ferro glanced in her direction.

"I thought this was a duel?" Ferro said.

"If you think I will risk it all in some showcase of bravado, you're wrong," Davin said. "We have a crew to protect. So talk, or she liquefies you."

Ferro hesitated, then dropped his gun. It hit the floor with a hollow thunk and bounced away.

"If you want to find Marl, she's at the terramorpher," Ferro said. "Waiting for her shuttle to come and carry her away."

"She's running? No faith in your protection?"

"Marl does what she needs to survive," Ferro said. "As we all do."

That was enough. Davin raised the stolen gun, swiped his index finger along the power setting, took a shot and hit Ferro in the knee. The low-powered bolt knocked Ferro into a crouch, but the man didn't make a noise, just looked at Davin hard.

"In the future, let's do this again. Without interruptions," Ferro said as Davin went by him.

"Yeah, I'll put that on my list. Way down at the bottom," Davin replied.

The skiffs, designed for those on-world showcase cruises, were docked nearby. Of the three Eden Prime maintained in the flat expanse used as a docking bay, one was missing. The other two, though, sat on their respective gray landing pads.

"Just waiting for us," Phyla commented as the two of them climbed the boarding stairs.

Because the skiffs were single-deck floating barges, there wasn't a ramp. A ladder, useful in emergencies or unscheduled landings, could be lowered from one of the sides. Otherwise, rolling stairs on the landing pads facilitated on and off-loading. Beyond that, the skiffs consisted of rails, a smattering of benches, and a pilot's console.

The things were so slow, security measures were non-existent. You get in a fight on a skiff, you were going to lose. Unless your opponent was another skiff, in which case Davin figured it would play out like an old pirate movie, both sides banging into each other and taking pot shots until one or the other called it quits.

Phyla triggered the jets, small-scale engines that turned on the movement of air rather than any propellant. The whole concept gave the skiff endless amounts of flight time, but its max speed barely beat out a jog. Not that this was a problem when you were using it to sell a moon. Marl had plenty of time to craft sales pitches, while the company reps could take a view of the place and run numbers to have a decision in hand by the time the skiff landed. They were purposefully boring.

"The computer says it'll take an hour," Phyla said. "These things are so slow."

"And you said you were jealous when I'd escort meetings on these things."
"Yeah, well, not anymore."

The Terramorpher

The machine filled the horizon. A massive metallic line painted over in parts with sold advertising, Eden Prime logos, and marred pieces where an unexpected piece of falling debris tore the color away. A ragged rainbow. Made in pieces on Earth and in space, then sent to Europa in a series of rocket-boosted boxes, contracted engineers and robots assembled the machine into the churning line of planetary remodeling it was now.

"Always forget how big these things are," Phyla said, staring.

"Too impatient to go any smaller," Davin replied.

The terramorpher would not win a race, but it churned over the ice and deposited plants engineered to build an atmosphere, to warm up the moon. To melt that icy surface. Eventually Europa would be a rock ball with oceans, and from there the road to a new paradise wasn't long.

"We've found Merc," Opal's voice came in over the comm. "They had a couple guys watching him. Took one look at Mox and ran. We're on our way back to the ship."

"Viola?" Davin asked. "You take care of those androids yet?"

"Fournine did," Viola replied a second later. "Blew them both up. And itself."

A pause. Viola sounded sad, but the turned bot had done better than it should have. A two for one android trade? He'd take that every time.

"Sorry to hear that," Davin said, unsure what else to say.

"Don't worry about it. I copied Fournine's data while it was turned off. We get a new body, I can bring it back."

"I'll put it on the shopping list," Davin said. "We're on our way to find Marl. Get the cargo hauler ready to go. We might need a pick-up."

Affirmatives were thrown around and a minute later Phyla guided the skiff into the docking bay on the terramorpher. Despite the size of the machine, actual room for people was minimal. The bay had room for two skiffs, one of which was already taken. From there a wide scaffolding stair led up to an observation deck and control panels. Only the bare essentials. Unlike the spectacular exterior, this part was a drab gray. Tourists didn't make it this far, so Eden Prime didn't bother sprucing things up.

Climbing off the skiff, Phyla and Davin drew their weapons again, edging up the stairs with Davin in the lead.

"How much you want to bet Marl's favorite flunky, Castor is here?" Davin said.

"All I've got," Phyla said, double-checking the energy on her rifle. "You know much about about him?"

"Only seen him spinning the words to gawking tourists. Our luck, the man's secretly a living weapon whose gonna take us both out before we know what's happening,"

"Seems like a good assumption," Phyla said.

The one landing before the observation deck, a platform there to give room for a stabilizing steel beam jutting through the terramorpher, held no answers in its empty flatness. Above, the observation deck hid behind the steep stairs and the plated inside of the big machine. The noise here, fifty feet above the ground, sounded like a grumbling stomach tied to an amplifier. Cracking ice.

"Here we go," Davin said, taking a breath and getting ready for a mad dash up the stairs.

He expected an okay from Phyla, a grunt of acknowledgment. What Davin heard instead was a stifled yell and the sound of a body hitting the platform behind him. Davin whirled around, bringing Melody up to fire, and caught Castor's kick in the jaw.

Davin bounced back into the stairs, splaying out against the metal steps, but hung on to the shotgun. Castor, holding his own gun in his left hand, gave Davin a leveling look, then pulled the trigger.

A green bolt lanced out, hit Davin's knee, and spreading around his leg like burning fire. A stun shot, meant to overload the nerves and trigger shock. Davin recognized the sensation - enough bar fights and he got pretty used to it - and swung the shotgun around, firing a round. Castor dove to the side, catching himself on the railing. Phyla brought herself back up to a crouch, reaching for her assault rifle.

"Two on one, Castor," Davin rasped as his left leg fell numb, the burning sensation rising through his stomach and spreading to his right side. "Drop the stunner and we won't kill you."

"You won't kill me anyway," Castor said, rolling to a crouch. "You're not a murderer."

"Then why is your boss claiming we are?"

Davin enunciated the last word with a blast from Melody. Castor anticipated it again, rolling out of the way, but came up right into a shot from Phyla's assault rifle. The white-hot bolt splashed into Castor's chest and fizzled out, a shower of sparks and then nothing. A personal shield. Damn things were expensive, finicky, and tended to let through the shots you really needed them to stop, but of course this guy had a working one.

Davin, now sitting on the steps and feeling his arm losing its ability to pull the trigger, popped off another round. It was nowhere near accurate, but Castor dove anyway. He was on the far side of the landing now.

Castor raised the stunner and squeezed off a second bolt. The green fire hit Davin in the chest and drove him back against the stairs. While stunners didn't interfere by design with the heart and lungs, Davin couldn't feel anymore if he was breathing or not.

"Leave him alone," Phyla said.

Another white bolt from Phyla's assault rifle hit Castor's shield, breaking apart. Then another, and a third. Phyla pressed harder on the trigger as she walked forward, sending dozens of shots at close range into Castor. He tried to move, tried to roll away, but he was too close.

A few seconds into the barrage, Castor's shield overloaded with a loud bang and the bodyguard took a couple unimpeded shots before Phyla lifted her hand from the trigger. Castor laid there on the landing, smoking and curled up on the metal floor.

"Come on," Phyla said, throwing Davin's arm over her shoulders. "Let's pay Marl a visit."

Davin would've nodded, but he seemed to have stopped working. Instead Davin let Phyla drag his numb body up the stairs and onto the open observation deck, where the frozen waters of Europa sat front and center.

Pain

The evening blaze of Jupiter splashed through the wide windows of the terramorpher's observation deck. It sat atop the long series of stairs, and Phyla was glad to see it. Davin wasn't exactly a light load. Draped over her shoulder and hanging limp, Phyla checked again to make sure the captain's eyes were still open. They were, and staring at the dark silhouette planted against the light.

"I always knew you were good, Davin, but I never realized just how good," Marl said, not bothering to turn around.

The flat floor of the observation deck ended with the window on one end and, on the sides, railings giving view to the churning inner workings of the terramorpher. Pistons pumped, conveyors shifted materials to chutes that would carry them to deposit points. The mechanical motions would have been hypnotizing in a calmer situation.

"Marl," Phyla said. "It's over. Drop the charges."

Marl glanced back, eyes wide. Not the voice she was expecting. Phyla hadn't met Marl. Only heard the woman over the *Jumper*'s comm every now and again. Seeing Marl now, in similar combat gear to Castor, the woman's backbone was clear. The straight-up shoulders, crossed arms, set mouth. Phyla had seen enough dealers in Vagrant's Hollow to know what someone looked like when they were certain.

"I assume Castor put our friend Davin into his current state?" Marl said.

"It doesn't matter. Just drop the charges so we can leave."

Phyla kept her distance. Wished there was somewhere to put Davin so she could draw her own rifle. Marl had at least one sidearm, and it wouldn't be much fun to dodge fire while still trying to keep the captain on her shoulders.

"I'm sorry that the inspectors contacted you," Marl said. "They were supposed to land and then be taken care of immediately thereafter. That's why I made sure we leaked the second ship, the one that turned its engines on your crew. Only, you weren't supposed to be there."

"Thanks for letting us know," Phyla said. She squatted to slip Davin off of her back, one hand staying on the assault rifle.

"I was trying to spare you."

"You were trying to keep a secret," Phyla replied. Davin hit the floor, crumpled to the ground. Phyla twisted, caught Davin's head before it slammed into the floor.

The sidearm didn't make a sound as it fired. The flash of the laser hit Phyla's eyes at the same time as the burn lashed her side. Pain bloomed and Phyla collapsed next to Davin. Breathing was inhaling fire. White lines played around the outside of her vision, threatening to expand and wipe away the universe in shock. The floor, her left hand touching it, was icy. That chill shoved her back from the edge. Couldn't collapse now. Had to create distance, use the rifle.

Fight back.

"Eden wants someone to take the fall for Clare and Ward," Marl said. She was walking towards Phyla now, her face haloed by Jupiter through the windows. The sidearm held out in front of her, stiff, as though Marl was conducting a ceremony. "And while I think Eden can rot, while I'm doing all I can to tear it apart, we aren't ready for its focused attention. Not yet."

Phyla used her legs, pressing herself back. The rifle dragged along the floor while her arms were busy pushing. Saw Marl's face tense up. Grabbed the rifle and swung it up in front of her face.

She couldn't see the laser, only the light it cast as the shot burrowed into the rifle. Nothing broke through the rifle's body. Bet its makers didn't think it would serve as a shield. Phyla swung the rifle back towards Marl, pressed the trigger, and the safety light blinked red. Malfunction. Marl wouldn't aim at her face again.

"Almost had me," Marl said, expression easing from stunned panic into an easy smile. "We would have tried to recruit all of you. Too bad."

"Recruit for what?" Phyla said. She had her own sidearm, there on her left thigh. Marl would kill her if Phyla went for it, but there wasn't any other option.

"It doesn't matter anymore," Marl replied. She raised the sidearm again. No time. Phyla made a reach for her own, the burn in her right side searing.

An End

Marl was only a meter away. About to shoot, body stance like a warrior delivering a summary execution to a bested opponent. Thing was, that attention meant she missed what Davin was doing. How he was struggling to move a hand he couldn't feel to grip the handle of Melody, how he only knew he'd found it in the fog of his perception when his arm didn't lift as easily as it did before.

How he pulled the trigger as soon as the shotgun flopped in front of his own eyes.

Melody wasn't stunned. The shotgun did what it was designed to do. Six balls of glowing green energy exploded out from the weapon and collapsed into Marl, bursting into gouts of flame. Melody's fire spread fast, the heat from each ball meeting the others halfway and igniting Marl's entire uniform.

Causing the head of Eden Prime to turn and backpedal, to hit the edge of the observation deck, to press over the railing and fall like an emerald meteor into the terramorpher's crunching depths.

Would have been nice to sigh right then. To feel the tension leak out of his muscles. To take a deep breath. But Davin was still floating in a half-conscious world where his body gave him no information. Where his lungs kept him breathing through an instinctual response, where his eyes blinked out of habit. The world a movie he was watching from inside his own head.

"Hey," Phyla said, her head appearing in front of his eyes. "Thanks for that."

A pause. A wait for an answer Davin wasn't able to give. He'd have nodded, declared that's what Marl had deserved, but his body wasn't listening.

"Right. I'm going to pick you up again, and we're going to get out of here," Phyla said. "I'm hurt, Davin, so if you can wake yourself up, the sooner the better. Or you will owe me so much for carrying you back to the ship, that—"

Davin was pretty sure Phyla kept talking. That she mixed in a series of curses as they went down the steps and Davin's full weight fell on her. But he couldn't really focus. Couldn't push back against the dead senses any more with the adrenaline dying. Couldn't do anything except greet the black hoping that when he woke up, he'd be somewhere else.

A New Contract

The blue moon never looked better than when Davin was leaving it behind. Glowing there in the dark field of stars, the edge of Jupiter sneaking into the window as the cargo hauler gathered speed in a gravity slingshot that would put them on target for Ganymede.

Old-style navigation aids like the slingshot were necessary as the hauler didn't have the fuel to brute-force its way through space. The maneuver meant it would take a few days to get around Jupiter's massive size and intersect with Ganymede. There, they'd get their ship back.

"And then where?" Phyla asked, lying on her cot. Erick had her chest all wrapped around with bandages, ointments spread across the section where Marl's shot struck home.

"Not sure yet. But I hear Neptune's beautiful this time of year," Davin said, sitting next to her. "The next wave of androids will have a hard time finding us out there."

Viola had the cockpit, with Opal giving the girl tips on astro-navigation. With the course already pre-programmed, there wasn't a whole lot of trouble they could get into. In fact, for the first time in what felt like months, Davin wasn't afraid something was going to go wrong.

A few hours later, getting ready to catch some much-desired sleep in the cramped crew quarters, Davin heard a buzz on the comm.

"Hey captain," Viola's voice. "Can you come up for a second?"

"Can I take a nap first?"

"Don't think you'll want to do that."

Up in the squat cockpit, where Davin had to duck his head to get to the deeper section with the chairs, Viola had the transmitter on the console. A video screen showing an active call, coming from Miner Prime.

"Mind ducking out for a few minutes?" Davin said to Viola, who squeezed past him with a glance and left the captain alone.

"It was harder to find this address than I thought," said the voice on the other end. "I learned that your ship was on Ganymede, but I couldn't reach you there. Then a friend mentioned your hijacking tendencies. Quite the downgrade."

"We'll have the *Jumper* back soon," Davin replied. The waiting game for transmissions from here gave Davin a chance to scan back through the headlines. A blip about Eden Prime, a fatal accident involving the base's manager. A second accidental explosion in the base itself, damaging some stores and a hotel. Eden's media team doing their work.

"Marl didn't drop the charges," Bosser's next communication said. "You're all still wanted for murder."

"You killed Lina. I ever see you again, I'll do whatever I can to justify that charge,"

"All of you are wanted, Davin. Your crew that you profess to care about so much. I'm calling to offer a solution," Bosser didn't even flinch in the transmission. Lina's death didn't cause the slightest surprise. No remorse. Davin hadn't realized what it was like to hate someone before this moment. The bubbling anger slicing through self restraint and begging Davin to find away to leap across space, take Bosser, and throw him out an airlock.

But Davin couldn't do that. Going back to Miner Prime wouldn't work either. Bosser would be ready, would drown the *Jumper* in laser fire before the ship could even dock. If the short-term was out of play, there was only one other way to go.

"You'll drop the charge?"

"I'll convince Eden to remove it. Tell them the truth."

"What do you want?" Davin asked, hating every word as it came out of his mouth.

The picture of Bosser's face, set in a grim line, flexed a minute later into a toothy grin as he described what the Wild Nines would need to do to clear their name. As he heard the words, Davin wondered if they were all going to die anyway.

Acknowledgements

This novel is the product of of my family and friends refusing to let a dream die. My fiancé Nicole, for letting me write in the early mornings and making sure I didn't starve. My brothers and parents for their continual comments, support, and enthusiasm.

Evan Aaseng, for being a constant sounding board and reeling me back in whenever my ideas went too far.

And, of course, you, the reader, for giving me a reason to write.

About the Author

A.R. Knight spins stories in a frosty house in Madison, WI, primarily owned by a pair of cats. After getting sucked into the working grind in the economic crash of the 2008, he found himself spending boring meetings soaring through space and going on grand adventures.

Eventually, spending time with podcasting, screenplays, short stories and other novels, he found a story he could fall into and a cast of characters both entertaining and full of heart.

The Wild Nines have more adventures to come, along with new plots, settings, and stories in the future. From there, A.R. Knight plans on jumping through to other worlds and finding new stories to tell in the limitless borders of our imagination.

Thanks, as always, for reading!

CPSIA information can be obtained
at www.ICGtesting.com
Printed in the USA
FFOW02n0502220817
39079FF